Mansfield Park

Nina Mitchell *and* Jane Austen

CRIMSON ROMANCE

F+W Media, Inc.

This edition published by
Crimson Romance
an imprint of F+W Media, Inc.
10151 Carver Road, Suite 200
Blue Ash, Ohio 45242
www.crimsonromance.com

ISBN 10: 1-4405-6822-7
ISBN 13: 978-1-4405-6822-0
eISBN 10: 1-4405-6823-5
eISBN 13: 978-1-4405-6823-7

Cover art © 123RF

Acknowledgments

Many thanks to fellow Wild and Wanton author Micah Persell, whose fine rendition of *Emma* inspired me to explore another side of Jane Austen; thanks to Jennifer Lawler for encouraging me to try this; thanks to Tara Gelsomino, Julie Sturgeon, and the editorial staff at Crimson for expertly guiding me through the process; and thanks most of all to Jane Austen for being her brilliant and wonderful self.

Prologue

It had been presumed by many that Mrs. Franny Price, formerly Miss Frances Ward, would find scarce comfort in the three sparsely furnished rooms she found herself occupying and sharing with Lieutenant Mr. Price following a hasty marriage about which it could be said the union was less cause for celebration than evidence of retribution of the sort that endures one's lifetime; the lifetime of the former Miss Frances Ward in particular. But while the dwelling was absent of adequate light and lacking the sort of comforts to which Mrs. Price had grown accustomed in her upbringing, it contained a warm and well-tended hearth—considered by many to be the true heart of a home—attended to solely by Mrs. Price, who had not only learnt to keep it burning; but to procure, without the sort of human assistance she had once depended upon in her youth, the source of its heat as well. It was customary for Mrs. Price to be found seated quite comfortably before the hearth, her firstborn swaddled at her breast, herself in contemplation of the life she had chosen for herself—a life she might have never imagined a mere twelvemonth prior—whilst her handsome husband snored softly under the bedcovers a few short paces away.

Mrs. Price found perhaps the majority of her comfort in watching her husband sleep, for it was in the quiet hours of the night that he held exceeding appeal. During daylight she found him to be like the hearth, in constant need of tending with tea to be made or toast or a wash, and it was during his daily demands that she found herself most doubtful of the decision that was beyond her abilities to change. It was during the moments of the day when Mr. Price demanded his boots polished that her thoughts would wander to her sister Maria's favourable match to Sir Thomas Bertram with a man of his own to polish his gentleman's boots. It was when Mr. Price's chamber pot needed a wash that even her sister Mrs. Norris's union with the stodgy Rev. Mr. Norris and his meager annual allowance, was imagined to be quite blissful. It was in the solitude of the darkness that Mrs. Price remembered her youthful conviction that her match would be one of the heart; and it was this memory that softened her feelings towards Mr. Price as she set the babe in his cradle and moved quietly under the bed covers to settle herself in the warmth of her husband's embrace.

Mr. Price's chest charmed her in every manner by which a lady could find herself charmed. Though she may also have admired his form in his tight breeches, it was his wide expanse of chest that she found herself dreaming of before she had known him as a wife knows a husband. It was his chest that she had first pressed her bosom against, his heart beating wildly beneath it, as she held tightly to his strong shoulders, her face buried in his neck, in stolen moments spent in the darkened corners of the library before she became Mrs. Price, moments when she delighted in the insistent prodding of his arousal against her belly and looked forward without question to the delicious mystery of finally feeling his manhood inside her after matrimony.

She delicately traced her fingertips across his chest as he breathed softly in slumber, and found herself once more aroused by the ripple of muscle beneath her touch. She reached for him under the bed linens and smiled at his quick attentiveness to her nearness even as he slept. She considered taking him in her mouth as he'd shewn her after returning from a sea excursion. A man of the sea is known to arrive home with many treasures to bequeath! The realisation that she had come to fancy bestowing such an act nearly as much as he took joy in being its recipient had surprized her and she had become a most eager pupil. But this night she had set her mind that she was ready to take pleasure in him as her husband once again. The skin of her belly had begun to tighten since birthing young William and the soreness between her legs had ceased, yearning once again to feel the heat and thrust of him inside her depths. She lifted her night-dress and slowly straddled him.

"Mrs. Price!" exclaimed he, now fully awake, his grey eyes gazing appreciatively at her form hovering above him.

"Quiet, Mr. Price! If the babe wakes you will soon find yourself alone under these quilts."

"It looks to me as though you are wanting to make another babe."

She imagined him winking in the darkness and smiled as he lifted her night-dress over her head; and a soft moan escaped her as his strong, calloused hands held her hips and guided her over the length of his arousal. She gasped when he held her there, slowly rubbing her most sensitive area with the tip of his manhood. She had to bite her bottom lip to stop from calling out his given name when he finally entered her—tenderly at first—before filling her fully.

"You have made me a happy man, Mrs. Price, and I do love you so," he said as he raised himself onto his elbows to better reach her hardened nipples with his tongue. The movement drove him farther into her depths and the friction against her sensitive parts increased and drove her deeper into their passion as she awaited her release. She ran her fingers through his golden curls and pulled him towards her.

His mouth found hers and his tongue brushed gently against her bottom lip. He pushed himself up to meet her as she rocked over him with more force, both of them surrendering at the same time, joyous tears of release streaming down her cheeks. She collapsed onto his exquisite chest. He stroked her back gently as she lay over him, not wanting yet to release him from inside her.

"Do you think we made another child?" whispered she as she felt his breathing slow and thought him to be asleep. She was not certain it was a question she wanted answered.

Her husband's hand brushed the hair from her cheek. "Perhaps a girl this time," said he.

She shook her head and sat up to look at him. "Only sons, Mr. Price. As my husband, I ask that you give me only sons." She did not offer more and felt him begin to harden again inside her as he gently pulled her beneath him so that he could rise above her, always willing to tend to her wishes in the darkness.

Chapter 1

About thirty years ago Miss Maria Ward, of Huntingdon, with only seven thousand pounds, had the good luck to captivate Sir Thomas Bertram, of Mansfield Park, in the county of Northampton, and to be thereby raised to the rank of a baronet's lady, with all the comforts and consequences of an handsome house and large income. All Huntingdon exclaimed on the greatness of the match, and her uncle, the lawyer, himself, allowed her to be at least three thousand pounds short of any equitable claim to it. Though it could be argued that it was quite the opposite with Sir Thomas Bertram being the one who captivated Miss Maria Ward who had become known by gentlemen throughout Huntingdon and beyond to be attached to a frequently slumbering chaperone and inviting of manly attentions—not so inviting as to render her impossible for marriage, but inviting and generous to the extent that many before Sir Thomas had whispered informal proposals in her ear with eager hope of a lifetime of her careful attention. It was in a coach between Northampton and Huntingdon that Sir Thomas himself whispered such an eager proposal whilst Miss Maria ardently pursued his breeches. It was not the first time Miss Maria had found herself in the position of her bosom exposed and her skirts lifted whilst her hands reached for areas where perhaps they should not have reached, but it was the first time she felt approval for her discovery. It was the surprising size and stock of Sir Thomas's manhood that she found most captivating and its character the only reason she responded to his proposal in the affirmative on the condition that the marriage be completed expeditiously. In that moment Sir Thomas felt himself to be of good luck and Miss Maria did not once contemplate the consequences of their union, though the effects on her family would be great.

She had two sisters to be benefited by her elevation; and such of their acquaintance as thought Miss Ward and Miss Frances quite as handsome as Miss Maria, did not scruple to predict their marrying with almost equal advantage. But there certainly are not so many men of large fortune in the world as there are pretty women to deserve them. Miss Ward, at the end of half a dozen years, found herself obliged to be attached to the Rev. Mr. Norris, a friend of her brother-in-law, with scarcely any private fortune, and Miss Frances fared yet worse. Miss Ward's match, indeed, when it came to the point, was not contemptible: Sir Thomas being happily able to give his friend an income in the living of Mansfield; and Mr. and Mrs. Norris began their career of conjugal felicity with very little less than a thousand a year. But Miss Frances married, in the common phrase, to disoblige her family, and by fixing on a lieutenant of marines, without education, fortune, or connexions, did it very thoroughly. She could hardly have made a more untoward choice. Sir Thomas Bertram had interest, which, from principle as well as pride—from a general wish of doing right, and a desire of seeing all that were connected with him in situations of respectability, he would have been glad to exert for the advantage of Lady Bertram's sister; but her husband's profession was such as no interest could reach; and before he had time to devise any other method of assisting them, an absolute breach between the sisters had taken place. It was the natural result of the conduct of each party, and such as a very imprudent marriage almost always produces. To save herself from useless remonstrance, Mrs. Price never wrote to her family on the subject till actually married. Lady Bertram, who was a woman of very tranquil feelings, and a temper remarkably easy and indolent, would have contented herself with merely giving up her sister, and thinking no more of the matter; but Mrs. Norris had a spirit of activity, which could not be satisfied till she had written a long and angry letter to Fanny, to point out the folly of her conduct, and threaten her with all its possible ill consequences. Mrs. Price, in her turn, was injured and angry; and an answer, which comprehended each sister in its bitterness, and bestowed such very disrespectful reflections on the pride of Sir Thomas as Mrs. Norris could not possibly keep to herself, put an end to all intercourse between them for a considerable period.

Their homes were so distant, and the circles in which they moved so distinct, as almost to preclude the means of ever hearing of each other's existence during the eleven following years, or, at least, to make it very wonderful to Sir Thomas that Mrs. Norris should ever have it in her power to tell them, as she now and then did, in an angry voice, that Fanny had got another child. By the end of eleven years, however, Mrs. Price could no longer afford to cherish pride or resentment, or to lose one connexion that might possibly assist her. A large and still increasing family, an husband disabled for active service, but not the less equal to company and good liquor, and a very small income to supply their wants, made her eager to regain the friends she had so carelessly sacrificed; and she addressed Lady Bertram in a letter which spoke so much contrition and despondence, such a superfluity of children, and such a want of almost everything else, as could not but dispose them all to a reconciliation. She was preparing for her ninth lying-in; and after bewailing the circumstance, and imploring their countenance as sponsors to the expected child, she could not conceal how important she felt they might be to the future maintenance of the eight already in being. Her eldest was a boy of ten years old, a fine spirited fellow, who longed to be out in the world; but what could she do? Was there any chance of his being hereafter useful to Sir Thomas in the concerns of his West Indian property? No situation would be beneath him; or what did Sir Thomas think of Woolwich? Or how could a boy be sent out to the East?

The letter was not unproductive. It re-established peace and kindness. Sir Thomas sent friendly advice and professions, Lady

Bertram dispatched money and baby-linen, and Mrs. Norris wrote the letters.

Such were its immediate effects, and within a twelvemonth a more important advantage to Mrs. Price resulted from it. Mrs. Norris was often observing to the others that she could not get her poor sister and her family out of her head, and that, much as they had all done for her, she seemed to be wanting to do more; and at length she could not but own it to be her wish that poor Mrs. Price should be relieved from the charge and expense of one child entirely out of her great number. "What if they were among them to undertake the care of her eldest daughter, a girl now nine years old, of an age to require more attention than her poor mother could possibly give? The trouble and expense of it to them would be nothing, compared with the benevolence of the action." Lady Bertram agreed with her instantly. "I think we cannot do better," said she; "let us send for the child."

Sir Thomas could not give so instantaneous and unqualified a consent. He debated and hesitated;—it was a serious charge;—a girl so brought up must be adequately provided for, or there would be cruelty instead of kindness in taking her from her family. He thought of his own four children, of his two sons, of cousins in love, etc.;—but no sooner had he deliberately begun to state his objections, than Mrs. Norris interrupted him with a reply to them all, whether stated or not.

"My dear Sir Thomas, I perfectly comprehend you, and do justice to the generosity and delicacy of your notions, which indeed are quite of a piece with your general conduct; and I entirely agree with you in the main as to the propriety of doing everything one could by way of providing for a child one had in a manner taken into one's own hands; and I am sure I should be the last person in the world to withhold my mite upon such an occasion. Having no children of my own, who should I look to in any little matter I may ever have to bestow, but the children of my sisters?—and

I am sure Mr. Norris is too just—but you know I am a woman of few words and professions. Do not let us be frightened from a good deed by a trifle. Give a girl an education, and introduce her properly into the world, and ten to one but she has the means of settling well, without farther expense to anybody. A niece of ours, Sir Thomas, I may say, or at least of *yours*, would not grow up in this neighbourhood without many advantages. I don't say she would be so handsome as her cousins. I dare say she would not; but she would be introduced into the society of this country under such very favourable circumstances as, in all human probability, would get her a creditable establishment. You are thinking of your sons—but do not you know that, of all things upon earth, *that* is the least likely to happen, brought up as they would be, always together like brothers and sisters? It is morally impossible. I never knew an instance of it. It is, in fact, the only sure way of providing against the connexion. Suppose her a pretty girl, and seen by Tom or Edmund for the first time seven years hence, and I dare say there would be mischief. The very idea of her having been suffered to grow up at a distance from us all in poverty and neglect, would be enough to make either of the dear, sweet-tempered boys in love with her. But breed her up with them from this time, and suppose her even to have the beauty of an angel, and she will never be more to either than a sister."

"There is a great deal of truth in what you say," replied Sir Thomas, "and far be it from me to throw any fanciful impediment in the way of a plan which would be so consistent with the relative situations of each. I only meant to observe that it ought not to be lightly engaged in, and that to make it really serviceable to Mrs. Price, and creditable to ourselves, we must secure to the child, or consider ourselves engaged to secure to her hereafter, as circumstances may arise, the provision of a gentlewoman, if no such establishment should offer as you are so sanguine in expecting."

"I thoroughly understand you," cried Mrs. Norris, "you are everything that is generous and considerate, and I am sure we shall never disagree on this point. Whatever I can do, as you well know, I am always ready enough to do for the good of those I love; and, though I could never feel for this little girl the hundredth part of the regard I bear your own dear children, nor consider her, in any respect, so much my own, I should hate myself if I were capable of neglecting her. Is not she a sister's child? And could I bear to see her want while I had a bit of bread to give her? My dear Sir Thomas, with all my faults I have a warm heart; and, poor as I am, would rather deny myself the necessaries of life than do an ungenerous thing. So, if you are not against it, I will write to my poor sister tomorrow, and make the proposal; and, as soon as matters are settled, *I* will engage to get the child to Mansfield; *you* shall have no trouble about it. My own trouble, you know, I never regard. I will send Nanny to London on purpose, and she may have a bed at her cousin the saddler's, and the child be appointed to meet her there. They may easily get her from Portsmouth to town by the coach, under the care of any creditable person that may chance to be going. I dare say there is always some reputable tradesman's wife or other going up."

Except to the attack on Nanny's cousin, Sir Thomas no longer made any objection, and a more respectable, though less economical rendezvous being accordingly substituted, everything was considered as settled, and the pleasures of so benevolent a scheme were already enjoyed. The division of gratifying sensations ought not, in strict justice, to have been equal; for Sir Thomas was fully resolved to be the real and consistent patron of the selected child, and Mrs. Norris had not the least intention of being at any expense whatever in her maintenance. As far as walking, talking, and contriving reached, she was thoroughly benevolent, and nobody knew better how to dictate liberality to others; but her love of money was equal to her love of directing, and she knew quite as well how to save her own as to spend that of her friends. Having married on a narrower income than she had been used to look forward to, she had, from the first, fancied a very strict line of economy necessary; and what was begun as a matter of prudence, soon grew into a matter of choice, as an object of that needful solicitude which there were no children to supply. Had there been a family to provide for, Mrs. Norris might never have saved her money; but having no care of that kind, there was nothing to impede her frugality, or lessen the comfort of making a yearly addition to an income which they had never lived up to. Under this infatuating principle, counteracted by no real affection for her sister, it was impossible for her to aim at more than the credit of projecting and arranging so expensive a charity; though perhaps she might so little know herself as to walk home to the Parsonage, after this conversation, in the happy belief of being the most liberal-minded sister and aunt in the world.

When the subject was brought forward again, her views were more fully explained; and, in reply to Lady Bertram's calm inquiry of "Where shall the child come to first, sister, to you or to us?" Sir Thomas heard with some surprise that it would be totally out of Mrs. Norris's power to take any share in the personal charge of her. He had been considering her as a particularly welcome addition at the Parsonage, as a desirable companion to an aunt who had no children of her own; but he found himself wholly mistaken. Mrs. Norris was sorry to say that the little girl's staying with them, at least as things then were, was quite out of the question. Poor Mr. Norris's indifferent state of health made it an impossibility: he could no more bear the noise of a child than he could fly; if, indeed, he should ever get well of his gouty complaints, it would be a different matter: she should then be glad to take her turn, and think nothing of the inconvenience; but just now, poor Mr. Norris took up every moment of her time, and the very mention of such a thing she was sure would distract him.

"Then she had better come to us," said Lady Bertram, with the utmost composure. After a short pause Sir Thomas added with dignity, "Yes, let her home be in this house. We will endeavour to do our duty by her, and she will, at least, have the advantage of companions of her own age, and of a regular instructress."

"Very true," cried Mrs. Norris, "which are both very important considerations; and it will be just the same to Miss Lee whether she has three girls to teach, or only two—there can be no difference. I only wish I could be more useful; but you see I do all in my power. I am not one of those that spare their own trouble; and Nanny shall fetch her, however it may put me to inconvenience to have my chief counsellor away for three days. I suppose, sister, you will put the child in the little white attic, near the old nurseries. It will be much the best place for her, so near Miss Lee, and not far from the girls, and close by the housemaids, who could either of them help to dress her, you know, and take care of her clothes, for I suppose you would not think it fair to expect Ellis to wait on her as well as the others. Indeed, I do not see that you could possibly place her anywhere else."

Lady Bertram made no opposition.

"I hope she will prove a well-disposed girl," continued Mrs. Norris, "and be sensible of her uncommon good fortune in having such friends."

"Should her disposition be really bad," said Sir Thomas, "we must not, for our own children's sake, continue her in the family; but there is no reason to expect so great an evil. We shall probably see much to wish altered in her, and must prepare ourselves for gross ignorance, some meanness of opinions, and very distressing vulgarity of manner; but these are not incurable faults; nor, I trust, can they be dangerous for her associates. Had my daughters been *younger* than herself, I should have considered the introduction of such a companion as a matter of very serious moment; but, as it is, I hope there can be nothing to fear for *them*, and everything to hope for *her*, from the association."

"That is exactly what I think," cried Mrs. Norris, "and what I was saying to my husband this morning. It will be an education for the child, said I, only being with her cousins; if Miss Lee taught her nothing, she would learn to be good and clever from *them*."

"I hope she will not tease my poor pug," said Lady Bertram; "I have but just got Julia to leave it alone."

"There will be some difficulty in our way, Mrs. Norris," observed Sir Thomas, "as to the distinction proper to be made between the girls as they grow up: how to preserve in the minds of my *daughters* the consciousness of what they are, without making them think too lowly of their cousin; and how, without depressing her spirits too far, to make her remember that she is not a *Miss Bertram*. I should wish to see them very good friends, and would, on no account, authorise in my girls the smallest degree of arrogance towards their relation; but still they cannot be equals. Their rank, fortune, rights, and expectations will always be different. It is a point of great delicacy, and you must assist us in our endeavours to choose exactly the right line of conduct."

Mrs. Norris was quite at his service; and though she perfectly agreed with him as to its being a most difficult thing, encouraged him to hope that between them it would be easily managed.

It will be readily believed that Mrs. Norris did not write to her sister in vain. Mrs. Price seemed rather surprised that a girl should be fixed on, when she had so many fine boys, but accepted the offer most thankfully, assuring them of her daughter's being a very well-disposed, good-humoured girl, and trusting they would never have cause to throw her off. She spoke of her farther as somewhat delicate and puny, but was sanguine in the hope of her being materially better for change of air. Poor woman! She probably thought change of air might agree with many of her children.

Chapter 2

The little girl performed her long journey in safety; and at Northampton was met by Mrs. Norris, who thus regaled in the credit of being foremost to welcome her, and in the importance of leading her in to the others, and recommending her to their kindness.

Fanny Price was at this time just ten years old, and though there might not be much in her first appearance to captivate, there was, at least, nothing to disgust her relations. She was small of her age, with no glow of complexion, nor any other striking beauty; exceedingly timid and shy, and shrinking from notice; but her air, though awkward, was not vulgar, her voice was sweet, and when she spoke her countenance was pretty. Sir Thomas and Lady Bertram received her very kindly; and Sir Thomas, seeing how much she needed encouragement, tried to be all that was conciliating: but he had to work against a most untoward gravity of deportment; and Lady Bertram, without taking half so much trouble, or speaking one word where he spoke ten, by the mere aid of a good-humoured smile, became immediately the less awful character of the two.

The young people were all at home, and sustained their share in the introduction very well, with much good humour, and no embarrassment, at least on the part of the sons, who, at seventeen and sixteen, and tall of their age, had all the grandeur of men in the eyes of their little cousin. The two girls were more at a loss from being younger and in greater awe of their father, who addressed them on the occasion with rather an injudicious particularity. But they were too much used to company and praise to have anything like natural shyness; and their confidence increasing from their cousin's total want of it, they were soon able to take a full survey of her face and her frock in easy indifference.

They were a remarkably fine family, the sons very well-looking, the daughters decidedly handsome, and all of them well-grown and forward of their age, which produced as striking a difference between the cousins in person, as education had given to their address; and no one would have supposed the girls so nearly of an age as they really were. There were in fact but two years between the youngest and Fanny. Julia Bertram was only twelve, and Maria but a year older. The little visitor meanwhile was as unhappy as possible. Afraid of everybody, ashamed of herself, and longing for the home she had left, she knew not how to look up, and could scarcely speak to be heard, or without crying. Mrs. Norris had been talking to her the whole way from Northampton of her wonderful good fortune, and the extraordinary degree of gratitude and good behaviour which it ought to produce, and her consciousness of misery was therefore increased by the idea of its being a wicked thing for her not to be happy. The fatigue, too, of so long a journey, became soon no trifling evil. In vain were the well-meant condescensions of Sir Thomas, and all the officious prognostications of Mrs. Norris that she would be a good girl; in vain did Lady Bertram smile and make her sit on the sofa with herself and Pug, and vain was even the sight of a gooseberry tart towards giving her comfort; she could scarcely swallow two mouthfuls before tears interrupted her, and sleep seeming to be her likeliest friend, she was taken to finish her sorrows in bed.

"This is not a very promising beginning," said Mrs. Norris, when Fanny had left the room. "After all that I said to her as we came along, I thought she would have behaved better; I told her how much might depend upon her acquitting herself well at first. I wish there may not be a little sulkiness of temper—her poor mother had a good deal; but we must make allowances for such a child—and I do not know that her being sorry to leave her home is really against her, for, with all its faults, it *was* her home, and she cannot as yet understand how much she has changed for the better; but then there is moderation in all things."

It required a longer time, however, than Mrs. Norris was inclined to allow, to reconcile Fanny to the novelty of Mansfield Park, and the separation from everybody she had been used to. Her feelings were very acute, and too little understood to be properly attended to. Nobody meant to be unkind, but nobody put themselves out of their way to secure her comfort.

The holiday allowed to the Miss Bertrams the next day, on purpose to afford leisure for getting acquainted with, and entertaining their young cousin, produced little union. They could not but hold her cheap on finding that she had but two sashes, and had never learned French; and when they perceived her to be little struck with the duet they were so good as to play, they could do no more than make her a generous present of some of their least valued toys, and leave her to herself, while they adjourned to whatever might be the favourite holiday sport of the moment, making artificial flowers or wasting gold paper.

Fanny, whether near or from her cousins, whether in the schoolroom, the drawing-room, or the shrubbery, was equally forlorn, finding something to fear in every person and place. She was disheartened by Lady Bertram's silence, awed by Sir Thomas's grave looks, and quite overcome by Mrs. Norris's admonitions. Her elder cousins mortified her by reflections on her size, and abashed her by noticing her shyness: Miss Lee wondered at her ignorance, and the maid-servants sneered at her clothes; and when to these sorrows was added the idea of the brothers and sisters among whom she had always been important as playfellow, instructress, and nurse, the despondence that sunk her little heart was severe.

The grandeur of the house astonished, but could not console her. The rooms were too large for her to move in with ease:

whatever she touched she expected to injure, and she crept about in constant terror of something or other; often retreating towards her own chamber to cry; and the little girl who was spoken of in the drawing-room when she left it at night as seeming so desirably sensible of her peculiar good fortune, ended every day's sorrows by sobbing herself to sleep. A week had passed in this way, and no suspicion of it conveyed by her quiet passive manner, when she was found one morning by her cousin Edmund, the youngest of the sons, sitting crying on the attic stairs.

"My dear little cousin," said he, with all the gentleness of an excellent nature, "what can be the matter?" And sitting down by her, he was at great pains to overcome her shame in being so surprised, and persuade her to speak openly. Was she ill? or was anybody angry with her? or had she quarrelled with Maria and Julia? or was she puzzled about anything in her lesson that he could explain? Did she, in short, want anything he could possibly get her, or do for her? For a long while no answer could be obtained beyond a "no, no—not at all—no, thank you"; but he still persevered; and no sooner had he begun to revert to her own home, than her increased sobs explained to him where the grievance lay. He tried to console her.

"You are sorry to leave Mama, my dear little Fanny," said he, "which shows you to be a very good girl; but you must remember that you are with relations and friends, who all love you, and wish to make you happy. Let us walk out in the park, and you shall tell me all about your brothers and sisters."

On pursuing the subject, he found that, dear as all these brothers and sisters generally were, there was one among them who ran more in her thoughts than the rest. It was William whom she talked of most, and wanted most to see. William, the eldest, a year older than herself, her constant companion and friend; her advocate with her mother (of whom he was the darling) in every distress. "William did not like she should come away; he had told her he should miss her very much indeed." "But William will write to you, I dare say." "Yes, he had promised he would, but he had told *her* to write first." "And when shall you do it?" She hung her head and answered hesitatingly, "she did not know; she had not any paper."

"If that be all your difficulty, I will furnish you with paper and every other material, and you may write your letter whenever you choose. Would it make you happy to write to William?"

"Yes, very."

"Then let it be done now. Come with me into the breakfast-room, we shall find everything there, and be sure of having the room to ourselves."

"But, cousin, will it go to the post?"

"Yes, depend upon me it shall: it shall go with the other letters; and, as your uncle will frank it, it will cost William nothing."

"My uncle!" repeated Fanny, with a frightened look.

"Yes, when you have written the letter, I will take it to my father to frank."

Fanny thought it a bold measure, but offered no further resistance; and they went together into the breakfast-room, where Edmund prepared her paper, and ruled her lines with all the goodwill that her brother could himself have felt, and probably with somewhat more exactness. He continued with her the whole time of her writing, to assist her with his penknife or his orthography, as either were wanted; and added to these attentions, which she felt very much, a kindness to her brother which delighted her beyond all the rest. He wrote with his own hand his love to his cousin William, and sent him half a guinea under the seal. Fanny's feelings on the occasion were such as she believed herself incapable of expressing; but her countenance and a few artless words fully conveyed all their gratitude and delight, and her cousin began to find her an interesting object. He talked to her more, and, from all that she said, was convinced of her having an affectionate heart, and a strong desire of doing right; and he could perceive her to be farther entitled to attention by great sensibility of her situation, and great timidity. He had never knowingly given her pain, but he now felt that she required more positive kindness; and with that view endeavoured, in the first place, to lessen her fears of them all, and gave her especially a great deal of good advice as to playing with Maria and Julia, and being as merry as possible.

From this day Fanny grew more comfortable. She felt that she had a friend, and the kindness of her cousin Edmund gave her better spirits with everybody else. The place became less strange, and the people less formidable; and if there were some amongst them whom she could not cease to fear, she began at least to know their ways, and to catch the best manner of conforming to them. The little rusticities and awkwardnesses which had at first made grievous inroads on the tranquillity of all, and not least of herself, necessarily wore away, and she was no longer materially afraid to appear before her uncle, nor did her aunt Norris's voice make her start very much. To her cousins she became occasionally an acceptable companion. Though unworthy, from inferiority of age and strength, to be their constant associate, their pleasures and schemes were sometimes of a nature to make a third very useful, especially when that third was of an obliging, yielding temper; and they could not but own, when their aunt inquired into her faults, or their brother Edmund urged her claims to their kindness, that "Fanny was good-natured enough."

Edmund was uniformly kind himself; and she had nothing worse to endure on the part of Tom than that sort of merriment which a young man of seventeen will always think fair with a child of ten. He was just entering into life, full of spirits, and with all the liberal dispositions of an eldest son, who feels born only for expense and enjoyment. His kindness to his little cousin was consistent with his situation and rights: he made her some very pretty presents, and laughed at her.

As her appearance and spirits improved, Sir Thomas and Mrs. Norris thought with greater satisfaction of their benevolent plan; and it was pretty soon decided between them that, though far from clever, she showed a tractable disposition, and seemed likely to give them little trouble. A mean opinion of her abilities was not confined to *them*. Fanny could read, work, and write, but she had been taught nothing more; and as her cousins found her ignorant of many things with which they had been long familiar, they thought her prodigiously stupid, and for the first two or three weeks were continually bringing some fresh report of it into the drawing-room. "Dear mama, only think, my cousin cannot put the map of Europe together—or my cousin cannot tell the principal rivers in Russia—or, she never heard of Asia Minor— or she does not know the difference between water-colours and crayons!—How strange!—Did you ever hear anything so stupid?"

"My dear," their considerate aunt would reply, "it is very bad, but you must not expect everybody to be as forward and quick at learning as yourself."

"But, aunt, she is really so very ignorant!—Do you know, we asked her last night which way she would go to get to Ireland; and she said, she should cross to the Isle of Wight. She thinks of nothing but the Isle of Wight, and she calls it *the Island*, as if there were no other island in the world. I am sure I should have been ashamed of myself, if I had not known better long before I was so old as she is. I cannot remember the time when I did not know a great deal that she has not the least notion of yet. How long ago it is, aunt, since we used to repeat the chronological order of the kings of England, with the dates of their accession, and most of the principal events of their reigns!"

"Yes," added the other; "and of the Roman emperors as low as Severus; besides a great deal of the heathen mythology, and all the metals, semi-metals, planets, and distinguished philosophers."

"Very true indeed, my dears, but you are blessed with wonderful memories, and your poor cousin has probably none at all. There is a vast deal of difference in memories, as well as in everything else, and therefore you must make allowance for your cousin, and pity her deficiency. And remember that, if you are ever so forward and clever yourselves, you should always be modest; for, much as you know already, there is a great deal more for you to learn."

"Yes, I know there is, till I am seventeen. But I must tell you another thing of Fanny, so odd and so stupid. Do you know, she says she does not want to learn either music or drawing."

"To be sure, my dear, that is very stupid indeed, and shows a great want of genius and emulation. But, all things considered, I do not know whether it is not as well that it should be so, for, though you know (owing to me) your papa and mama are so good as to bring her up with you, it is not at all necessary that she should be as accomplished as you are;—on the contrary, it is much more desirable that there should be a difference."

Such were the counsels by which Mrs. Norris assisted to form her nieces' minds; and it is not very wonderful that, with all their promising talents and early information, they should be entirely deficient in the less common acquirements of self-knowledge, generosity and humility. In everything but disposition they were admirably taught. Sir Thomas did not know what was wanting, because, though a truly anxious father, he was not outwardly affectionate, and the reserve of his manner repressed all the flow of their spirits before him.

To the education of her daughters Lady Bertram paid not the smallest attention. She had not time for such cares. She was a woman who spent her days in sitting, nicely dressed, on a sofa, doing some long piece of needlework, of little use and no beauty, thinking more of her pug than her children, but very indulgent to the latter when it did not put herself to inconvenience, guided in everything important by Sir Thomas, and in smaller concerns by her sister. Had she possessed greater leisure for the service of her girls, she would probably have supposed it unnecessary, for they were under the care of a governess, with proper masters, and could want nothing more. As for Fanny's being stupid at learning, "she could only say it was very unlucky, but some people *were* stupid, and Fanny must take more pains: she did not know what else was to be done; and, except her being so dull, she must add she saw no harm in the poor little thing, and always found her very handy and quick in carrying messages, and fetching what she wanted."

Fanny, with all her faults of ignorance and timidity, was fixed at Mansfield Park, and learning to transfer in its favour much of her attachment to her former home, grew up there not unhappily among her cousins. There was no positive ill-nature in Maria or Julia; and though Fanny was often mortified by their treatment of her, she thought too lowly of her own claims to feel injured by it.

From about the time of her entering the family, Lady Bertram, in consequence of a little ill-health, and a great deal of indolence, gave up the house in town, which she had been used to occupy every spring, and remained wholly in the country, leaving Sir Thomas to attend his duty in Parliament, with whatever increase or diminution of comfort might arise from her absence. In the country, therefore, the Miss Bertrams continued to exercise their memories, practise their duets, and grow tall and womanly: and their father saw them becoming in person, manner, and accomplishments, everything that could satisfy his anxiety. His eldest son was careless and extravagant, and had already given him much uneasiness; but his other children promised him nothing but good. His daughters, he felt, while they retained the name of Bertram, must be giving it new grace, and in quitting it, he trusted, would extend its respectable alliances; and the character of Edmund, his strong good sense and uprightness of mind, bid most fairly for utility, honour, and happiness to himself and all his connexions. He was to be a clergyman.

Amid the cares and the complacency which his own children suggested, Sir Thomas did not forget to do what he could for the children of Mrs. Price: he assisted her liberally in the education and disposal of her sons as they became old enough for a determinate pursuit; and Fanny, though almost totally separated from her family, was sensible of the truest satisfaction in hearing of any kindness towards them, or of anything at all promising in their situation or conduct. Once, and once only, in the course of many years, had she the happiness of being with William. Of the rest she saw nothing: nobody seemed to think of her ever going amongst them again, even for a visit, nobody at home seemed to want her; but William determining, soon after her removal, to be a sailor, was invited to spend a week with his sister in Northamptonshire before he went to sea. Their eager affection in meeting, their exquisite delight in being together, their hours of happy mirth, and moments of serious conference, may be imagined; as well as the sanguine views and spirits of the boy even to the last, and the misery of the girl when he left her. Luckily the visit happened in the Christmas holidays, when she could directly look for comfort to her cousin Edmund; and he told her such charming things of what William was to do, and be hereafter, in consequence of his profession, as made her gradually admit that the separation might have some use. Edmund's friendship never failed her: his leaving Eton for Oxford made no change in his kind dispositions, and only afforded more frequent opportunities of proving them. Without any display of doing more than the rest, or any fear of doing too much, he was always true to her interests, and considerate of her feelings, trying to make her good qualities understood, and to conquer the diffidence which prevented their being more apparent; giving her advice, consolation, and encouragement.

Kept back as she was by everybody else, his single support could not bring her forward; but his attentions were otherwise of the highest importance in assisting the improvement of her mind, and extending its pleasures. He knew her to be clever, to have a quick apprehension as well as good sense, and a fondness for reading, which, properly directed, must be an education in itself. Miss Lee taught her French, and heard her read the daily portion of history; but he recommended the books which charmed her leisure hours, he encouraged her taste, and corrected her judgment: he made reading useful by talking to her of what she read, and heightened its attraction by judicious praise. In return for such services she loved him better than anybody in the world except William: her heart was divided between the two.

Chapter 3

The first event of any importance in the family was the death of Mr. Norris, which happened when Fanny was about fifteen, and necessarily introduced alterations and novelties. Mrs. Norris, on quitting the Parsonage, removed first to the Park, and afterwards to a small house of Sir Thomas's in the village, and consoled herself for the loss of her husband by considering that she could do very well without him; and for her reduction of income by the evident necessity of stricter economy.

The living was hereafter for Edmund; and, had his uncle died a few years sooner, it would have been duly given to some friend to hold till he were old enough for orders. But Tom's extravagance had, previous to that event, been so great as to render a different disposal of the next presentation necessary, and the younger brother must help to pay for the pleasures of the elder. There was another family living actually held for Edmund; but though this circumstance had made the arrangement somewhat easier to Sir Thomas's conscience, he could not but feel it to be an act of injustice, and he earnestly tried to impress his eldest son with the same conviction, in the hope of its producing a better effect than anything he had yet been able to say or do.

"I blush for you, Tom," said he, in his most dignified manner; "I blush for the expedient which I am driven on, and I trust I may pity your feelings as a brother on the occasion. You have robbed Edmund for ten, twenty, thirty years, perhaps for life, of more than half the income which ought to be his. It may hereafter be in my power, or in yours (I hope it will), to procure him better preferment; but it must not be forgotten that no benefit of that sort would have been beyond his natural claims on us, and that nothing can, in fact, be an equivalent for the certain advantage which he is now obliged to forego through the urgency of your debts."

Tom listened with some shame and some sorrow; but escaping as quickly as possible, could soon with cheerful selfishness reflect, firstly, that he had not been half so much in debt as some of his friends; secondly, that his father had made a most tiresome piece of work of it; and, thirdly, that the future incumbent, whoever he might be, would, in all probability, die very soon.

On Mr. Norris's death the presentation became the right of a Dr. Grant, who came consequently to reside at Mansfield; and on proving to be a hearty man of forty-five, seemed likely to disappoint Mr. Bertram's calculations. But "no, he was a short-necked, apoplectic sort of fellow, and, plied well with good things, would soon pop off."

He had a wife about fifteen years his junior, but no children; and they entered the neighbourhood with the usual fair report of being very respectable, agreeable people.

The time was now come when Sir Thomas expected his sister-in-law to claim her share in their niece, the change in Mrs. Norris's situation, and the improvement in Fanny's age, seeming not merely to do away any former objection to their living together, but even to give it the most decided eligibility; and as his own circumstances were rendered less fair than heretofore, by some recent losses on his West India estate, in addition to his eldest son's extravagance, it became not undesirable to himself to be relieved from the expense of her support, and the obligation of her future provision. In the fullness of his belief that such a thing must be, he mentioned its probability to his wife; and the first time of the subject's occurring to her again happening to be when Fanny was present, she calmly observed to her, "So, Fanny, you are going to leave us, and live with my sister. How shall you like it?"

Fanny was too much surprised to do more than repeat her aunt's words, "Going to leave you?"

"Yes, my dear; why should you be astonished? You have been five years with us, and my sister always meant to take you when Mr. Norris died. But you must come up and tack on my patterns all the same."

The news was as disagreeable to Fanny as it had been unexpected. She had never received kindness from her aunt Norris, and could not love her.

"I shall be very sorry to go away," said she, with a faltering voice.

"Yes, I dare say you will; *that's* natural enough. I suppose you have had as little to vex you since you came into this house as any creature in the world."

"I hope I am not ungrateful, aunt," said Fanny modestly.

"No, my dear; I hope not. I have always found you a very good girl."

"And am I never to live here again?"

"Never, my dear; but you are sure of a comfortable home. It can make very little difference to you, whether you are in one house or the other."

Fanny left the room with a very sorrowful heart; she could not feel the difference to be so small, she could not think of living with her aunt with anything like satisfaction. As soon as she met with Edmund she told him her distress.

"Cousin," said she, "something is going to happen which I do not like at all; and though you have often persuaded me into being reconciled to things that I disliked at first, you will not be able to do it now. I am going to live entirely with my aunt Norris."

"Indeed!"

"Yes; my aunt Bertram has just told me so. It is quite settled. I am to leave Mansfield Park, and go to the White House, I suppose, as soon as she is removed there."

"Well, Fanny, and if the plan were not unpleasant to you, I should call it an excellent one."

"Oh, cousin!"

Edmund reached for Fanny's hands and brought them nearer his heart, a gesture to which she had grown familiar as her cousin was known for his caring ways, though as she had grown into a young woman, she did find she felt differently under his touch. She found the difference difficult to describe other than it lacked the ease of her youth, and she often felt the colour rise to her face when he was close.

"It has everything else in its favour. My aunt is acting like a sensible woman in wishing for you. She is choosing a friend and companion exactly where she ought, and I am glad her love of money does not interfere. You will be what you ought to be to her. I hope it does not distress you very much, Fanny?"

"Indeed it does: I cannot like it. I love this house and everything in it: I shall love nothing there. You know how uncomfortable I feel with her."

"I can say nothing for her manner to you as a child; but it was the same with us all, or nearly so. She never knew how to be pleasant to children. But you are now of an age to be treated better; I think she is behaving better already; and when you are her only companion, you *must* be important to her."

"I can never be important to any one."

"What is to prevent you?"

"Everything. My situation, my foolishness and awkwardness."

"As to your foolishness and awkwardness, my dear Fanny, believe me, you never have a shadow of either, but in using the words so improperly. There is no reason in the world why you should not be important where you are known. You have good sense, and a sweet temper, and I am sure you have a grateful heart, that could never receive kindness without wishing to return it. I do not know any better qualifications for a friend and companion."

"You are too kind," said Fanny, colouring further at such praise and the manner in which he continued to gaze upon her; "how shall I ever thank you as I ought, for thinking so well of me. Oh! cousin, if I am to go away, I shall remember your goodness to the last moment of my life."

"Why, indeed, Fanny, I should hope to be remembered at such a distance as the White House. You speak as if you were going two hundred miles off instead of only across the park; but you will belong to us almost as much as ever. The two families will be meeting every day in the year. The only difference will be that, living with your aunt, you will necessarily be brought forward as you ought to be. *Here* there are too many whom you can hide behind; but with *her* you will be forced to speak for yourself."

"Oh! I do not say so."

Edmund released her hands but in the same moment used his own to lift her chin so he could see her eyes more carefully. "I must say it, and say it with pleasure. Mrs. Norris is much better fitted than my mother for having the charge of you now. She is of a temper to do a great deal for anybody she really interests herself about, and she will force you to do justice to your natural powers."

Fanny sighed as she turned away, and said, "I cannot see things as you do; but I ought to believe you to be right rather than myself, and I am very much obliged to you for trying to reconcile me to what must be. If I could suppose my aunt really to care for me, it would be delightful to feel myself of consequence to anybody. *Here*, I know, I am of none, and yet I love the place so well."

"The place, Fanny, is what you will not quit, though you quit the house. You will have as free a command of the park and gardens as ever. Even *your* constant little heart need not take fright at such a nominal change. You will have the same walks to frequent, the same library to choose from, the same people to look at, the same horse to ride."

"Very true. Yes, dear old grey pony! Ah! cousin, when I remember how much I used to dread riding, what terrors it gave me to hear it talked of as likely to do me good (oh! how I have trembled at my uncle's opening his lips if horses were talked of), and then think of the kind pains you took to reason and persuade me out of my fears, and convince me that I should like it after a little while, and feel how right you proved to be, I am inclined to hope you may always prophesy as well." And she considered once more how fortunate she was in her circumstances; how fortunate was she to have the love and care of her relatives.

"And I am quite convinced that your being with Mrs. Norris will be as good for your mind as riding has been for your health, and as much for your ultimate happiness too."

So ended their discourse, which, for any very appropriate service it could render Fanny, might as well have been spared, for Mrs. Norris had not the smallest intention of taking her. It had never occurred to her, on the present occasion, but as a thing to be carefully avoided. To prevent its being expected, she had fixed on the smallest habitation which could rank as genteel among the buildings of Mansfield parish, the White House being only just large enough to receive herself and her servants, and allow a spare room for a friend, of which she made a very particular point. The spare rooms at the Parsonage had never been wanted, but the absolute necessity of a spare room for a friend was now never forgotten. Not all her precautions, however, could save her from being suspected of something better; or, perhaps, her very display of the importance of a spare room might have misled Sir Thomas to suppose it really intended for Fanny. Lady Bertram soon brought the matter to a certainty by carelessly observing to Mrs. Norris —

"I think, sister, we need not keep Miss Lee any longer, when Fanny goes to live with you."

Mrs. Norris almost started. "Live with me, dear Lady Bertram! what do you mean?"

"Is she not to live with you? I thought you had settled it with Sir Thomas."

"Me! Never. I never spoke a syllable about it to Sir Thomas, nor he to me. Fanny live with me! The last thing in the world for me to think of, or for anybody to wish that really knows us both. Good heaven! what could I do with Fanny? Me! a poor, helpless, forlorn widow, unfit for anything, my spirits quite broke down; what could I do with a girl at her time of life? A girl of fifteen! the very age of all others to need most attention and care, and put the cheerfullest spirits to the test! Sure Sir Thomas could not seriously expect such a thing! Sir Thomas is too much my friend. Nobody that wishes me well, I am sure, would propose it. How came Sir Thomas to speak to you about it?"

"Indeed, I do not know. I suppose he thought it best."

"But what did he say? He could not say he *wished* me to take Fanny. I am sure in his heart he could not wish me to do it."

"No; he only said he thought it very likely; and I thought so too. We both thought it would be a comfort to you. But if you do not like it, there is no more to be said. She is no encumbrance here."

"Dear sister, if you consider my unhappy state, how can she be any comfort to me? Here am I, a poor desolate widow, deprived of the best of husbands, my health gone in attending and nursing him, my spirits still worse, all my peace in this world destroyed, with hardly enough to support me in the rank of a gentlewoman, and enable me to live so as not to disgrace the memory of the dear departed—what possible comfort could I have in taking such a charge upon me as Fanny? If I could wish it for my own sake, I would not do so unjust a thing by the poor girl. She is in good hands, and sure of doing well. I must struggle through my sorrows and difficulties as I can."

"Then you will not mind living by yourself quite alone?"

"Lady Bertram, I do not complain. I know I cannot live as I have done, but I must retrench where I can, and learn to be a better manager. I *have been* a liberal housekeeper enough, but I shall not be ashamed to practise economy now. My situation is as much altered as my income. A great many things were due from poor Mr. Norris, as clergyman of the parish, that cannot be expected from me. It is unknown how much was consumed in our kitchen by odd comers and goers. At the White House, matters must be better looked after. I *must* live within my income, or I shall be miserable; and I own it would give me great satisfaction to be able to do rather more, to lay by a little at the end of the year."

"I dare say you will. You always do, don't you?"

"My object, Lady Bertram, is to be of use to those that come after me. It is for your children's good that I wish to be richer. I have nobody else to care for, but I should be very glad to think I could leave a little trifle among them worth their having."

"You are very good, but do not trouble yourself about them. They are sure of being well provided for. Sir Thomas will take care of that."

"Why, you know, Sir Thomas's means will be rather straitened if the Antigua estate is to make such poor returns."

"Oh! *that* will soon be settled. Sir Thomas has been writing about it, I know."

"Well, Lady Bertram," said Mrs. Norris, moving to go, "I can only say that my sole desire is to be of use to your family: and so, if Sir Thomas should ever speak again about my taking Fanny, you will be able to say that my health and spirits put it quite out of the question; besides that, I really should not have a bed to give her, for I must keep a spare room for a friend."

It was as they lay in bed with the light of the moon streaming through the window that Lady Bertram repeated enough of this conversation to her husband to convince him how much he had mistaken his sister-in-law's views; and she was from that moment perfectly safe from all expectation, or the slightest allusion to it from him. He began to speak his objections to his wife when she in turn moved to persuade him that words were not necessary as she lifted his nightclothes and reached for him. It had been many years since they first formed their union and, indeed, he knew himself to be fortunate her eagerness for him had never dulled; but he found himself desiring for once to complete a discussion. As he opened his mouth to assert as much, she covered it with her own while rising up to straddle him. The feel of her warm tongue in his mouth and the soft thickness of her legs and the roundness of her bottom over him became a distraction for which he found himself most willing. She moved her mouth to brush it gently across his chest. "My dearest, Sir Thomas. Is not this activity much more pleasant than the discussion of family matters?" asked she. "I cannot be certain of that, Lady Bertram," he replied, pretending ignorance, "for I have no knowledge of this activity for which you advocate." She laughed softly and while doing so looked twenty years younger, as he himself felt twenty years younger when she reached for him and brought him inside her. They both gasped as he entered her fully. "Perhaps this will awaken your memory," she said as she began to ride him. He closed his eyes while she lifted herself up and then down, and he moved his own hips to match her soft rhythm. He rose on his elbows to fleck her dark and hardened nipples with his tongue. She moaned in soft ecstasy as she continued to rock her hips over him. He considered allowing himself the satisfaction of spending himself inside her right there, but the sight of her fullness above him—her stomach soft and plump from birthing their children, her bosom heavy with her years—and the remembrance of the many night she stroked him to ecstasy whilst asking nothing for herself other than his pleasure, stirred him to offer her more on this moonlit night. He reached up and gently lifted her from him. She began to object, and then he turned her around and swiftly entered her from behind, the sound of her eager cries and the sight of her ample bottom beneath him nearly leading to his swift release. He forced himself to steady his breathing as he reached around her to find her most sensitive place, his touch steady and rhythmic as he continued to thrust within her whilst she called out his given name. "This activity is most familiar to me now," he whispered before teasing the back of her ear with his tongue. "Let go, my darling Maria. Let go." And she did, collapsing onto the sheet as he filled her. They lay together with their breaths in harmony before Sir Thomas pulled himself from her and gently guided her towards a pillow. Lady Bertram smiled sleepily. Sir Thomas kissed her brow and allowed himself to drift into slumber.

Upon first light, Sir Thomas's wished his thoughts could rest on the warmth of his wife who lay sleeping next to him. But as he rose, he found that he must think again of his sister-in-law. He could not but wonder at her refusing to do anything for a niece whom she had been so forward to adopt; but, as she took early care to make him, as well as Lady Bertram, understand that whatever she possessed was designed for their family, he soon grew reconciled to a distinction which, at the same time that it was advantageous and complimentary to them, would enable him better to provide for Fanny himself.

Fanny soon learnt how unnecessary had been her fears of a removal; and her spontaneous, untaught felicity on the discovery, conveyed some consolation to Edmund for his disappointment in what he had expected to be so essentially serviceable to her. Mrs. Norris took possession of the White House, the Grants arrived at the Parsonage, and these events over, everything at Mansfield went on for some time as usual.

The Grants showing a disposition to be friendly and sociable, gave great satisfaction in the main among their new acquaintance. They had their faults, and Mrs. Norris soon found them out. The Doctor was very fond of eating, and would have a good dinner every day; and Mrs. Grant, instead of contriving to gratify him at little expense, gave her cook as high wages as they did at Mansfield Park, and was scarcely ever seen in her offices. Mrs. Norris could not speak with any temper of such grievances, nor of the quantity of butter and eggs that were regularly consumed in the house. "Nobody loved plenty and hospitality more than herself; nobody more hated pitiful doings; the Parsonage, she believed, had never been wanting in comforts of any sort, had never borne a bad character in *her time*, but this was a way of going on that she could not understand. A fine lady in a country parsonage was quite out of place. *Her* store-room, she thought, might have been good enough for Mrs. Grant to go into. Inquire where she would, she could not find out that Mrs. Grant had ever had more than five thousand pounds."

Lady Bertram listened without much interest to this sort of invective. She could not enter into the wrongs of an economist, but she felt all the injuries of beauty in Mrs. Grant's being so well settled in life without being handsome, and expressed her astonishment on that point almost as often, though not so diffusely, as Mrs. Norris discussed the other.

These opinions had been hardly canvassed a year before another event arose of such importance in the family, as might fairly claim some place in the thoughts and conversation of the ladies. Sir Thomas found it expedient to go to Antigua himself, for the better arrangement of his affairs, and he took his eldest son with him, in the hope of detaching him from some bad connexions at home. They left England with the probability of being nearly a twelvemonth absent.

The necessity of the measure in a pecuniary light, and the hope of its utility to his son, reconciled Sir Thomas to the effort of quitting the rest of his family, and of leaving his daughters to the direction of others at their present most interesting time of life. He could not think Lady Bertram quite equal to supply his place with them, or rather, to perform what should have been her own; but, in Mrs. Norris's watchful attention, and in Edmund's judgment, he had sufficient confidence to make him go without fears for their conduct.

Lady Bertram did not at all like to have her husband leave her; whom else could she reach towards in the moonlight? But she was not disturbed by any alarm for his safety, or solicitude for his comfort, being one of those persons who think nothing can be dangerous, or difficult, or fatiguing to anybody but themselves.

The Miss Bertrams were much to be pitied on the occasion: not for their sorrow, but for their want of it. Their father was no object of love to them; he had never seemed the friend of their pleasures, and his absence was unhappily most welcome. They were relieved by it from all restraint; and without aiming at one gratification that would probably have been forbidden by Sir Thomas, they felt themselves immediately at their own disposal, and to have every indulgence within their reach. Fanny's relief, and her consciousness of it, were quite equal to her cousins'; but a more tender nature suggested that her feelings were ungrateful, and she really grieved because she could not grieve. "Sir Thomas, who had done so much for her and her brothers, and who was gone perhaps never to return! that she should see him go without a tear! it was a shameful insensibility." He had said to her, moreover, on the very last morning, that he hoped she might see William again in the course of the ensuing winter, and had charged her to write and invite him to Mansfield as soon as the squadron to which he belonged should be known to be in England. "This was so thoughtful and kind!" and would he only have smiled upon her, and called her "my dear Fanny," while he said it, every former frown or cold address might have been forgotten. But he had ended his speech in a way to sink her in sad mortification, by adding, "If William does come to Mansfield, I hope you may be able to convince him that the many years which have passed since you parted have not been spent on your side entirely without improvement; though, I fear, he must find his sister at sixteen in some respects too much like his sister at ten." She cried bitterly over this reflection when her uncle was gone; and her cousins, on seeing her with red eyes, set her down as a hypocrite.

Chapter 4

Tom Bertram had of late spent so little of his time at home that he could be only nominally missed; and Lady Bertram was soon astonished to find how very well they did even without his father, how well Edmund could supply his place in carving, talking to the steward, writing to the attorney, settling with the servants, and equally saving her from all possible fatigue or exertion in every particular but that of directing her letters.

The earliest intelligence of the travellers' safe arrival at Antigua, after a favourable voyage, was received; though not before Mrs. Norris had been indulging in very dreadful fears, and trying to make Edmund participate them whenever she could get him alone; and as she depended on being the first person made acquainted with any fatal catastrophe, she had already arranged the manner of breaking it to all the others, when Sir Thomas's assurances of their both being alive and well made it necessary to lay by her agitation and affectionate preparatory speeches for a while.

The winter came and passed without their being called for; the accounts continued perfectly good; and Mrs. Norris, in promoting gaieties for her nieces, assisting their toilets, displaying their accomplishments, and looking about for their future husbands, had so much to do as, in addition to all her own household cares, some interference in those of her sister, and Mrs. Grant's wasteful doings to overlook, left her very little occasion to be occupied in fears for the absent.

The Miss Bertrams were now fully established among the belles of the neighbourhood; and as they joined to beauty and brilliant acquirements a manner naturally easy, and carefully formed to general civility and obligingness, they possessed its favour as well as its admiration. Their vanity was in such good order that they seemed to be quite free from it, and gave themselves no airs; while the praises attending such behaviour, secured and brought round by their aunt, served to strengthen them in believing they had no faults.

Lady Bertram did not go into public with her daughters. She was too indolent even to accept a mother's gratification in witnessing their success and enjoyment at the expense of any personal trouble, and the charge was made over to her sister, who desired nothing better than a post of such honourable representation, and very thoroughly relished the means it afforded her of mixing in society without having horses to hire.

Fanny had no share in the festivities of the season; but she enjoyed being avowedly useful as her aunt's companion when they called away the rest of the family; and, as Miss Lee had left Mansfield, she naturally became everything to Lady Bertram during the night of a ball or a party. She talked to her, listened to her, read to her; and the tranquillity of such evenings, her perfect security in such a *tete-a-tete* from any sound of unkindness, was unspeakably welcome to a mind which had seldom known a pause in its alarms or embarrassments. As to her cousins' gaieties, she loved to hear an account of them, especially of the balls, and whom Edmund had danced with; but thought too lowly of her own situation to imagine she should ever be admitted to the same, and listened, therefore, without an idea of any nearer concern in them. It would be contrary to presume that Fanny could not picture herself dancing for she had been well instructed on the steps growing up with her cousins. It was most likely that she could not conceive, even in the deepest recesses of her imagination, what it would be to dance with one not attached to Mansfield. But upon the whole, it was a comfortable winter to her, even though it brought no opportunity for her own dancing; for though it brought no William to England, the never-failing hope of his arrival was worth much.

The ensuing spring deprived her of her valued friend, the old grey pony; and for some time she was in danger of feeling the loss in her health as well as in her affections; for in spite of the acknowledged importance of her riding on horse-back, no measures were taken for mounting her again, "because," as it was observed by her aunts, "she might ride one of her cousin's horses at any time when they did not want them," and as the Miss Bertrams regularly wanted their horses every fine day, and had no idea of carrying their obliging manners to the sacrifice of any real pleasure, that time, of course, never came. They took their cheerful rides in the fine mornings of April and May; and Fanny either sat at home the whole day with one aunt, or walked beyond her strength at the instigation of the other: Lady Bertram holding exercise to be as unnecessary for everybody as it was unpleasant to herself; and Mrs. Norris, who was walking all day, thinking everybody ought to walk as much. Edmund was absent at this time, or the evil would have been earlier remedied. When he returned, to understand how Fanny was situated, and perceived its ill effects, there seemed with him but one thing to be done; and that "Fanny must have a horse" was the resolute declaration with which he opposed whatever could be urged by the supineness of his mother, or the economy of his aunt, to make it appear unimportant. Mrs. Norris could not help thinking that some steady old thing might be found among the numbers belonging to the Park that would do vastly well; or that one might be borrowed of the steward; or that perhaps Dr. Grant might now and then lend them the pony he sent to the post. She could not but consider it as absolutely unnecessary, and even improper, that Fanny should have a regular lady's horse of her own, in the style of her cousins. She was sure Sir Thomas had never intended it: and she must say that, to be making such a purchase in his absence, and adding to the great expenses of his stable, at a time when a large part of his income was unsettled, seemed to her very unjustifiable. "Fanny must have a horse," was Edmund's only reply. Mrs. Norris could not see it in the same light. Lady Bertram did: she entirely agreed with her son as to the necessity of it, and as to its being considered necessary by his father; she only pleaded against there being any hurry; she only wanted him to wait till Sir Thomas's return, and then Sir Thomas might settle it all himself. He would be at home in September, and where would be the harm of only waiting till September?

Though Edmund was much more displeased with his aunt than with his mother, as evincing least regard for her niece, he could not help paying more attention to what she said; and at length determined on a method of proceeding which would obviate the risk of his father's thinking he had done too much, and at the same time procure for Fanny the immediate means of exercise, which he could not bear she should be without. He had three horses of his own, but not one that would carry a woman. Two of them were hunters; the third, a useful road-horse: this third he resolved to exchange for one that his cousin might ride; he knew where such a one was to be met with; and having once made up his mind, the whole business was soon completed. The new mare proved a treasure; with a very little trouble she became exactly calculated for the purpose, and Fanny was then put in almost full possession of her. She had not supposed before that anything could ever suit her like the old grey pony; but her delight in Edmund's mare was far beyond any former pleasure of the sort; and the addition it was ever receiving in the consideration of that kindness from which her pleasure sprung, was beyond all her words to express. She regarded her cousin as an example of everything good and great, as possessing worth which no one but herself could ever appreciate, and as entitled to such gratitude from her as no feelings could be strong enough to pay. Her sentiments towards him were compounded of all that was respectful, grateful, confiding, and tender.

As the horse continued in name, as well as fact, the property of Edmund, Mrs. Norris could tolerate its being for Fanny's use;

and had Lady Bertram ever thought about her own objection again, he might have been excused in her eyes for not waiting till Sir Thomas's return in September, for when September came Sir Thomas was still abroad, and without any near prospect of finishing his business. Unfavourable circumstances had suddenly arisen at a moment when he was beginning to turn all his thoughts towards England; and the very great uncertainty in which everything was then involved determined him on sending home his son, and waiting the final arrangement by himself. Tom arrived safely, bringing an excellent account of his father's health; but to very little purpose, as far as Mrs. Norris was concerned. Sir Thomas's sending away his son seemed to her so like a parent's care, under the influence of a foreboding of evil to himself, that she could not help feeling dreadful presentiments; and as the long evenings of autumn came on, was so terribly haunted by these ideas, in the sad solitariness of her cottage, as to be obliged to take daily refuge in the dining-room of the Park. The return of winter engagements, however, was not without its effect; and in the course of their progress, her mind became so pleasantly occupied in superintending the fortunes of her eldest niece, as tolerably to quiet her nerves. "If poor Sir Thomas were fated never to return, it would be peculiarly consoling to see their dear Maria well married," she very often thought; always when they were in the company of men of fortune, and particularly on the introduction of a young man who had recently succeeded to one of the largest estates and finest places in the country.

Mr. Rushworth was from the first struck with the beauty of Miss Bertram, and, being inclined to marry, soon fancied himself in love. He was a heavy young man, with not more than common sense; but as there was nothing disagreeable in his figure or address, the young lady was well pleased with her conquest. Being now in her twenty-first year, Maria Bertram was beginning to think matrimony a duty; and as a marriage with Mr. Rushworth would give her the enjoyment of a larger income than her father's, as well as ensure her the house in town, which was now a prime object, it became, by the same rule of moral obligation, her evident duty to marry Mr. Rushworth if she could. Mrs. Norris was most zealous in promoting the match, by every suggestion and contrivance likely to enhance its desirableness to either party; and, among other means, by seeking an intimacy with the gentleman's mother, who at present lived with him, and to whom she even forced Lady Bertram to go through ten miles of indifferent road to pay a morning visit. It was not long before a good understanding took place between this lady and herself. Mrs. Rushworth acknowledged herself very desirous that her son should marry, and declared that of all the young ladies she had ever seen, Miss Bertram seemed, by her amiable qualities and accomplishments, the best adapted to make him happy. Mrs. Norris accepted the compliment, and admired the nice discernment of character which could so well distinguish merit. Maria was indeed the pride and delight of them all—perfectly faultless—an angel; and, of course, so surrounded by admirers, must be difficult in her choice: but yet, as far as Mrs. Norris could allow herself to decide on so short an acquaintance, Mr. Rushworth appeared precisely the young man to deserve and attach her.

After dancing with each other at a proper number of balls, the young people justified these opinions, and an engagement, with a due reference to the absent Sir Thomas, was entered into, much to the satisfaction of their respective families, and of the general lookers-on of the neighbourhood, who had, for many weeks past, felt the expediency of Mr. Rushworth's marrying Miss Bertram.

It was some months before Sir Thomas's consent could be received; but, in the meanwhile, as no one felt a doubt of his most cordial pleasure in the connexion, the intercourse of the two families was carried on without restraint, and no other attempt made at secrecy than Mrs. Norris's talking of it everywhere as a matter not to be talked of at present.

Edmund was the only one of the family who could see a fault in the business; but no representation of his aunt's could induce him to find Mr. Rushworth a desirable companion. He could allow his sister to be the best judge of her own happiness, but he was not pleased that her happiness should centre in a large income; nor could he refrain from often saying to himself, in Mr. Rushworth's company—"If this man had not twelve thousand a year, he would be a very stupid fellow."

Sir Thomas, however, was truly happy in the prospect of an alliance so unquestionably advantageous, and of which he heard nothing but the perfectly good and agreeable. It was a connexion exactly of the right sort—in the same county, and the same interest—and his most hearty concurrence was conveyed as soon as possible. He only conditioned that the marriage should not take place before his return, which he was again looking eagerly forward to. He wrote in April, and had strong hopes of settling everything to his entire satisfaction, and leaving Antigua before the end of the summer.

Such was the state of affairs in the month of July; and Fanny had just reached her eighteenth year, when the society of the village received an addition in the brother and sister of Mrs. Grant, a Mr. and Miss Crawford, the children of her mother by a second marriage. They were young people of fortune. The son had a good estate in Norfolk, the daughter twenty thousand pounds. As children, their sister had been always very fond of them; but, as her own marriage had been soon followed by the death of their common parent, which left them to the care of a brother of their father, of whom Mrs. Grant knew nothing, she had scarcely seen them since. In their uncle's house they had found a kind home. Admiral and Mrs. Crawford, though agreeing in nothing else, were united in affection for these children, or, at least, were no farther adverse in their feelings than that each had their favourite, to whom they showed the greatest fondness of the two. The Admiral delighted in the boy, Mrs. Crawford doted on the girl; and it was the lady's death which now obliged her *protégée*, after some months' further trial at her uncle's house, to find another home. Admiral Crawford was a man of vicious conduct, who chose, instead of retaining his niece, to bring his mistress under his own roof; and to this Mrs. Grant was indebted for her sister's proposal of coming to her, a measure quite as welcome on one side as it could be expedient on the other; for Mrs. Grant, having by this time run through the usual resources of ladies residing in the country without a family of children—having more than filled her favourite sitting-room with pretty furniture, and made a choice collection of plants and poultry—was very much in want of some variety at home. The arrival, therefore, of a sister whom she had always loved, and now hoped to retain with her as long as she remained single, was highly agreeable; and her chief anxiety was lest Mansfield should not satisfy the habits of a young woman who had been mostly used to London.

Miss Crawford was not entirely free from similar apprehensions, though they arose principally from doubts of her sister's style of living and tone of society; and it was not till after she had tried in vain to persuade her brother to settle with her at his own country house, that she could resolve to hazard herself among her other relations. To anything like a permanence of abode, or limitation of society, Henry Crawford had, unluckily, a great dislike: he could not accommodate his sister in an article of such importance; but he escorted her, with the utmost kindness, into Northamptonshire, and as readily engaged to fetch her away again, at half an hour's notice, whenever she were weary of the place.

The meeting was very satisfactory on each side. Miss Crawford found a sister without preciseness or rusticity, a sister's husband who looked the gentleman, and a house commodious and well fitted up; and Mrs. Grant received in those whom she hoped to love better than ever a young man and woman of very prepossessing appearance. Mary Crawford was remarkably pretty with dark hair and eyes, and a fine figure; Henry, with the same dark eyes, though not handsome, had air and countenance; the manners of both were lively and pleasant, and Mrs. Grant immediately gave them credit for everything else. She was delighted with each, but Mary was her dearest object; and having never been able to glory in beauty of her own, she thoroughly enjoyed the power of being proud of her sister's. She had not waited her arrival to look out for a suitable match for her: she had fixed on Tom Bertram; the eldest son of a baronet was not too good for a girl of twenty thousand pounds, with all the elegance and accomplishments which Mrs. Grant foresaw in her; and being a warm-hearted, unreserved woman, Mary had not been three hours in the house before she told her what she had planned.

Miss Crawford was glad to find a family of such consequence so very near them, and not at all displeased either at her sister's early care, or the choice it had fallen on. Matrimony was her object, provided she could marry well: and having seen Mr. Bertram in town, she knew that objection could no more be made to his person than to his situation in life. While she treated it as a joke, therefore, she did not forget to think of it seriously. The scheme was soon repeated to Henry.

"And now," added Mrs. Grant, "I have thought of something to make it complete. I should dearly love to settle you both in this country; and therefore, Henry, you shall marry the youngest Miss Bertram, a nice, handsome, good-humoured, accomplished girl, who will make you very happy."

Henry bowed and thanked her.

"My dear sister," said Mary, "if you can persuade him into anything of the sort, it will be a fresh matter of delight to me to find myself allied to anybody so clever, and I shall only regret that you have not half a dozen daughters to dispose of. If you can persuade Henry to marry, you must have the address of a Frenchwoman. All that English abilities can do has been tried already. I have three very particular friends who have been all dying for him in their turn; and the pains which they, their mothers (very clever women), as well as my dear aunt and myself, have taken to reason, coax, or trick him into marrying, is inconceivable! He is the most horrible flirt that can be imagined. If your Miss Bertrams do not like to have their hearts broke, let them avoid Henry."

"My dear brother, I will not believe this of you."

"No, I am sure you are too good. You will be kinder than Mary. You will allow for the doubts of youth and inexperience. I am of a cautious temper, and unwilling to risk my happiness in a hurry. Nobody can think more highly of the matrimonial state than myself. I consider the blessing of a wife as most justly described in those discreet lines of the poet—'Heaven's *last* best gift.'"

"There, Mrs. Grant, you see how he dwells on one word, and only look at his smile. I assure you he is very detestable; the Admiral's lessons have quite spoiled him."

"I pay very little regard," said Mrs. Grant, "to what any young person says on the subject of marriage. If they profess a disinclination for it, I only set it down that they have not yet seen the right person."

Dr. Grant laughingly congratulated Miss Crawford on feeling no disinclination to the state herself.

"Oh yes! I am not at all ashamed of it. I would have everybody marry if they can do it properly: I do not like to have people throw themselves away; but everybody should marry as soon as they can do it to advantage."

Chapter 5

The young people were pleased with each other from the first. On each side there was much to attract, and their acquaintance soon promised as early an intimacy as good manners would warrant. Miss Crawford's beauty did her no disservice with the Miss Bertrams. They were too handsome themselves to dislike any woman for being so too, and were almost as much charmed as their brothers with her lively dark eye, clear brown complexion, and general prettiness. Had she been tall, full formed, and fair, it might have been more of a trial: but as it was, there could be no comparison; and she was most allowably a sweet, pretty girl, while they were the finest young women in the country.

Her brother was not handsome: no, when they first saw him he was absolutely plain, black and plain; but still he was the gentleman, with a pleasing address. The second meeting proved him not so very plain: he was plain, to be sure, but then he had so much countenance, and his teeth were so good, and he was so well made, his shoulders broad and his breeches well fitting, that one soon forgot he was plain; and after a third interview, after dining in company with him at the Parsonage, he was no longer allowed to be called so by anybody. He was, in fact, the most agreeable young man the sisters had ever known, and they were equally delighted with him. Miss Bertram's engagement made him in equity the property of Julia, of which Julia was fully aware; and before he had been at Mansfield a week, she was quite ready to be fallen in love with.

Maria's notions on the subject were more confused and indistinct. She did not want to see or understand. "There could be no harm in her liking an agreeable man—everybody knew her situation—Mr. Crawford must take care of himself." Mr.

Crawford did not mean to be in any danger! the Miss Bertrams were worth pleasing, and were ready to be pleased; and he began with no object but of making them like him. He did not want them to die of love; but with sense and temper which ought to have made him judge and feel better, he allowed himself great latitude on such points.

"I like your Miss Bertrams exceedingly, sister," said he, as he returned from attending them to their carriage after the said dinner visit; "they are very elegant, agreeable girls."

"So they are indeed, and I am delighted to hear you say it. But you like Julia best."

"Oh yes! I like Julia best."

"But do you really? for Miss Bertram is in general thought the handsomest."

"So I should suppose. She has the advantage in every feature, and I prefer her countenance; but I like Julia best; Miss Bertram is certainly the handsomest, and I have found her the most agreeable, but I shall always like Julia best, because you order me."

"I shall not talk to you, Henry, but I know you *will* like her best at last."

"Do not I tell you that I like her best *at first?*"

"And besides, Miss Bertram is engaged. Remember that, my dear brother. Her choice is made."

"Yes, and I like her the better for it. An engaged woman is always more agreeable than a disengaged. She is satisfied with herself. Her cares are over, and she feels that she may exert all her powers of pleasing without suspicion. All is safe with a lady engaged: no harm can be done."

"Why, as to that, Mr. Rushworth is a very good sort of young man, and it is a great match for her."

"But Miss Bertram does not care three straws for him; *that* is your opinion of your intimate friend. *I* do not subscribe to it. I am sure Miss Bertram is very much attached to Mr. Rushworth. I could see it in her eyes, when he was mentioned. I think too well of Miss Bertram to suppose she would ever give her hand without her heart."

"Mary, how shall we manage him?"

"We must leave him to himself, I believe. Talking does no good. He will be taken in at last."

"But I would not have him *taken in*; I would not have him duped; I would have it all fair and honourable."

"Oh dear! let him stand his chance and be taken in. It will do just as well. Everybody is taken in at some period or other."

"Not always in marriage, dear Mary."

"In marriage especially. With all due respect to such of the present company as chance to be married, my dear Mrs. Grant, there is not one in a hundred of either sex who is not taken in when they marry. Look where I will, I see that it *is* so; and I feel that it *must* be so, when I consider that it is, of all transactions, the one in which people expect most from others, and are least honest themselves."

"Ah! You have been in a bad school for matrimony, in Hill Street."

"My poor aunt had certainly little cause to love the state; but, however, speaking from my own observation, it is a manoeuvring business. I know so many who have married in the full expectation and confidence of some one particular advantage in the connexion, or accomplishment, or good quality in the person, who have found themselves entirely deceived, and been obliged to put up with exactly the reverse. What is this but a take in?"

"My dear child, there must be a little imagination here. I beg your pardon, but I cannot quite believe you. Depend upon it, you see but half. You see the evil, but you do not see the consolation. There will be little rubs and disappointments everywhere, and we are all apt to expect too much; but then, if one scheme of happiness fails, human nature turns to another; if the first calculation is wrong, we make a second better: we find comfort somewhere—and those evil-minded observers, dearest Mary, who make much of a little, are more taken in and deceived than the parties themselves."

"Well done, sister! I honour your *esprit du corps*. When I am a wife, I mean to be just as staunch myself; and I wish my friends in general would be so too. It would save me many a heartache."

"You are as bad as your brother, Mary; but we will cure you both. Mansfield shall cure you both, and without any taking in. Stay with us, and we will cure you."

The Crawfords, without wanting to be cured, were very willing to stay. Mary was satisfied with the Parsonage as a present home, and Henry equally ready to lengthen his visit. He had come, intending to spend only a few days with them; but Mansfield promised well, and there was nothing to call him elsewhere. It delighted Mrs. Grant to keep them both with her, and Dr. Grant was exceedingly well contented to have it so: a talking pretty young woman like Miss Crawford is always pleasant society to an indolent, stay-at-home man; and Mr. Crawford's being his guest was an excuse for drinking claret every day.

The Miss Bertrams' admiration of Mr. Crawford was more rapturous than anything which Miss Crawford's habits made her likely to feel. She acknowledged, however, that the Mr. Bertrams were very fine young men, that two such young men were not often seen together even in London, and that their manners, particularly those of the eldest, were very good. *He* had been much in London, and had more liveliness and gallantry than Edmund, and must, therefore, be preferred; and, indeed, his being the eldest was another strong claim. She had felt an early presentiment that she *should* like the eldest best. She knew it was her way.

Tom Bertram must have been thought pleasant, indeed, at any rate; he was the sort of young man to be generally liked, his agreeableness was of the kind to be oftener found agreeable than some endowments of a higher stamp, for he had easy manners, excellent spirits, a large acquaintance, and a great deal to say; and the reversion of Mansfield Park, and a baronetcy, did no harm to all this. Miss Crawford soon felt that he and his situation might do. She looked about her with due consideration, and found almost everything in his favour: a park, a real park, five miles round, a spacious modern-built house, so well placed and well screened as to deserve to be in any collection of engravings of gentlemen's seats in the kingdom, and wanting only to be completely new furnished—pleasant sisters, a quiet mother, and an agreeable man himself—with the advantage of being tied up from much gaming at present by a promise to his father, and of being Sir Thomas hereafter. It might do very well; she believed she should accept him; and she began accordingly to interest herself a little about the horse which he had to run at the B—— races.

These races were to call him away not long after their acquaintance began; and as it appeared that the family did not, from his usual goings on, expect him back again for many weeks, it would bring his passion to an early proof. Much was said on his side to induce her to attend the races, and schemes were made for a large party to them, with all the eagerness of inclination, but it would only do to be talked of.

And Fanny, what was *she* doing and thinking all this while? and what was *her* opinion of the newcomers? Few young ladies of eighteen could be less called on to speak their opinion than Fanny. In a quiet way, very little attended to, she paid her tribute of admiration to Miss Crawford's beauty; but as she still continued to think Mr. Crawford very plain, in spite of her two cousins having repeatedly proved the contrary, she never mentioned *him*. The notice, which she excited herself, was to this effect. "I begin now to understand you all, except Miss Price," said Miss Crawford, as she was walking with the Mr. Bertrams. "Pray, is she out, or is she not? I am puzzled. She dined at the Parsonage, with the rest of you, which seemed like being *out*; and yet she says so little, that I can hardly suppose she *is*."

Edmund, to whom this was chiefly addressed, replied, "I believe I know what you mean, but I will not undertake to answer the question. My cousin is grown up. She has the age and sense of a woman, but the outs and not outs are beyond me." And indeed he did find himself in a silent state of perturbation, for if Fanny was not out and needed to be out, he was not certain such a status was within his means to acquire.

"And yet, in general, nothing can be more easily ascertained. The distinction is so broad. Manners as well as appearance are, generally speaking, so totally different. Till now, I could not have supposed it possible to be mistaken as to a girl's being out or not. A girl not out has always the same sort of dress: a close bonnet, for instance; looks very demure, and never says a word. You may smile, but it is so, I assure you; and except that it is sometimes carried a little too far, it is all very proper. Girls should be quiet and modest. The most objectionable part is, that the alteration of manners on being introduced into company is frequently too sudden. They sometimes pass in such very little time from reserve to quite the opposite—to confidence! *That* is the faulty part of the present system. One does not like to see a girl of eighteen or nineteen so immediately up to every thing—and perhaps when one has seen her hardly able to speak the year before. Mr. Bertram, I dare say *you* have sometimes met with such changes."

"I believe I have, but this is hardly fair; I see what you are at. You are quizzing me and Miss Anderson."

"No, indeed. Miss Anderson! I do not know who or what you mean. I am quite in the dark. But I *will* quiz you with a great deal of pleasure, if you will tell me what about."

"Ah! you carry it off very well, but I cannot be quite so far imposed on. You must have had Miss Anderson in your eye, in describing an altered young lady. You paint too accurately for mistake. It was exactly so. The Andersons of Baker Street. We were speaking of them the other day, you know. Edmund, you have heard me mention Charles Anderson. The circumstance was precisely as this lady has represented it. When Anderson first introduced me to his family, about two years ago, his sister was not *out*, and I could not get her to speak to me. I sat there an hour one morning waiting for Anderson, with only her and a little girl or two in the room, the governess being sick or run away, and the mother in and out every moment with letters of business, and I could hardly get a word or a look from the young lady—nothing like a civil answer—she screwed up her mouth, and turned from me with such an air! I did not see her again for a twelvemonth. She was then *out*. I met her at Mrs. Holford's, and did not recollect her. She came up to me, claimed me as an acquaintance, stared me out of countenance; and talked and laughed till I did not know which way to look. I felt that I must be the jest of the room at the time, and Miss Crawford, it is plain, has heard the story."

"And a very pretty story it is, and with more truth in it, I dare say, than does credit to Miss Anderson. It is too common a fault. Mothers certainly have not yet got quite the right way of managing their daughters. I do not know where the error lies. I do not pretend to set people right, but I do see that they are often wrong."

"Those who are showing the world what female manners *should* be," said Mr. Bertram gallantly, "are doing a great deal to set them right."

"The error is plain enough," said the less courteous Edmund; "such girls are ill brought up. They are given wrong notions from the beginning. They are always acting upon motives of vanity, and there is no more real modesty in their behaviour *before* they appear in public than afterwards."

"I do not know," replied Miss Crawford hesitatingly. "Yes, I cannot agree with you there. It is certainly the modestest part of the business. It is much worse to have girls not out give themselves the same airs and take the same liberties as if they were, which I have seen done. That is worse than anything—quite disgusting!"

"Yes, *that* is very inconvenient indeed," said Mr. Bertram. "It leads one astray; one does not know what to do. The close bonnet and demure air you describe so well (and nothing was ever juster), tell one what is expected; but I got into a dreadful scrape last year from the want of them. I went down to Ramsgate for a week with a friend last September, just after my return from the West Indies. My friend Sneyd—you have heard me speak of Sneyd, Edmund—his father, and mother, and sisters, were there, all new to me. When we reached Albion Place they were out; we went after them, and found them on the pier: Mrs. and the two Miss Sneyds, with others of their acquaintance. I made my bow in form; and as Mrs. Sneyd was surrounded by men, attached myself to one of her daughters, walked by her side all the way home, and made myself as agreeable as I could; the young lady perfectly easy in her manners, and as ready to talk as to listen. I had not a suspicion that I could be doing anything wrong. They looked just the same: both well-dressed, with veils and parasols like other girls; but I afterwards found that I had been giving all my attention to the youngest, who was not *out*, and had most excessively offended the eldest. Miss Augusta ought not to have been noticed for the next six months; and Miss Sneyd, I believe, has never forgiven me."

"That was bad indeed. Poor Miss Sneyd. Though I have no younger sister, I feel for her. To be neglected before one's time must be very vexatious; but it was entirely the mother's fault. Miss Augusta should have been with her governess. Such half-and-half doings never prosper. But now I must be satisfied about Miss Price. Does she go to balls? Does she dine out every where, as well as at my sister's?"

"No," replied Edmund; "I do not think she has ever been to a ball. My mother seldom goes into company herself, and dines nowhere but with Mrs. Grant, and Fanny stays at home with *her*."

"Oh! then the point is clear. Miss Price is not out."

Chapter 6

Mr. Bertram set off for _________ , and Miss Crawford was prepared to find a great chasm in their society, and to miss him decidedly in the meetings which were now becoming almost daily between the families; and on their all dining together at the Park soon after his going, she retook her chosen place near the bottom of the table, fully expecting to feel a most melancholy difference in the change of masters. It would be a very flat business, she was sure. In comparison with his brother, Edmund would have nothing to say. The soup would be sent round in a most spiritless manner, wine drank without any smiles or agreeable trifling, and the venison cut up without supplying one pleasant anecdote of any former haunch, or a single entertaining story, about "my friend such a one." She must try to find amusement in what was passing at the upper end of the table, and in observing Mr. Rushworth, who was now making his appearance at Mansfield for the first time since the Crawfords' arrival. He had been visiting a friend in the neighbouring county, and that friend having recently had his grounds laid out by an improver, Mr. Rushworth was returned with his head full of the subject, and very eager to be improving his own place in the same way; and though not saying much to the purpose, could talk of nothing else. The subject had been already handled in the drawing-room; it was revived in the dining-parlour. Miss Bertram's attention and opinion was evidently his chief aim; and though her deportment showed rather conscious superiority than any solicitude to oblige him, the mention of Sotherton Court, and the ideas attached to it, gave her a feeling of complacency, which prevented her from being very ungracious.

"I wish you could see Compton," said he; "it is the most complete thing! I never saw a place so altered in my life. I told

Smith I did not know where I was. The approach *now*, is one of the finest things in the country: you see the house in the most surprising manner. I declare, when I got back to Sotherton yesterday, it looked like a prison—quite a dismal old prison."

"Oh, for shame!" cried Mrs. Norris. "A prison indeed? Sotherton Court is the noblest old place in the world."

"It wants improvement, ma'am, beyond anything. I never saw a place that wanted so much improvement in my life; and it is so forlorn that I do not know what can be done with it."

"No wonder that Mr. Rushworth should think so at present," said Mrs. Grant to Mrs. Norris, with a smile; "but depend upon it, Sotherton will have *every* improvement in time which his heart can desire."

"I must try to do something with it," said Mr. Rushworth, "but I do not know what. I hope I shall have some good friend to help me."

"Your best friend upon such an occasion," said Miss Bertram calmly, "would be Mr. Repton, I imagine."

"That is what I was thinking of. As he has done so well by Smith, I think I had better have him at once. His terms are five guineas a day."

"Well, and if they were *ten*," cried Mrs. Norris, "I am sure *you* need not regard it. The expense need not be any impediment. If I were you, I should not think of the expense. I would have everything done in the best style, and made as nice as possible. Such a place as Sotherton Court deserves everything that taste and money can do. You have space to work upon there, and grounds that will well reward you. For my own part, if I had anything within the fiftieth part of the size of Sotherton, I should be always planting and improving, for naturally I am excessively fond of it. It would be too ridiculous for me to attempt anything where I am now, with my little half acre. It would be quite a burlesque. But if I had more room, I should take a prodigious delight in improving and planting. We did a vast deal in that way at the Parsonage: we made it quite a different place from what it was when we first had it. You young ones do not remember much about it, perhaps; but if dear Sir Thomas were here, he could tell you what improvements we made: and a great deal more would have been done, but for poor Mr. Norris's sad state of health. He could hardly ever get out, poor man, to enjoy anything, and *that* disheartened me from doing several things that Sir Thomas and I used to talk of. If it had not been for *that*, we should have carried on the garden wall, and made the plantation to shut out the churchyard, just as Dr. Grant has done. We were always doing something as it was. It was only the spring twelvemonth before Mr. Norris's death that we put in the apricot against the stable wall, which is now grown such a noble tree, and getting to such perfection, sir," addressing herself then to Dr. Grant.

"The tree thrives well, beyond a doubt, madam," replied Dr. Grant. "The soil is good; and I never pass it without regretting that the fruit should be so little worth the trouble of gathering."

"Sir, it is a Moor Park, we bought it as a Moor Park, and it cost us—that is, it was a present from Sir Thomas, but I saw the bill— and I know it cost seven shillings, and was charged as a Moor Park."

"You were imposed on, ma'am," replied Dr. Grant: "these potatoes have as much the flavour of a Moor Park apricot as the fruit from that tree. It is an insipid fruit at the best; but a good apricot is eatable, which none from my garden are."

"The truth is, ma'am," said Mrs. Grant, pretending to whisper across the table to Mrs. Norris, "that Dr. Grant hardly knows what the natural taste of our apricot is: he is scarcely ever indulged with one, for it is so valuable a fruit; with a little assistance, and ours is such a remarkably large, fair sort, that what with early tarts and preserves, my cook contrives to get them all."

Mrs. Norris, who had begun to redden, was appeased; and, for a little while, other subjects took place of the improvements of Sotherton. Dr. Grant and Mrs. Norris were seldom good friends; their acquaintance had begun in dilapidations, and their habits were totally dissimilar.

After a short interruption Mr. Rushworth began again. "Smith's place is the admiration of all the country; and it was a mere nothing before Repton took it in hand. I think I shall have Repton."

"Mr. Rushworth," said Lady Bertram, "if I were you, I would have a very pretty shrubbery. One likes to get out into a shrubbery in fine weather."

Mr. Rushworth was eager to assure her ladyship of his acquiescence, and tried to make out something complimentary; but, between his submission to *her* taste, and his having always intended the same himself, with the superadded objects of professing attention to the comfort of ladies in general, and of insinuating that there was one only whom he was anxious to please, he grew puzzled, and Edmund was glad to put an end to his speech by a proposal of wine. Mr. Rushworth, however, though not usually a great talker, had still more to say on the subject next his heart. "Smith has not much above a hundred acres altogether in his grounds, which is little enough, and makes it more surprising that the place can have been so improved. Now, at Sotherton we have a good seven hundred, without reckoning the water meadows; so that I think, if so much could be done at Compton, we need not despair. There have been two or three fine old trees cut down, that grew too near the house, and it opens the prospect amazingly, which makes me think that Repton, or anybody of that sort, would certainly have the avenue at Sotherton down: the avenue that leads from the west front to the top of the hill, you know," turning to Miss Bertram particularly as he spoke. But Miss Bertram thought it most becoming to reply —

"The avenue! Oh! I do not recollect it. I really know very little of Sotherton."

Fanny, who was sitting on the other side of Edmund, exactly opposite Miss Crawford, and who had been attentively listening, now looked at him, and said in a low voice —

"Cut down an avenue! What a pity! Does it not make you think of Cowper? 'Ye fallen avenues, once more I mourn your fate unmerited.'"

He smiled as he answered, and turned towards her, and she smiled in return as their eyes met. "I am afraid the avenue stands a bad chance, Fanny."

"I should like to see Sotherton before it is cut down, to see the place as it is now, in its old state; but I do not suppose I shall."

"Have you never been there? No, you never can; and, unluckily, it is out of distance for a ride. I wish we could contrive it." He continued to hold her gaze and she felt her cheeks flush, which was undoubtedly the result of the warm meal they were consuming and for no other reason besides.

"Oh! it does not signify. Whenever I do see it, you will tell me how it has been altered." But poor Fanny was scarcely able to calm herself and utter a brief reply before losing her place of importance in the discussion.

"I collect," said Miss Crawford, "that Sotherton is an old place, and a place of some grandeur. In any particular style of building?"

"The house was built in Elizabeth's time, and is a large, regular, brick building; heavy, but respectable looking, and has many good rooms. It is ill placed. It stands in one of the lowest spots of the park; in that respect, unfavourable for improvement. But the woods are fine, and there is a stream, which, I dare say, might be made a good deal of. Mr. Rushworth is quite right, I think, in meaning to give it a modern dress, and I have no doubt that it will be all done extremely well."

Miss Crawford listened with submission, and said to herself, "He is a well-bred man; he makes the best of it."

"I do not wish to influence Mr. Rushworth," he continued; "but, had I a place to new fashion, I should not put myself into the hands of an improver. I would rather have an inferior degree of beauty, of my own choice, and acquired progressively. I would rather abide by my own blunders than by his."

"*You* would know what you were about, of course; but that would not suit *me*. I have no eye or ingenuity for such matters, but as they are before me; and had I a place of my own in the country, I should be most thankful to any Mr. Repton who would undertake it, and give me as much beauty as he could for my money; and I should never look at it till it was complete."

"It would be delightful to *me* to see the progress of it all," said Fanny.

"Ay, you have been brought up to it. It was no part of my education; and the only dose I ever had, being administered by not the first favourite in the world, has made me consider improvements *in hand* as the greatest of nuisances. Three years ago the Admiral, my honoured uncle, bought a cottage at Twickenham for us all to spend our summers in; and my aunt and I went down to it quite in raptures; but it being excessively pretty, it was soon found necessary to be improved, and for three months we were all dirt and confusion, without a gravel walk to step on, or a bench fit for use. I would have everything as complete as possible in the country, shrubberies and flower-gardens, and rustic seats innumerable: but it must all be done without my care. Henry is different; he loves to be doing."

Edmund was sorry to hear Miss Crawford, whom he was much disposed to admire, speak so freely of her uncle. It did not suit his sense of propriety, and he was silenced, till induced by further smiles and liveliness to put the matter by for the present.

"Mr. Bertram," said she, "I have tidings of my harp at last. I am assured that it is safe at Northampton; and there it has probably been these ten days, in spite of the solemn assurances we have so often received to the contrary." Edmund expressed his pleasure and surprise. "The truth is, that our inquiries were too direct; we sent a servant, we went ourselves: this will not do seventy miles from London; but this morning we heard of it in the right way. It was seen by some farmer, and he told the miller, and the miller told the butcher, and the butcher's son-in-law left word at the shop."

"I am very glad that you have heard of it, by whatever means, and hope there will be no further delay."

"I am to have it to-morrow; but how do you think it is to be conveyed? Not by a wagon or cart: oh no! nothing of that kind could be hired in the village. I might as well have asked for porters and a handbarrow."

"You would find it difficult, I dare say, just now, in the middle of a very late hay harvest, to hire a horse and cart?"

"I was astonished to find what a piece of work was made of it! To want a horse and cart in the country seemed impossible, so I told my maid to speak for one directly; and as I cannot look out of my dressing-closet without seeing one farmyard, nor walk in the shrubbery without passing another, I thought it would be only ask and have, and was rather grieved that I could not give the advantage to all. Guess my surprise, when I found that I had been asking the most unreasonable, most impossible thing in the world; had offended all the farmers, all the labourers, all the hay in the parish! As for Dr. Grant's bailiff, I believe I had better keep out of *his* way; and my brother-in-law himself, who is all kindness in general, looked rather black upon me when he found what I had been at."

"You could not be expected to have thought on the subject before; but when you *do* think of it, you must see the importance of getting in the grass. The hire of a cart at any time might not be so easy as you suppose: our farmers are not in the habit of letting them out; but, in harvest, it must be quite out of their power to spare a horse."

"I shall understand all your ways in time; but, coming down with the true London maxim, that everything is to be got with money, I was a little embarrassed at first by the sturdy independence of your country customs. However, I am to have my harp fetched to-morrow. Henry, who is good-nature itself, has offered to fetch it in his barouche. Will it not be honourably conveyed?"

Edmund spoke of the harp as his favourite instrument, and hoped to be soon allowed to hear her. Fanny had never heard the harp at all, and wished for it very much.

"I shall be most happy to play to you both," said Miss Crawford; "at least as long as you can like to listen: probably much longer, for I dearly love music myself, and where the natural taste is equal the player must always be best off, for she is gratified in more ways than one. Now, Mr. Bertram, if you write to your brother, I entreat you to tell him that my harp is come: he heard so much of my misery about it. And you may say, if you please, that I shall prepare my most plaintive airs against his return, in compassion to his feelings, as I know his horse will lose."

"If I write, I will say whatever you wish me; but I do not, at present, foresee any occasion for writing."

"No, I dare say, nor if he were to be gone a twelvemonth, would you ever write to him, nor he to you, if it could be helped. The occasion would never be foreseen. What strange creatures brothers are! You would not write to each other but upon the most urgent necessity in the world; and when obliged to take up the pen to say that such a horse is ill, or such a relation dead, it is done in the fewest possible words. You have but one style among you. I know it perfectly. Henry, who is in every other respect exactly what a brother should be, who loves me, consults me, confides in me, and will talk to me by the hour together, has never yet turned the page in a letter; and very often it is nothing more than—'Dear Mary, I am just arrived. Bath seems full, and everything as usual. Yours sincerely.' That is the true manly style; that is a complete brother's letter."

"When they are at a distance from all their family," said Fanny, colouring for William's sake, "they can write long letters."

"Miss Price has a brother at sea," said Edmund, "whose excellence as a correspondent makes her think you too severe upon us."

"At sea, has she? In the king's service, of course?"

Fanny would rather have had Edmund tell the story, but his determined silence obliged her to relate her brother's situation: her voice was animated in speaking of his profession, and the foreign stations he had been on; but she could not mention the number of years that he had been absent without tears in her eyes. Miss Crawford civilly wished him an early promotion.

"Do you know anything of my cousin's captain?" said Edmund; "Captain Marshall? You have a large acquaintance in the navy, I conclude?"

"Among admirals, large enough; but," with an air of grandeur, "we know very little of the inferior ranks. Post-captains may be very good sort of men, but they do not belong to *us*. Of various admirals I could tell you a great deal: of them and their flags, and the gradation of their pay, and their bickerings and jealousies. But, in general, I can assure you that they are all passed over, and all very ill used. Certainly, my home at my uncle's brought me acquainted with a circle of admirals. Of *Rears* and *Vices* I saw enough. Now do not be suspecting me of a pun, I entreat."

Edmund again felt grave, and only replied, "It is a noble profession."

"Yes, the profession is well enough under two circumstances: if it make the fortune, and there be discretion in spending it; but, in short, it is not a favourite profession of mine. It has never worn an amiable form to *me*."

Edmund reverted to the harp, and was again very happy in the prospect of hearing her play.

The subject of improving grounds, meanwhile, was still under consideration among the others; and Mrs. Grant could not help addressing her brother, though it was calling his attention from Miss Julia Bertram.

"My dear Henry, have *you* nothing to say? You have been an improver yourself, and from what I hear of Everingham, it may vie with any place in England. Its natural beauties, I am sure, are great. Everingham, as it *used* to be, was perfect in my estimation: such a happy fall of ground, and such timber! What would I not give to see it again?"

"Nothing could be so gratifying to me as to hear your opinion of it," was his answer; "but I fear there would be some disappointment: you would not find it equal to your present ideas. In extent, it is a mere nothing; you would be surprised at its insignificance; and, as for improvement, there was very little for me to do—too little: I should like to have been busy much longer."

"You are fond of the sort of thing?" said Julia.

"Excessively; but what with the natural advantages of the ground, which pointed out, even to a very young eye, what little remained to be done, and my own consequent resolutions, I had not been of age three months before Everingham was all that it is now. My plan was laid at Westminster, a little altered, perhaps, at Cambridge, and at one-and-twenty executed. I am inclined to envy Mr. Rushworth for having so much happiness yet before him. I have been a devourer of my own."

"Those who see quickly, will resolve quickly, and act quickly," said Julia. "*You* can never want employment. Instead of envying Mr. Rushworth, you should assist him with your opinion."

Mrs. Grant, hearing the latter part of this speech, enforced it warmly, persuaded that no judgment could be equal to her brother's; and as Miss Bertram caught at the idea likewise, and gave it her full support, declaring that, in her opinion, it was infinitely better to consult with friends and disinterested advisers, than immediately to throw the business into the hands of a professional man, Mr. Rushworth was very ready to request the favour of Mr. Crawford's assistance; and Mr. Crawford, after properly depreciating his own abilities, was quite at his service in any way that could be useful. Mr. Rushworth then began to propose Mr. Crawford's doing him the honour of coming over to Sotherton, and taking a bed there; when Mrs. Norris, as if reading in her two nieces' minds their little approbation of a plan which was to take Mr. Crawford away, interposed with an amendment.

"There can be no doubt of Mr. Crawford's willingness; but why should not more of us go? Why should not we make a little party? Here are many that would be interested in your improvements, my dear Mr. Rushworth, and that would like to hear Mr. Crawford's opinion on the spot, and that might be of some small use to you with *their* opinions; and, for my own part, I have been long wishing to wait upon your good mother again; nothing but having no horses of my own could have made me so remiss; but now I could go and sit a few hours with Mrs. Rushworth, while the rest of you walked about and settled things, and then we could all return to a late dinner here, or dine at Sotherton, just as might be most agreeable to your mother, and have a pleasant drive home by moonlight. I dare say Mr. Crawford would take my two nieces and me in his barouche, and Edmund can go on horseback, you know, sister, and Fanny will stay at home with you."

Lady Bertram made no objection; and every one concerned in the going was forward in expressing their ready concurrence, excepting Edmund, who heard it all and said nothing for he found his thoughts taking a different journey and arriving at Miss Crawford—most specifically her brown eyes—and considering whether while Fanny's light eyes resembled purity, Miss Crawford's could be considered by some to be exotic; and finally concluding that her eyes were indeed exotic and wondering what his conclusion meant exactly, if anything. Not that he was one to find himself concerned with such thoughts, though he did wonder where a journey toward the exotic would take him and he found himself delighting in the many possibilities.

Chapter 7

"Well, Fanny, and how do you like Miss Crawford *now*?" said Edmund the next day, after thinking some time on the subject himself. "How did you like her yesterday?"

"Very well—very much. I like to hear her talk. She entertains me; and she is so extremely pretty, that I have great pleasure in looking at her."

"It is her countenance that is so attractive. She has a wonderful play of feature! But was there nothing in her conversation that struck you, Fanny, as not quite right?"

"Oh yes! she ought not to have spoken of her uncle as she did. I was quite astonished. An uncle with whom she has been living so many years, and who, whatever his faults may be, is so very fond of her brother, treating him, they say, quite like a son. I could not have believed it!"

"I thought you would be struck. It was very wrong; very indecorous."

"And very ungrateful, I think."

"Ungrateful is a strong word. I do not know that her uncle has any claim to her *gratitude*; his wife certainly had; and it is the warmth of her respect for her aunt's memory which misleads her here. She is awkwardly circumstanced. With such warm feelings and lively spirits it must be difficult to do justice to her affection for Mrs. Crawford, without throwing a shade on the Admiral. I do not pretend to know which was most to blame in their disagreements, though the Admiral's present conduct might incline one to the side of his wife; but it is natural and amiable that Miss Crawford should acquit her aunt entirely. I do not censure her *opinions*; but there certainly *is* impropriety in making them public."

"Do not you think," said Fanny, after a little consideration, "that this impropriety is a reflection itself upon Mrs. Crawford, as her niece has been entirely brought up by her? She cannot have given her right notions of what was due to the Admiral."

"That is a fair remark. Yes, we must suppose the faults of the niece to have been those of the aunt; and it makes one more sensible of the disadvantages she has been under. But I think her present home must do her good. Mrs. Grant's manners are just what they ought to be. She speaks of her brother with a very pleasing affection."

"Yes, except as to his writing her such short letters. She made me almost laugh; but I cannot rate so very highly the love or good-nature of a brother who will not give himself the trouble of writing anything worth reading to his sisters, when they are separated. I am sure William would never have used *me* so, under any circumstances. And what right had she to suppose that *you* would not write long letters when you were absent?"

"The right of a lively mind, Fanny, seizing whatever may contribute to its own amusement or that of others; perfectly allowable, when untinctured by ill-humour or roughness; and there is not a shadow of either in the countenance or manner of Miss Crawford: nothing sharp, or loud, or coarse. She is perfectly feminine, except in the instances we have been speaking of. There she cannot be justified. I am glad you saw it all as I did."

Having formed her mind and gained her affections, he had a good chance of her thinking like him; though at this period, and on this subject, there began now to be some danger of dissimilarity, for he was in a line of admiration of Miss Crawford, which might lead him where Fanny could not follow. Miss Crawford's attractions did not lessen. The harp arrived, and rather added to her beauty, wit, and good-humour; for she played with the greatest obligingness, with an expression and taste which were peculiarly becoming, and there was something clever to be said at the close of every air. Edmund was at the Parsonage every day, to be indulged with his favourite instrument: one morning secured an invitation for the next; for the lady could not be unwilling to have a listener, and every thing was soon in a fair train.

A young woman, pretty, lively, with a harp as elegant as herself, and both placed near a window, cut down to the ground, and opening on a little lawn, surrounded by shrubs in the rich foliage of summer, was enough to catch any man's heart. The season, the scene, the air, were all favourable to tenderness and sentiment. Mrs. Grant and her tambour frame were not without their use: it was all in harmony; and as everything will turn to account when love is once set going, even the sandwich tray, and Dr. Grant doing the honours of it, were worth looking at. Without studying the business, however, or knowing what he was about, Edmund was beginning, at the end of a week of such intercourse, to be a good deal in love; and to the credit of the lady it may be added that, without his being a man of the world or an elder brother, without any of the arts of flattery or the gaieties of small talk, he began to be agreeable to her. She felt it to be so, though she had not foreseen, and could hardly understand it; for he was not pleasant by any common rule: he talked no nonsense; he paid no compliments; his opinions were unbending, his attentions tranquil and simple. There was a charm, perhaps, in his sincerity, his steadiness, his integrity, which Miss Crawford might be equal to feel, though not equal to discuss with herself. She did not think very much about it, however: he pleased her for the present; she liked to have him near her; it was enough.

Fanny could not wonder that Edmund was at the Parsonage every morning; she would gladly have been there too, might she have gone in uninvited and unnoticed, to hear the harp; neither could she wonder that, when the evening stroll was over, and the two families parted again, he should think it right to attend Mrs. Grant and her sister to their home, while Mr. Crawford was devoted to the ladies of the Park; but she thought it a very bad exchange; and if Edmund were not there to mix the wine and water for her, would rather go without it than not. She was a little surprised that he could spend so many hours with Miss Crawford, and not see more of the sort of fault which he had already observed, and of which *she* was almost always reminded by a something of the same nature whenever she was in her company; but so it was. Edmund was fond of speaking to her of Miss Crawford, but he seemed to think it enough that the Admiral had since been spared; and she scrupled to point out her own remarks to him, lest it should appear like ill-nature. The first actual pain which Miss Crawford occasioned her was the consequence of an inclination to learn to ride, which the former caught, soon after her being settled at Mansfield, from the example of the young ladies at the Park, and which, when Edmund's acquaintance with her increased, led to his encouraging the wish, and the offer of his own quiet mare for the purpose of her first attempts, as the best fitted for a beginner that either stable could furnish. No pain, no injury, however, was designed by him to his cousin in this offer: *she* was not to lose a day's exercise by it. The mare was only to be taken down to the Parsonage half an hour before her ride were to begin; and Fanny, on its being first proposed, so far from feeling slighted, was almost over-powered with gratitude that he should be asking her leave for it.

Miss Crawford made her first essay with great credit to herself, and no inconvenience to Fanny. Edmund, who had taken down the mare and presided at the whole, returned with it in excellent time, before either Fanny or the steady old coachman, who always attended her when she rode without her cousins, were ready to set forward. The second day's trial was not so guiltless. Miss Crawford's enjoyment of riding was such that she did not know how to leave off. Active and fearless, and though rather small, strongly made, she seemed formed for a horsewoman; and to the pure genuine pleasure of the exercise, something was probably added in Edmund's attendance and instructions, and something more in the conviction of very much surpassing her sex in general by her early progress, to make her unwilling to dismount. Fanny was ready and waiting, and Mrs. Norris was beginning to scold her for not being gone, and still no horse was announced, no Edmund appeared. To avoid her aunt, and look for him, she went out.

The houses, though scarcely half a mile apart, were not within sight of each other; but, by walking fifty yards from the hall door, she could look down the park, and command a view of the Parsonage and all its demesnes, gently rising beyond the village road; and in Dr. Grant's meadow she immediately saw the group—Edmund and Miss Crawford both on horse-back, riding side by side, Dr. and Mrs. Grant, and Mr. Crawford, with two or three grooms, standing about and looking on. A happy party it appeared to her, all interested in one object: cheerful beyond a doubt, for the sound of merriment ascended even to her. It was a sound which did not make *her* cheerful; she wondered that Edmund should forget her, and felt a pang. She could not turn her eyes from the meadow; she could not help watching all that passed. At first Miss Crawford and her companion made the circuit of the field, which was not small, at a foot's pace; then, at *her* apparent suggestion, they rose into a canter; and to Fanny's timid nature it was most astonishing to see how well she sat. After a few minutes they stopped entirely. Edmund was close to her; he was speaking to her; he was evidently directing her management of the bridle; he had hold of her hand; she saw it, or the imagination supplied what the eye could not reach. She must not wonder at all this; what could be more natural than that Edmund should be making himself useful, and proving his good-nature by any one? She could not but think, indeed, that Mr. Crawford might as well have saved him the trouble; that it would have been particularly proper and becoming in a brother to have done it himself; but Mr. Crawford, with all his boasted good-nature, and all his coachmanship, probably knew nothing of the matter, and had no active kindness in comparison of Edmund. She began to think it rather hard upon the mare to have such double duty; if she were forgotten, the poor mare should be remembered. And she could not but think what it would be for Edmund to hold her own hand as they rode together and was pleased not to have the opportunity to consider as much before being thankfully distracted.

Her feelings for one and the other were soon a little tranquillised by seeing the party in the meadow disperse, and Miss Crawford still on horseback, but attended by Edmund on foot, pass through a gate into the lane, and so into the park, and make towards the spot where she stood. She began then to be afraid of appearing rude and impatient; and walked to meet them with a great anxiety to avoid the suspicion.

"My dear Miss Price," said Miss Crawford, as soon as she was at all within hearing, "I am come to make my own apologies for keeping you waiting; but I have nothing in the world to say for myself—I knew it was very late, and that I was behaving extremely ill; and therefore, if you please, you must forgive me. Selfishness must always be forgiven, you know, because there is no hope of a cure."

Fanny's answer was extremely civil, and Edmund added his conviction that she could be in no hurry. "For there is more than time enough for my cousin to ride twice as far as she ever goes," said he, "and you have been promoting her comfort by preventing her from setting off half an hour sooner: clouds are now coming up, and she will not suffer from the heat as she would have done then. I wish *you* may not be fatigued by so much exercise. I wish you had saved yourself this walk home."

"No part of it fatigues me but getting off this horse, I assure you," said she, as she sprang down with his help; "I am very strong. Nothing ever fatigues me but doing what I do not like. Miss Price,

I give way to you with a very bad grace; but I sincerely hope you will have a pleasant ride, and that I may have nothing but good to hear of this dear, delightful, beautiful animal."

The old coachman, who had been waiting about with his own horse, now joining them, Fanny was lifted on hers, and they set off across another part of the park; her feelings of discomfort not lightened by seeing, as she looked back, that the others were walking down the hill together to the village; nor did her attendant do her much good by his comments on Miss Crawford's great cleverness as a horse-woman, which he had been watching with an interest almost equal to her own.

"It is a pleasure to see a lady with such a good heart for riding!" said he. "I never see one sit a horse better. She did not seem to have a thought of fear. Very different from you, miss, when you first began, six years ago come next Easter. Lord bless you! how you did tremble when Sir Thomas first had you put on!"

In the drawing-room Miss Crawford was also celebrated. Her merit in being gifted by Nature with strength and courage was fully appreciated by the Miss Bertrams; her delight in riding was like their own; her early excellence in it was like their own, and they had great pleasure in praising it.

"I was sure she would ride well," said Julia; "she has the make for it. Her figure is as neat as her brother's."

"Yes," added Maria, "and her spirits are as good, and she has the same energy of character. I cannot but think that good horsemanship has a great deal to do with the mind."

When they parted at night Edmund asked Fanny whether she meant to ride the next day.

"No, I do not know—not if you want the mare," was her answer.

"I do not want her at all for myself," said he; "but whenever you are next inclined to stay at home, I think Miss Crawford would be glad to have her a longer time—for a whole morning, in short.

She has a great desire to get as far as Mansfield Common: Mrs. Grant has been telling her of its fine views, and I have no doubt of her being perfectly equal to it. But any morning will do for this. She would be extremely sorry to interfere with you. It would be very wrong if she did. *She* rides only for pleasure; *you* for health."

"I shall not ride to-morrow, certainly," said Fanny; "I have been out very often lately, and would rather stay at home. You know I am strong enough now to walk very well."

Edmund looked pleased, which must be Fanny's comfort, and the ride to Mansfield Common took place the next morning: the party included all the young people but herself, and was much enjoyed at the time, and doubly enjoyed again in the evening discussion. A successful scheme of this sort generally brings on another; and the having been to Mansfield Common disposed them all for going somewhere else the day after. There were many other views to be shewn; and though the weather was hot, there were shady lanes wherever they wanted to go. A young party is always provided with a shady lane. Four fine mornings successively were spent in this manner, in shewing the Crawfords the country, and doing the honours of its finest spots. Everything answered; it was all gaiety and good-humour, the heat only supplying inconvenience enough to be talked of with pleasure— till the fourth day, when the happiness of one of the party was exceedingly clouded. Miss Bertram was the one. Edmund and Julia were invited to dine at the Parsonage, and *she* was excluded. It was meant and done by Mrs. Grant, with perfect good-humour, on Mr. Rushworth's account, who was partly expected at the Park that day; but it was felt as a very grievous injury, and her good manners were severely taxed to conceal her vexation and anger till she reached home. As Mr. Rushworth did *not* come, the injury was increased, and she had not even the relief of shewing her power over him; she could only be sullen to her mother, aunt, and cousin, and throw as great a gloom as possible over their dinner and dessert.

Between ten and eleven Edmund and Julia walked into the drawing-room, fresh with the evening air, glowing and cheerful, the very reverse of what they found in the three ladies sitting there, for Maria would scarcely raise her eyes from her book, and Lady Bertram was half-asleep; and even Mrs. Norris, discomposed by her niece's ill-humour, and having asked one or two questions about the dinner, which were not immediately attended to, seemed almost determined to say no more. For a few minutes the brother and sister were too eager in their praise of the night and their remarks on the stars, to think beyond themselves; but when the first pause came, Edmund, looking around, said, "But where is Fanny? Is she gone to bed?"

"No, not that I know of," replied Mrs. Norris; "she was here a moment ago."

Her own gentle voice speaking from the other end of the room, which was a very long one, told them that she was on the sofa. Mrs. Norris began scolding.

"That is a very foolish trick, Fanny, to be idling away all the evening upon a sofa. Why cannot you come and sit here, and employ yourself as *we* do? If you have no work of your own, I can supply you from the poor basket. There is all the new calico, that was bought last week, not touched yet. I am sure I almost broke my back by cutting it out. You should learn to think of other people; and, take my word for it, it is a shocking trick for a young person to be always lolling upon a sofa."

Before half this was said, Fanny was returned to her seat at the table, and had taken up her work again; and Julia, who was in high good-humour, from the pleasures of the day, did her the justice of exclaiming, "I must say, ma'am, that Fanny is as little upon the sofa as anybody in the house."

"Fanny," said Edmund, after looking at her attentively, "I am sure you have the headache."

She could not deny it, but said it was not very bad.

"I can hardly believe you," he replied; "I know your looks too well. How long have you had it?"

"Since a little before dinner. It is nothing but the heat."

"Did you go out in the heat?"

"Go out! to be sure she did," said Mrs. Norris: "would you have her stay within such a fine day as this? Were not we *all* out? Even your mother was out to-day for above an hour."

"Yes, indeed, Edmund," added her ladyship, who had been thoroughly awakened by Mrs. Norris's sharp reprimand to Fanny; "I was out above an hour. I sat three-quarters of an hour in the flower-garden, while Fanny cut the roses; and very pleasant it was, I assure you, but very hot. It was shady enough in the alcove, but I declare I quite dreaded the coming home again."

"Fanny has been cutting roses, has she?"

"Yes, and I am afraid they will be the last this year. Poor thing! *She* found it hot enough; but they were so full-blown that one could not wait."

"There was no help for it, certainly," rejoined Mrs. Norris, in a rather softened voice; "but I question whether her headache might not be caught *then*, sister. There is nothing so likely to give it as standing and stooping in a hot sun; but I dare say it will be well to-morrow. Suppose you let her have your aromatic vinegar; I always forget to have mine filled."

"She has got it," said Lady Bertram; "she has had it ever since she came back from your house the second time."

"What!" cried Edmund; "has she been walking as well as cutting roses; walking across the hot park to your house, and doing it twice, ma'am? No wonder her head aches."

Mrs. Norris was talking to Julia, and did not hear.

"I was afraid it would be too much for her," said Lady Bertram; "but when the roses were gathered, your aunt wished to have them, and then you know they must be taken home."

"But were there roses enough to oblige her to go twice?"

"No; but they were to be put into the spare room to dry; and, unluckily, Fanny forgot to lock the door of the room and bring away the key, so she was obliged to go again."

Edmund got up and walked about the room, saying, "And could nobody be employed on such an errand but Fanny? Upon my word, ma'am, it has been a very ill-managed business."

"I am sure I do not know how it was to have been done better," cried Mrs. Norris, unable to be longer deaf; "unless I had gone myself, indeed; but I cannot be in two places at once; and I was talking to Mr. Green at that very time about your mother's dairymaid, by *her* desire, and had promised John Groom to write to Mrs. Jefferies about his son, and the poor fellow was waiting for me half an hour. I think nobody can justly accuse me of sparing myself upon any occasion, but really I cannot do everything at once. And as for Fanny's just stepping down to my house for me—it is not much above a quarter of a mile—I cannot think I was unreasonable to ask it. How often do I pace it three times a day, early and late, ay, and in all weathers too, and say nothing about it?"

"I wish Fanny had half your strength, ma'am."

"If Fanny would be more regular in her exercise, she would not be knocked up so soon. She has not been out on horseback now this long while, and I am persuaded that, when she does not ride, she ought to walk. If she had been riding before, I should not have asked it of her. But I thought it would rather do her good after being stooping among the roses; for there is nothing so refreshing as a walk after a fatigue of that kind; and though the sun was strong, it was not so very hot. Between ourselves, Edmund," nodding significantly at his mother, "it was cutting the roses, and dawdling about in the flower-garden, that did the mischief."

"I am afraid it was, indeed," said the more candid Lady Bertram, who had overheard her; "I am very much afraid she caught the headache there, for the heat was enough to kill anybody. It was as much as I could bear myself. Sitting and calling to Pug, and trying to keep him from the flower-beds, was almost too much for me."

Edmund said no more to either lady; but going quietly to another table, on which the supper-tray yet remained, brought a glass of Madeira to Fanny, and obliged her to drink the greater part. She wished to be able to decline it; but the tears, which a variety of feelings created, made it easier to swallow than to speak.

Vexed as Edmund was with his mother and aunt, he was still more angry with himself. His own forgetfulness of her was worse than anything which they had done. Nothing of this would have happened had she been properly considered; but she had been left four days together without any choice of companions or exercise, and without any excuse for avoiding whatever her unreasonable aunts might require. He was ashamed to think that for four days together she had not had the power of riding, and very seriously resolved, however unwilling he must be to check a pleasure of Miss Crawford's, that it should never happen again.

Fanny went to bed with her heart as full as on the first evening of her arrival at the Park. The state of her spirits had probably had its share in her indisposition; for she had been feeling neglected, and been struggling against discontent and envy for some days past. As she leant on the sofa, to which she had retreated that she might not be seen, the pain of her mind had been much beyond that in her head; and the sudden change which Edmund's kindness had then occasioned, made her hardly know how to support herself.

Chapter 8

Fanny's rides recommenced the very next day; and as it was a pleasant fresh-feeling morning, less hot than the weather had lately been, Edmund trusted that her losses, both of health and pleasure, would be soon made good. While she was gone Mr. Rushworth arrived, escorting his mother, who came to be civil and to shew her civility especially, in urging the execution of the plan for visiting Sotherton, which had been started a fortnight before, and which, in consequence of her subsequent absence from home, had since lain dormant. Mrs. Norris and her nieces were all well pleased with its revival, and an early day was named and agreed to, provided Mr. Crawford should be disengaged: the young ladies did not forget that stipulation, and though Mrs. Norris would willingly have answered for his being so, they would neither authorise the liberty nor run the risk; and at last, on a hint from Miss Bertram, Mr. Rushworth discovered that the properest thing to be done was for him to walk down to the Parsonage directly, and call on Mr. Crawford, and inquire whether Wednesday would suit him or not.

Before his return Mrs. Grant and Miss Crawford came in. Having been out some time, and taken a different route to the house, they had not met him. Comfortable hopes, however, were given that he would find Mr. Crawford at home. The Sotherton scheme was mentioned of course. It was hardly possible, indeed, that anything else should be talked of, for Mrs. Norris was in high spirits about it; and Mrs. Rushworth, a well-meaning, civil, prosing, pompous woman, who thought nothing of consequence, but as it related to her own and her son's concerns, had not yet given over pressing Lady Bertram to be of the party. Lady Bertram constantly declined it; but her placid manner of refusal made Mrs.

Rushworth still think she wished to come, till Mrs. Norris's more numerous words and louder tone convinced her of the truth.

"The fatigue would be too much for my sister, a great deal too much, I assure you, my dear Mrs. Rushworth. Ten miles there, and ten back, you know. You must excuse my sister on this occasion, and accept of our two dear girls and myself without her. Sotherton is the only place that could give her a *wish* to go so far, but it cannot be, indeed. She will have a companion in Fanny Price, you know, so it will all do very well; and as for Edmund, as he is not here to speak for himself, I will answer for his being most happy to join the party. He can go on horseback, you know."

Mrs. Rushworth being obliged to yield to Lady Bertram's staying at home, could only be sorry. "The loss of her ladyship's company would be a great drawback, and she should have been extremely happy to have seen the young lady too, Miss Price, who had never been at Sotherton yet, and it was a pity she should not see the place."

"You are very kind, you are all kindness, my dear madam," cried Mrs. Norris; "but as to Fanny, she will have opportunities in plenty of seeing Sotherton. She has time enough before her; and her going now is quite out of the question. Lady Bertram could not possibly spare her."

"Oh no! I cannot do without Fanny."

Mrs. Rushworth proceeded next, under the conviction that everybody must be wanting to see Sotherton, to include Miss Crawford in the invitation; and though Mrs. Grant, who had not been at the trouble of visiting Mrs. Rushworth, on her coming into the neighbourhood, civilly declined it on her own account, she was glad to secure any pleasure for her sister; and Mary, properly pressed and persuaded, was not long in accepting her share of the civility. Mr. Rushworth came back from the Parsonage successful; and Edmund made his appearance just in time to learn what had been settled for Wednesday, to attend Mrs. Rushworth to her carriage, and walk half-way down the park with the two other ladies.

On his return to the breakfast-room, he found Mrs. Norris trying to make up her mind as to whether Miss Crawford's being of the party were desirable or not, or whether her brother's barouche would not be full without her. The Miss Bertrams laughed at the idea, assuring her that the barouche would hold four perfectly well, independent of the box, on which *one* might go with him.

"But why is it necessary," said Edmund, "that Crawford's carriage, or his *only*, should be employed? Why is no use to be made of my mother's chaise? I could not, when the scheme was first mentioned the other day, understand why a visit from the family were not to be made in the carriage of the family."

"What!" cried Julia: "go boxed up three in a postchaise in this weather, when we may have seats in a barouche! No, my dear Edmund, that will not quite do."

"Besides," said Maria, "I know that Mr. Crawford depends upon taking us. After what passed at first, he would claim it as a promise."

"And, my dear Edmund," added Mrs. Norris, "taking out *two* carriages when *one* will do, would be trouble for nothing; and, between ourselves, coachman is not very fond of the roads between this and Sotherton: he always complains bitterly of the narrow lanes scratching his carriage, and you know one should not like to have dear Sir Thomas, when he comes home, find all the varnish scratched off."

"That would not be a very handsome reason for using Mr. Crawford's," said Maria; "but the truth is, that Wilcox is a stupid old fellow, and does not know how to drive. I will answer for it that we shall find no inconvenience from narrow roads on Wednesday."

"There is no hardship, I suppose, nothing unpleasant," said Edmund, "in going on the barouche box."

"Unpleasant!" cried Maria: "oh dear! I believe it would be generally thought the favourite seat. There can be no comparison as to one's view of the country. Probably Miss Crawford will choose the barouche-box herself."

"There can be no objection, then, to Fanny's going with you; there can be no doubt of your having room for her."

"Fanny!" repeated Mrs. Norris; "my dear Edmund, there is no idea of her going with us. She stays with her aunt. I told Mrs. Rushworth so. She is not expected."

"You can have no reason, I imagine, madam," said he, addressing his mother, "for wishing Fanny *not* to be of the party, but as it relates to yourself, to your own comfort. If you could do without her, you would not wish to keep her at home?"

"To be sure not, but I *cannot* do without her."

"You can, if I stay at home with you, as I mean to do."

There was a general cry out at this. "Yes," he continued, "there is no necessity for my going, and I mean to stay at home. Fanny has a great desire to see Sotherton. I know she wishes it very much. She has not often a gratification of the kind, and I am sure, ma'am, you would be glad to give her the pleasure now?"

"Oh yes! very glad, if your aunt sees no objection."

Mrs. Norris was very ready with the only objection which could remain—their having positively assured Mrs. Rushworth that Fanny could not go, and the very strange appearance there would consequently be in taking her, which seemed to her a difficulty quite impossible to be got over. It must have the strangest appearance! It would be something so very unceremonious, so bordering on disrespect for Mrs. Rushworth, whose own manners were such a pattern of good-breeding and attention, that she really did not feel equal to it. Mrs. Norris had no affection for Fanny, and no wish of procuring her pleasure at any time; but her opposition to Edmund *now*, arose more from partiality for her own scheme, because it *was* her own, than from anything else. She felt that she had arranged everything extremely well, and that any alteration must be for the worse. When Edmund, therefore, told her in reply, as he did when she would give him the hearing, that she need not distress herself on Mrs. Rushworth's account, because he had taken the opportunity, as he walked with her through the hall, of mentioning Miss Price as one who would probably be of the party, and had directly received a very sufficient invitation for his cousin, Mrs. Norris was too much vexed to submit with a very good grace, and would only say, "Very well, very well, just as you chuse, settle it your own way, I am sure I do not care about it."

"It seems very odd," said Maria, "that you should be staying at home instead of Fanny."

"I am sure she ought to be very much obliged to you," added Julia, hastily leaving the room as she spoke, from a consciousness that she ought to offer to stay at home herself.

"Fanny will feel quite as grateful as the occasion requires," was Edmund's only reply, and the subject dropt.

Fanny's gratitude, when she heard the plan, was, in fact, much greater than her pleasure. She felt Edmund's kindness with all, and more than all, the sensibility which he, unsuspicious of her fond attachment, could be aware of; but that he should forego any enjoyment on her account gave her pain, and her own satisfaction in seeing Sotherton would be nothing without him.

The next meeting of the two Mansfield families produced another alteration in the plan, and one that was admitted with general approbation. Mrs. Grant offered herself as companion for the day to Lady Bertram in lieu of her son, and Dr. Grant was to join them at dinner. Lady Bertram was very well pleased to have it so, and the young ladies were in spirits again. Even Edmund was very thankful for an arrangement which restored him to his share of the party; and Mrs. Norris thought it an excellent plan, and had it at her tongue's end, and was on the point of proposing it, when Mrs. Grant spoke.

Wednesday was fine, and soon after breakfast the barouche arrived, Mr. Crawford driving his sisters; and as everybody was ready, there was nothing to be done but for Mrs. Grant to alight and the others to take their places. The place of all places, the envied seat, the post of honour, was unappropriated. To whose happy lot was it to fall? While each of the Miss Bertrams were meditating how best, and with the most appearance of obliging the others, to secure it, the matter was settled by Mrs. Grant's saying, as she stepped from the carriage, "As there are five of you, it will be better that one should sit with Henry; and as you were saying lately that you wished you could drive, Julia, I think this will be a good opportunity for you to take a lesson."

Happy Julia! Unhappy Maria! The former was on the barouche-box in a moment, the latter took her seat within, in gloom and mortification; and the carriage drove off amid the good wishes of the two remaining ladies, and the barking of Pug in his mistress's arms.

Their road was through a pleasant country; and Fanny, whose rides had never been extensive, was soon beyond her knowledge, and was very happy in observing all that was new, and admiring all that was pretty. She was not often invited to join in the conversation of the others, nor did she desire it. Her own thoughts and reflections were habitually her best companions; and, in observing the appearance of the country, the bearings of the roads, the difference of soil, the state of the harvest, the cottages, the cattle, the children, she found entertainment that could only have been heightened by having Edmund to speak to of what she felt. That was the only point of resemblance between her and the lady who sat by her: in everything but a value for Edmund, Miss Crawford was very unlike her. She had none of Fanny's delicacy of taste, of mind, of feeling; she saw Nature, inanimate Nature, with little observation; her attention was all for men and women, her talents for the light and lively. In looking back after Edmund, however, when there was any stretch of road behind them, or when he gained on them in ascending a considerable hill, they were united, and a "there he is" broke at the same moment from them both, more than once. And it was during these moments that Fanny could not help but feel herself perhaps even lighter of heart than her companion, for when Fanny saw Edmund, a fluttering sensation began in her middle, caused her heart to jolt, and ended with what she felt to be an expression on her face of pure heaven. In these moments she found herself gazing in curious comparison at Miss Crawford and saw no evidence of similar rapture in her countenance, but rather noted nothing more than recognition at seeing a familiar acquaintance; indeed it could be said that Miss Crawford's expression upon seeing Edmund was quite similar to the expression she wore when greeting Fanny or even her own brother. There was no evidence of pure mirth, no innocence of heart detected whatever; and Fanny took some vain satisfaction in its observation.

For the first seven miles Miss Bertram had very little real comfort: her prospect always ended in Mr. Crawford and her sister sitting side by side, full of conversation and merriment; and to see only his expressive profile as he turned with a smile to Julia, or to catch the laugh of the other, was a perpetual source of irritation, which her own sense of propriety could but just smooth over. When Julia looked back, it was with a countenance of delight, and whenever she spoke to them, it was in the highest spirits: "her view of the country was charming, she wished they could all see it," etc.; but her only offer of exchange was addressed to Miss Crawford, as they gained the summit of a long hill, and was not more inviting than this: "Here is a fine burst of country. I wish you had my seat, but I dare say you will not take it, let me press you ever so much;" and Miss Crawford could hardly answer before they were moving again at a good pace.

When they came within the influence of Sotherton associations, it was better for Miss Bertram, who might be said to have two strings to her bow. She had Rushworth feelings, and Crawford feelings, and in the vicinity of Sotherton the former had considerable effect. Mr. Rushworth's consequence was hers. She could not tell Miss Crawford that "those woods belonged to Sotherton," she could not carelessly observe that "she believed that it was now all Mr. Rushworth's property on each side of the road," without elation of heart; and it was a pleasure to increase with their approach to the capital freehold mansion, and ancient manorial residence of the family, with all its rights of court-leet and court-baron.

"Now we shall have no more rough road, Miss Crawford; our difficulties are over. The rest of the way is such as it ought to be. Mr. Rushworth has made it since he succeeded to the estate. Here begins the village. Those cottages are really a disgrace. The church spire is reckoned remarkably handsome. I am glad the church is not so close to the great house as often happens in old places. The annoyance of the bells must be terrible. There is the parsonage: a tidy-looking house, and I understand the clergyman and his wife are very decent people. Those are almshouses, built by some of the family. To the right is the steward's house; he is a very respectable man. Now we are coming to the lodge-gates; but we have nearly a mile through the park still. It is not ugly, you see, at this end; there is some fine timber, but the situation of the house is dreadful. We go down hill to it for half a mile, and it is a pity, for it would not be an ill-looking place if it had a better approach."

Miss Crawford was not slow to admire; she pretty well guessed Miss Bertram's feelings, and made it a point of honour to promote her enjoyment to the utmost. Mrs. Norris was all delight and volubility; and even Fanny had something to say in admiration, and might be heard with complacency. Her eye was eagerly taking in everything within her reach; and after being at some pains to get a view of the house, and observing that "it was a sort of building which she could not look at but with respect," she added, "Now, where is the avenue? The house fronts the east, I perceive. The avenue, therefore, must be at the back of it. Mr. Rushworth talked of the west front."

"Yes, it is exactly behind the house; begins at a little distance, and ascends for half a mile to the extremity of the grounds. You may see something of it here—something of the more distant trees. It is oak entirely."

Miss Bertram could now speak with decided information of what she had known nothing about when Mr. Rushworth had asked her opinion; and her spirits were in as happy a flutter as vanity and pride could furnish, when they drove up to the spacious stone steps before the principal entrance.

Chapter 9

Mr. Rushworth was at the door to receive his fair lady; and the whole party were welcomed by him with due attention. In the drawing-room they were met with equal cordiality by the mother, and Miss Bertram had all the distinction with each that she could wish. After the business of arriving was over, it was first necessary to eat, and the doors were thrown open to admit them through one or two intermediate rooms into the appointed dining-parlour, where a collation was prepared with abundance and elegance. Much was said, and much was ate, and all went well. The particular object of the day was then considered. How would Mr. Crawford like, in what manner would he chuse, to take a survey of the grounds? Mr. Rushworth mentioned his curricle. Mr. Crawford suggested the greater desirableness of some carriage which might convey more than two. "To be depriving themselves of the advantage of other eyes and other judgments, might be an evil even beyond the loss of present pleasure."

Mrs. Rushworth proposed that the chaise should be taken also; but this was scarcely received as an amendment: the young ladies neither smiled nor spoke. Her next proposition, of shewing the house to such of them as had not been there before, was more acceptable, for Miss Bertram was pleased to have its size displayed, and all were glad to be doing something.

The whole party rose accordingly, and under Mrs. Rushworth's guidance were shewn through a number of rooms, all lofty, and many large, and amply furnished in the taste of fifty years back, with shining floors, solid mahogany, rich damask, marble, gilding, and carving, each handsome in its way. Of pictures there were abundance, and some few good, but the larger part were family portraits, no longer anything to anybody but Mrs. Rushworth, who had been at great pains to learn all that the housekeeper could teach, and was now almost equally well qualified to shew the house. On the present occasion she addressed herself chiefly to Miss Crawford and Fanny, but there was no comparison in the willingness of their attention; for Miss Crawford, who had seen scores of great houses, and cared for none of them, had only the appearance of civilly listening, while Fanny, to whom everything was almost as interesting as it was new, attended with unaffected earnestness to all that Mrs. Rushworth could relate of the family in former times, its rise and grandeur, regal visits and loyal efforts, delighted to connect anything with history already known, or warm her imagination with scenes of the past.

The situation of the house excluded the possibility of much prospect from any of the rooms; and while Fanny and some of the others were attending Mrs. Rushworth, Henry Crawford was looking grave and shaking his head at the windows. Every room on the west front looked across a lawn to the beginning of the avenue immediately beyond tall iron palisades and gates.

Having visited many more rooms than could be supposed to be of any other use than to contribute to the window-tax, and find employment for housemaids, "Now," said Mrs. Rushworth, "we are coming to the chapel, which properly we ought to enter from above, and look down upon; but as we are quite among friends, I will take you in this way, if you will excuse me."

They entered. Fanny's imagination had prepared her for something grander than a mere spacious, oblong room, fitted up for the purpose of devotion: with nothing more striking or more solemn than the profusion of mahogany, and the crimson velvet cushions appearing over the ledge of the family gallery above. "I am disappointed," said she, in a low voice, to Edmund. "This is not my idea of a chapel. There is nothing awful here, nothing melancholy, nothing grand. Here are no aisles, no arches, no inscriptions, no banners. No banners, cousin, to be 'blown by the night wind of heaven.' No signs that a 'Scottish monarch sleeps below.'"

"You forget, Fanny, how lately all this has been built, and for how confined a purpose, compared with the old chapels of castles and monasteries. It was only for the private use of the family. They have been buried, I suppose, in the parish church. *There* you must look for the banners and the achievements."

"It was foolish of me not to think of all that; but I am disappointed."

Mrs. Rushworth began her relation. "This chapel was fitted up as you see it, in James the Second's time. Before that period, as I understand, the pews were only wainscot; and there is some reason to think that the linings and cushions of the pulpit and family seat were only purple cloth; but this is not quite certain. It is a handsome chapel, and was formerly in constant use both morning and evening. Prayers were always read in it by the domestic chaplain, within the memory of many; but the late Mr. Rushworth left it off."

"Every generation has its improvements," said Miss Crawford, with a smile, to Edmund.

Mrs. Rushworth was gone to repeat her lesson to Mr. Crawford; and Edmund, Fanny, and Miss Crawford remained in a cluster together.

"It is a pity," cried Fanny, "that the custom should have been discontinued. It was a valuable part of former times. There is something in a chapel and chaplain so much in character with a great house, with one's ideas of what such a household should be! A whole family assembling regularly for the purpose of prayer is fine!"

"Very fine indeed," said Miss Crawford, laughing. "It must do the heads of the family a great deal of good to force all the poor housemaids and footmen to leave business and pleasure, and say their prayers here twice a day, while they are inventing excuses themselves for staying away."

"*That* is hardly Fanny's idea of a family assembling," said Edmund. "If the master and mistress do *not* attend themselves, there must be more harm than good in the custom."

"At any rate, it is safer to leave people to their own devices on such subjects. Everybody likes to go their own way—to chuse their own time and manner of devotion. The obligation of attendance, the formality, the restraint, the length of time—altogether it is a formidable thing, and what nobody likes; and if the good people who used to kneel and gape in that gallery could have foreseen that the time would ever come when men and women might lie another ten minutes in bed, when they woke with a headache, without danger of reprobation, because chapel was missed, they would have jumped with joy and envy. Cannot you imagine with what unwilling feelings the former belles of the house of Rushworth did many a time repair to this chapel? The young Mrs. Eleanors and Mrs. Bridgets—starched up into seeming piety, but with heads full of something very different—especially if the poor chaplain were not worth looking at—and, in those days, I fancy parsons were very inferior even to what they are now."

For a few moments she was unanswered. Fanny coloured and looked at Edmund, but felt too angry for speech; and he needed a little recollection before he could say, "Your lively mind can hardly be serious even on serious subjects. You have given us an amusing sketch, and human nature cannot say it was not so. We must all feel *at times* the difficulty of fixing our thoughts as we could wish; but if you are supposing it a frequent thing, that is to say, a weakness grown into a habit from neglect, what could be expected from the *private* devotions of such persons? Do you think the minds which are suffered, which are indulged in wanderings in a chapel, would be more collected in a closet?"

"Yes, very likely. They would have two chances at least in their favour. There would be less to distract the attention from without, and it would not be tried so long."

"The mind which does not struggle against itself under *one* circumstance, would find objects to distract it in the *other*, I believe; and the influence of the place and of example may often rouse better feelings than are begun with. The greater length of the service, however, I admit to be sometimes too hard a stretch upon the mind. One wishes it were not so; but I have not yet left Oxford long enough to forget what chapel prayers are."

While this was passing, the rest of the party being scattered about the chapel, Julia called Mr. Crawford's attention to her sister, by saying, "Do look at Mr. Rushworth and Maria, standing side by side, exactly as if the ceremony were going to be performed. Have not they completely the air of it?"

Mr. Crawford smiled his acquiescence, and stepping forward to Maria, said, in a voice which she only could hear, "I do not like to see Miss Bertram so near the altar."

Starting, the lady instinctively moved a step or two, but recovering herself in a moment, affected to laugh, and asked him, in a tone not much louder, "If he would give her away?"

"I am afraid I should do it very awkwardly," was his reply, with a look of meaning.

Julia, joining them at the moment, carried on the joke.

"Upon my word, it is really a pity that it should not take place directly, if we had but a proper licence, for here we are altogether, and nothing in the world could be more snug and pleasant." And she talked and laughed about it with so little caution as to catch the comprehension of Mr. Rushworth and his mother, and expose her sister to the whispered gallantries of her lover, while Mrs. Rushworth spoke with proper smiles and dignity of its being a most happy event to her whenever it took place.

"If Edmund were but in orders!" cried Julia, and running to where he stood with Miss Crawford and Fanny: "My dear Edmund, if you were but in orders now, you might perform the ceremony directly. How unlucky that you are not ordained; Mr. Rushworth and Maria are quite ready."

Miss Crawford's countenance, as Julia spoke, might have amused a disinterested observer. She looked almost aghast under the new idea she was receiving. Fanny pitied her. "How distressed she will be at what she said just now," passed across her mind.

"Ordained!" said Miss Crawford; "what, are you to be a clergyman?"

"Yes; I shall take orders soon after my father's return—probably at Christmas."

Miss Crawford, rallying her spirits, and recovering her complexion, replied only, "If I had known this before, I would have spoken of the cloth with more respect," and turned the subject.

The chapel was soon afterwards left to the silence and stillness which reigned in it, with few interruptions, throughout the year. Miss Bertram, displeased with her sister, led the way, and all seemed to feel that they had been there long enough.

The lower part of the house had been now entirely shewn, and Mrs. Rushworth, never weary in the cause, would have proceeded towards the principal staircase, and taken them through all the rooms above, if her son had not interposed with a doubt of there being time enough. "For if," said he, with the sort of self-evident proposition which many a clearer head does not always avoid, "we are *too* long going over the house, we shall not have time for what is to be done out of doors. It is past two, and we are to dine at five."

Mrs. Rushworth submitted; and the question of surveying the grounds, with the who and the how, was likely to be more fully agitated, and Mrs. Norris was beginning to arrange by what junction of carriages and horses most could be done, when the young people, meeting with an outward door, temptingly open on a flight of steps which led immediately to turf and shrubs, and all the sweets of pleasure-grounds, as by one impulse, one wish for air and liberty, all walked out.

"Suppose we turn down here for the present," said Mrs. Rushworth, civilly taking the hint and following them. "Here are the greatest number of our plants, and here are the curious pheasants."

"Query," said Mr. Crawford, looking round him, "whether we may not find something to employ us here before we go farther? I see walls of great promise. Mr. Rushworth, shall we summon a council on this lawn?"

"James," said Mrs. Rushworth to her son, "I believe the wilderness will be new to all the party. The Miss Bertrams have never seen the wilderness yet."

No objection was made, but for some time there seemed no inclination to move in any plan, or to any distance. All were attracted at first by the plants or the pheasants, and all dispersed about in happy independence. Mr. Crawford was the first to move forward to examine the capabilities of that end of the house. The lawn, bounded on each side by a high wall, contained beyond the first planted area a bowling-green, and beyond the bowling-green a long terrace walk, backed by iron palisades, and commanding a view over them into the tops of the trees of the wilderness immediately adjoining. It was a good spot for fault-finding. Mr. Crawford was soon followed by Miss Bertram and Mr. Rushworth; and when, after a little time, the others began to form into parties, these three were found in busy consultation on the terrace by Edmund, Miss Crawford, and Fanny, who seemed as naturally to unite, and who, after a short participation of their regrets and difficulties, left them and walked on. The remaining three, Mrs. Rushworth, Mrs. Norris, and Julia, were still far behind;

for Julia, whose happy star no longer prevailed, was obliged to keep by the side of Mrs. Rushworth, and restrain her impatient feet to that lady's slow pace, while her aunt, having fallen in with the housekeeper, who was come out to feed the pheasants, was lingering behind in gossip with her. Poor Julia, the only one out of the nine not tolerably satisfied with their lot, was now in a state of complete penance, and as different from the Julia of the barouche-box as could well be imagined. The politeness which she had been brought up to practise as a duty made it impossible for her to escape; while the want of that higher species of self-command, that just consideration of others, that knowledge of her own heart, that principle of right, which had not formed any essential part of her education, made her miserable under it.

"This is insufferably hot," said Miss Crawford, when they had taken one turn on the terrace, and were drawing a second time to the door in the middle which opened to the wilderness. "Shall any of us object to being comfortable? Here is a nice little wood, if one can but get into it. What happiness if the door should not be locked! but of course it is; for in these great places the gardeners are the only people who can go where they like."

The door, however, proved not to be locked, and they were all agreed in turning joyfully through it, and leaving the unmitigated glare of day behind. A considerable flight of steps landed them in the wilderness, which was a planted wood of about two acres, and though chiefly of larch and laurel, and beech cut down, and though laid out with too much regularity, was darkness and shade, and natural beauty, compared with the bowling-green and the terrace. They all felt the refreshment of it, and for some time could only walk and admire. At length, after a short pause, Miss Crawford began with, "So you are to be a clergyman, Mr. Bertram. This is rather a surprise to me."

"Why should it surprise you? You must suppose me designed for some profession, and might perceive that I am neither a lawyer, nor a soldier, nor a sailor."

"Very true; but, in short, it had not occurred to me. And you know there is generally an uncle or a grandfather to leave a fortune to the second son."

"A very praiseworthy practice," said Edmund, "but not quite universal. I am one of the exceptions, and *being* one, must do something for myself."

"But why are you to be a clergyman? I thought *that* was always the lot of the youngest, where there were many to chuse before him."

"Do you think the church itself never chosen, then?"

"*Never* is a black word. But yes, in the *never* of conversation, which means *not very often*, I do think it. For what is to be done in the church? Men love to distinguish themselves, and in either of the other lines distinction may be gained, but not in the church. A clergyman is nothing."

"The *nothing* of conversation has its gradations, I hope, as well as the *never*. A clergyman cannot be high in state or fashion. He must not head mobs, or set the ton in dress. But I cannot call that situation nothing which has the charge of all that is of the first importance to mankind, individually or collectively considered, temporally and eternally, which has the guardianship of religion and morals, and consequently of the manners which result from their influence. No one here can call the *office* nothing. If the man who holds it is so, it is by the neglect of his duty, by foregoing its just importance, and stepping out of his place to appear what he ought not to appear."

"*You* assign greater consequence to the clergyman than one has been used to hear given, or than I can quite comprehend. One does not see much of this influence and importance in society, and how can it be acquired where they are so seldom seen themselves? How can two sermons a week, even supposing them worth hearing, supposing the preacher to have the sense to prefer Blair's to his own, do all that you speak of? govern the conduct and fashion the manners of a large congregation for the rest of the week? One scarcely sees a clergyman out of his pulpit."

"*You* are speaking of London, *I* am speaking of the nation at large."

"The metropolis, I imagine, is a pretty fair sample of the rest."

"Not, I should hope, of the proportion of virtue to vice throughout the kingdom. We do not look in great cities for our best morality. It is not there that respectable people of any denomination can do most good; and it certainly is not there that the influence of the clergy can be most felt. A fine preacher is followed and admired; but it is not in fine preaching only that a good clergyman will be useful in his parish and his neighbourhood, where the parish and neighbourhood are of a size capable of knowing his private character, and observing his general conduct, which in London can rarely be the case. The clergy are lost there in the crowds of their parishioners. They are known to the largest part only as preachers. And with regard to their influencing public manners, Miss Crawford must not misunderstand me, or suppose I mean to call them the arbiters of good-breeding, the regulators of refinement and courtesy, the masters of the ceremonies of life. The *manners* I speak of might rather be called *conduct*, perhaps, the result of good principles; the effect, in short, of those doctrines which it is their duty to teach and recommend; and it will, I believe, be everywhere found, that as the clergy are, or are not what they ought to be, so are the rest of the nation."

"Certainly," said Fanny, with gentle earnestness.

"There," cried Miss Crawford, "you have quite convinced Miss Price already."

"I wish I could convince Miss Crawford too."

"I do not think you ever will," said she, with an arch smile; "I am just as much surprised now as I was at first that you should intend to take orders. You really are fit for something better. Come, do change your mind. It is not too late. Go into the law."

"Go into the law! With as much ease as I was told to go into this wilderness."

"Now you are going to say something about law being the worst wilderness of the two, but I forestall you; remember, I have forestalled you."

"You need not hurry when the object is only to prevent my saying a *bon mot*, for there is not the least wit in my nature. I am a very matter-of-fact, plain-spoken being, and may blunder on the borders of a repartee for half an hour together without striking it out."

A general silence succeeded. Each was thoughtful. Fanny made the first interruption by saying, "I wonder that I should be tired with only walking in this sweet wood; but the next time we come to a seat, if it is not disagreeable to you, I should be glad to sit down for a little while."

"My dear Fanny," cried Edmund, immediately drawing her arm within his, "how thoughtless I have been! I hope you are not very tired. Perhaps," turning to Miss Crawford, "my other companion may do me the honour of taking an arm."

"Thank you, but I am not at all tired." She took it, however, as she spoke, and the gratification of having her do so, of feeling such a connexion for the first time, made him a little forgetful of Fanny. "You scarcely touch me," said he. "You do not make me of any use. What a difference in the weight of a woman's arm from that of a man! At Oxford I have been a good deal used to have a man lean on me for the length of a street, and you are only a fly in the comparison."

"I am really not tired, which I almost wonder at; for we must have walked at least a mile in this wood. Do not you think we have?"

"Not half a mile," was his sturdy answer; for he was not yet so much in love as to measure distance, or reckon time, with feminine lawlessness.

"Oh! you do not consider how much we have wound about. We have taken such a very serpentine course, and the wood itself must be half a mile long in a straight line, for we have never seen the end of it yet since we left the first great path."

"But if you remember, before we left that first great path, we saw directly to the end of it. We looked down the whole vista, and saw it closed by iron gates, and it could not have been more than a furlong in length."

"Oh! I know nothing of your furlongs, but I am sure it is a very long wood, and that we have been winding in and out ever since we came into it; and therefore, when I say that we have walked a mile in it, I must speak within compass."

"We have been exactly a quarter of an hour here," said Edmund, taking out his watch. "Do you think we are walking four miles an hour?"

"Oh! do not attack me with your watch. A watch is always too fast or too slow. I cannot be dictated to by a watch."

A few steps farther brought them out at the bottom of the very walk they had been talking of; and standing back, well shaded and sheltered, and looking over a ha-ha into the park, was a comfortable-sized bench, on which they all sat down.

"I am afraid you are very tired, Fanny," said Edmund, observing her; "why would not you speak sooner? This will be a bad day's amusement for you if you are to be knocked up. Every sort of exercise fatigues her so soon, Miss Crawford, except riding."

"How abominable in you, then, to let me engross her horse as I did all last week! I am ashamed of you and of myself, but it shall never happen again."

"*Your* attentiveness and consideration makes me more sensible of my own neglect. Fanny's interest seems in safer hands with you than with me."

"That she should be tired now, however, gives me no surprise; for there is nothing in the course of one's duties so fatiguing as what we have been doing this morning: seeing a great house, dawdling from one room to another, straining one's eyes and one's attention, hearing what one does not understand, admiring what one does not care for. It is generally allowed to be the greatest bore in the world, and Miss Price has found it so, though she did not know it."

"I shall soon be rested," said Fanny; "to sit in the shade on a fine day, and look upon verdure, is the most perfect refreshment."

After sitting a little while Miss Crawford was up again. "I must move," said she; "resting fatigues me. I have looked across the ha-ha till I am weary. I must go and look through that iron gate at the same view, without being able to see it so well."

Edmund left the seat likewise. "Now, Miss Crawford, if you will look up the walk, you will convince yourself that it cannot be half a mile long, or half half a mile."

"It is an immense distance," said she; "I see *that* with a glance."

He still reasoned with her, but in vain. She would not calculate, she would not compare. She would only smile and assert. The greatest degree of rational consistency could not have been more engaging, and they talked with mutual satisfaction. At last it was agreed that they should endeavour to determine the dimensions of the wood by walking a little more about it. They would go to one end of it, in the line they were then in—for there was a straight green walk along the bottom by the side of the ha-ha— and perhaps turn a little way in some other direction, if it seemed likely to assist them, and be back in a few minutes. Fanny said she was rested, and would have moved too, but this was not suffered. Edmund urged her remaining where she was with an earnestness which she could not resist, and she was left on the bench to think with pleasure of her cousin's care, but with great regret that she was not stronger. She watched them till they had turned the corner, and listened till all sound of them had ceased. And as memory is known to present itself at the most unfortunate of moments,

Fanny's thoughts brought to mind an afternoon not so long ago; a twelvemonth or more prior to the introduction of Mr. and Miss Crawford, when she was presented the fortune of taking a walk beyond the garden gate at Mansfield. It is not to be presumed that she was given such time to spend freely on her own, but rather should be noted its occurrence owing to chance as both her aunts were otherwise occupied as were the Miss Bertrams. Were it under usual circumstances, Fanny might have been given to concern about walking about the woods on the other side of the gate, but she had only moments prior seen from her attic window both Tom and Edmund approaching the perimeter of the park and the dense forest beyond. It was near the end of her seventeenth year and she was at an age when she was too young to be satisfied with the mundane, yet perhaps too old to be interested in a frolic amongst the trees with her cousins. But she found herself most curious to know what they were about, and she gave cook the odd excuse of foraging for wild asparagus as she set out to follow Tom and Edmund.

Fanny might not have known immediately where they were if not for the great gales of laughter and sounds of water splashing about. Not many years before she had played near the same pond as a girl new to Mansfield. She expected they were bathing and began to turn away and offer them privacy when she heard Edmund's exclamation of laughter and could not help but lower herself deep into the shrubbery and follow the direction of his voice, only to discover herself most unprepared for the sight before her.

She had seen images of unclothed men as statues or renderings in the books found in Sir Thomas's library; indeed Maria and Julia had routinely shared their excitement at the discovery of such images more than once during her childhood. But it turned out seeing an unclothed man in the pages of a book and seeing one a few feet before her were for Fanny two very different circumstances, so much so that she began to feel as if her very breath had stopt. Thankfully Edmund stood in the water and his only exposure was above the waist, but she found his torso to be everything of magnificence. He was smooth as the marble of the statues and his broad expanse of back and shoulders were most remarkable, but it was the dark and shining hairs that caught her attention as they spread across his beautiful chest and down his fine arms. She could not take her eyes from him, even to look at Tom who was calling towards his brother whilst spraying him with water. It was as she watched Edmund manouevre his body in different poses to block his brother's friendly attack that she saw more of him, and as she managed a glimpse at the trail of dark hairs leading downward from his navel, she turned to leave them for fear she might faint and thus be discovered, but it was at that very moment of her attempted escape Edmund began to remove himself from the water.

Fanny found herself motionless as she studied Edmund's backside and the dark hairs clinging wetly to his long and well-shaped legs. When he turned she saw the front of him,—all of him,—Edmund and his manhood in all its brilliance. Her throat became dry, her heart-beat rang in her ears, and she could not recall even how she managed to find her way out of the woods that afternoon with tears pouring hotly over her cheeks, so certain was she that she had committed the greatest of sins by seeing Edmund—by seeing so much of him!

Fanny vowed never to think on Edmund again in such a way and upon this most recent reflection vowed the same once more. He had been chusing carefully concerning his future and Fanny must secure her own; and as she sat waiting, hoping most impatiently for a distraction, she attempted to control her thoughts with a list of the fortunes in her life for which she was most grateful.

Chapter 10

A quarter of an hour, twenty minutes, passed away, and Fanny was still thinking of Edmund, Miss Crawford, and herself, without interruption from any one. She began to be surprised at being left so long, and to listen with an anxious desire of hearing their steps and their voices again. She listened, and at length she heard; she heard voices and feet approaching; but she had just satisfied herself that it was not those she wanted, when Miss Bertram, Mr. Rushworth, and Mr. Crawford issued from the same path which she had trod herself, and were before her.

"Miss Price all alone" and "My dear Fanny, how comes this?" were the first salutations. She told her story. "Poor dear Fanny," cried her cousin, "how ill you have been used by them! You had better have staid with us."

Then seating herself with a gentleman on each side, she resumed the conversation which had engaged them before, and discussed the possibility of improvements with much animation. Nothing was fixed on; but Henry Crawford was full of ideas and projects, and, generally speaking, whatever he proposed was immediately approved, first by her, and then by Mr. Rushworth, whose principal business seemed to be to hear the others, and who scarcely risked an original thought of his own beyond a wish that they had seen his friend Smith's place.

After some minutes spent in this way, Miss Bertram, observing the iron gate, expressed a wish of passing through it into the park, that their views and their plans might be more comprehensive. It was the very thing of all others to be wished, it was the best, it was the only way of proceeding with any advantage, in Henry Crawford's opinion; and he directly saw a knoll not half a mile off, which would give them exactly the requisite command of the house. Go therefore they must to that knoll, and through that gate; but the gate was locked. Mr. Rushworth wished he had brought the key; he had been very near thinking whether he should not bring the key; he was determined he would never come without the key again; but still this did not remove the present evil. They could not get through; and as Miss Bertram's inclination for so doing did by no means lessen, it ended in Mr. Rushworth's declaring outright that he would go and fetch the key. He set off accordingly.

"It is undoubtedly the best thing we can do now, as we are so far from the house already," said Mr. Crawford, when he was gone.

"Yes, there is nothing else to be done. But now, sincerely, do not you find the place altogether worse than you expected?"

"No, indeed, far otherwise. I find it better, grander, more complete in its style, though that style may not be the best. And to tell you the truth," speaking rather lower, "I do not think that *I* shall ever see Sotherton again with so much pleasure as I do now. Another summer will hardly improve it to me."

After a moment's embarrassment the lady replied, "You are too much a man of the world not to see with the eyes of the world. If other people think Sotherton improved, I have no doubt that you will."

"I am afraid I am not quite so much the man of the world as might be good for me in some points. My feelings are not quite so evanescent, nor my memory of the past under such easy dominion as one finds to be the case with men of the world."

This was followed by a short silence. Miss Bertram began again. "You seemed to enjoy your drive here very much this morning. I was glad to see you so well entertained. You and Julia were laughing the whole way."

"Were we? Yes, I believe we were; but I have not the least recollection at what. Oh! I believe I was relating to her some ridiculous stories of an old Irish groom of my uncle's. Your sister loves to laugh."

"You think her more light-hearted than I am?"

"More easily amused," he replied; "consequently, you know," smiling, "better company. I could not have hoped to entertain you with Irish anecdotes during a ten miles' drive."

"Naturally, I believe, I am as lively as Julia, but I have more to think of now."

"You have, undoubtedly; and there are situations in which very high spirits would denote insensibility. Your prospects, however, are too fair to justify want of spirits. You have a very smiling scene before you."

"Do you mean literally or figuratively? Literally, I conclude. Yes, certainly, the sun shines, and the park looks very cheerful. But unluckily that iron gate, that ha-ha, give me a feeling of restraint and hardship. 'I cannot get out,' as the starling said." As she spoke, and it was with expression, she walked to the gate: he followed her. "Mr. Rushworth is so long fetching this key!"

"And for the world you would not get out without the key and without Mr. Rushworth's authority and protection, or I think you might with little difficulty pass round the edge of the gate, here, with my assistance; I think it might be done, if you really wished to be more at large, and could allow yourself to think it not prohibited."

"Prohibited! nonsense! I certainly can get out that way, and I will. Mr. Rushworth will be here in a moment, you know; we shall not be out of sight."

"Or if we are, Miss Price will be so good as to tell him that he will find us near that knoll: the grove of oak on the knoll."

Fanny, feeling all this to be wrong, could not help making an effort to prevent it. "You will hurt yourself, Miss Bertram," she cried; "you will certainly hurt yourself against those spikes; you will tear your gown; you will be in danger of slipping into the ha-ha. You had better not go."

Her cousin was safe on the other side while these words were spoken, and, smiling with all the good-humour of success, she said, "Thank you, my dear Fanny, but I and my gown are alive and well, and so good-bye."

Fanny was again left to her solitude, and with no increase of pleasant feelings, for she was sorry for almost all that she had seen and heard, astonished at Miss Bertram, and angry with Mr. Crawford. By taking a circuitous route, and, as it appeared to her, very unreasonable direction to the knoll, they were soon beyond her eye; and for some minutes longer she remained without sight or sound of any companion. She seemed to have the little wood all to herself. She could almost have thought that Edmund and Miss Crawford had left it, but that it was impossible for Edmund to forget her so entirely.

She was again roused from disagreeable musings by sudden footsteps: somebody was coming at a quick pace down the principal walk. She expected Mr. Rushworth, but it was Julia, who, hot and out of breath, and with a look of disappointment, cried out on seeing her, "Heyday! Where are the others? I thought Maria and Mr. Crawford were with you."

Fanny explained.

"A pretty trick, upon my word! I cannot see them anywhere," looking eagerly into the park. "But they cannot be very far off, and I think I am equal to as much as Maria, even without help."

"But, Julia, Mr. Rushworth will be here in a moment with the key. Do wait for Mr. Rushworth."

"Not I, indeed. I have had enough of the family for one morning. Why, child, I have but this moment escaped from his horrible mother. Such a penance as I have been enduring, while you were sitting here so composed and so happy! It might have been as well, perhaps, if you had been in my place, but you always contrive to keep out of these scrapes."

This was a most unjust reflection, but Fanny could allow for it, and let it pass: Julia was vexed, and her temper was hasty; but she felt that it would not last, and therefore, taking no notice, only asked her if she had not seen Mr. Rushworth.

"Yes, yes, we saw him. He was posting away as if upon life and death, and could but just spare time to tell us his errand, and where you all were."

"It is a pity he should have so much trouble for nothing."

"*That* is Miss Maria's concern. I am not obliged to punish myself for *her* sins. The mother I could not avoid, as long as my tiresome aunt was dancing about with the housekeeper, but the son I *can* get away from."

And she immediately scrambled across the fence, and walked away, not attending to Fanny's last question of whether she had seen anything of Miss Crawford and Edmund. The sort of dread in which Fanny now sat of seeing Mr. Rushworth prevented her thinking so much of their continued absence, however, as she might have done. She felt that he had been very ill-used, and was quite unhappy in having to communicate what had passed. He joined her within five minutes after Julia's exit; and though she made the best of the story, he was evidently mortified and displeased in no common degree. At first he scarcely said anything; his looks only expressed his extreme surprise and vexation, and he walked to the gate and stood there, without seeming to know what to do.

"They desired me to stay—my cousin Maria charged me to say that you would find them at that knoll, or thereabouts."

"I do not believe I shall go any farther," said he sullenly; "I see nothing of them. By the time I get to the knoll they may be gone somewhere else. I have had walking enough."

And he sat down with a most gloomy countenance by Fanny.

"I am very sorry," said she; "it is very unlucky." And she longed to be able to say something more to the purpose.

After an interval of silence, "I think they might as well have staid for me," said he.

"Miss Bertram thought you would follow her."

"I should not have had to follow her if she had staid."

This could not be denied, and Fanny was silenced. After another pause, he went on—"Pray, Miss Price, are you such a great admirer of this Mr. Crawford as some people are? For my part, I can see nothing in him."

"I do not think him at all handsome."

"Handsome! Nobody can call such an undersized man handsome. He is not five foot nine. I should not wonder if he is not more than five foot eight. I think he is an ill-looking fellow. In my opinion, these Crawfords are no addition at all. We did very well without them."

A small sigh escaped Fanny here, and she did not know how to contradict him.

"If I had made any difficulty about fetching the key, there might have been some excuse, but I went the very moment she said she wanted it."

"Nothing could be more obliging than your manner, I am sure, and I dare say you walked as fast as you could; but still it is some distance, you know, from this spot to the house, quite into the house; and when people are waiting, they are bad judges of time, and every half minute seems like five."

He got up and walked to the gate again, and "wished he had had the key about him at the time." Fanny thought she discerned in his standing there an indication of relenting, which encouraged her to another attempt, and she said, therefore, "It is a pity you should not join them. They expected to have a better view of the house from that part of the park, and will be thinking how it may be improved; and nothing of that sort, you know, can be settled without you."

She found herself more successful in sending away than in retaining a companion. Mr. Rushworth was worked on. "Well," said he, "if you really think I had better go: it would be foolish to bring the key for nothing." And letting himself out, he walked off without farther ceremony.

Fanny's thoughts were now all engrossed by the two who had left her so long ago, and getting quite impatient, she resolved to go in search of them. She followed their steps along the bottom walk, and had just turned up into another, when the voice and the laugh of Miss Crawford once more caught her ear; the sound approached, and a few more windings brought them before her. They were just returned into the wilderness from the park, to which a sidegate, not fastened, had tempted them very soon after their leaving her, and they had been across a portion of the park into the very avenue which Fanny had been hoping the whole morning to reach at last, and had been sitting down under one of the trees. This was their history. It was evident that they had been spending their time pleasantly, and were not aware of the length of their absence. Fanny's best consolation was in being assured that Edmund had wished for her very much, and that he should certainly have come back for her, had she not been tired already; but this was not quite sufficient to do away with the pain of having been left a whole hour, when he had talked of only a few minutes, nor to banish the sort of curiosity she felt to know what they had been conversing about all that time; and the result of the whole was to her disappointment and depression, as they prepared by general agreement to return to the house.

On reaching the bottom of the steps to the terrace, Mrs. Rushworth and Mrs. Norris presented themselves at the top, just ready for the wilderness, at the end of an hour and a half from their leaving the house. Mrs. Norris had been too well employed to move faster. Whatever cross-accidents had occurred to intercept the pleasures of her nieces, she had found a morning of complete enjoyment; for the housekeeper, after a great many courtesies on the subject of pheasants, had taken her to the dairy, told her all about their cows, and given her the receipt for a famous cream cheese; and since Julia's leaving them they had been met by the gardener, with whom she had made a most satisfactory acquaintance, for she had set him right as to his grandson's illness, convinced him that it was an ague, and promised him a charm for it; and he, in return, had shewn her all his choicest nursery of plants, and actually presented her with a very curious specimen of heath.

On this *rencontre* they all returned to the house together, there to lounge away the time as they could with sofas, and chit-chat, and Quarterly Reviews, till the return of the others, and the arrival of dinner. It was late before the Miss Bertrams and the two gentlemen came in, and their ramble did not appear to have been more than partially agreeable, or at all productive of anything useful with regard to the object of the day. By their own accounts they had been all walking after each other, and the junction which had taken place at last seemed, to Fanny's observation, to have been as much too late for re-establishing harmony, as it confessedly had been for determining on any alteration. She felt, as she looked at Julia and Mr. Rushworth, that hers was not the only dissatisfied bosom amongst them: there was gloom on the face of each. Mr. Crawford and Miss Bertram were much more gay, and she thought that he was taking particular pains, during dinner, to do away any little resentment of the other two, and restore general good-humour.

Dinner was soon followed by tea and coffee, a ten miles' drive home allowed no waste of hours; and from the time of their sitting down to table, it was a quick succession of busy nothings till the carriage came to the door, and Mrs. Norris, having fidgeted about, and obtained a few pheasants' eggs and a cream cheese from the housekeeper, and made abundance of civil speeches to Mrs. Rushworth, was ready to lead the way. At the same moment Mr. Crawford, approaching Julia, said, "I hope I am not to lose my companion, unless she is afraid of the evening air in so exposed a seat." The request had not been foreseen, but was very graciously received, and Julia's day was likely to end almost as well as it began. Miss Bertram had made up her mind to something different, and was a little disappointed; but her conviction of being really the one preferred comforted her under it, and enabled her to receive Mr. Rushworth's parting attentions as she ought. He was certainly better pleased to hand her into the barouche than to assist her in ascending the box, and his complacency seemed confirmed by the arrangement.

"Well, Fanny, this has been a fine day for you, upon my word," said Mrs. Norris, as they drove through the park. "Nothing but pleasure from beginning to end! I am sure you ought to be very much obliged to your aunt Bertram and me for contriving to let you go. A pretty good day's amusement you have had!"

Maria was just discontented enough to say directly, "I think *you* have done pretty well yourself, ma'am. Your lap seems full of good things, and here is a basket of something between us which has been knocking my elbow unmercifully."

"My dear, it is only a beautiful little heath, which that nice old gardener would make me take; but if it is in your way, I will have it in my lap directly. There, Fanny, you shall carry that parcel for me; take great care of it: do not let it fall; it is a cream cheese, just like the excellent one we had at dinner. Nothing would satisfy that good old Mrs. Whitaker, but my taking one of the cheeses. I stood out as long as I could, till the tears almost came into her eyes, and I knew it was just the sort that my sister would be delighted with. That Mrs. Whitaker is a treasure! She was quite shocked when I asked her whether wine was allowed at the second table, and she has turned away two housemaids for wearing white gowns. Take care of the cheese, Fanny. Now I can manage the other parcel and the basket very well."

"What else have you been spunging?" said Maria, half-pleased that Sotherton should be so complimented.

"Spunging, my dear! It is nothing but four of those beautiful pheasants' eggs, which Mrs. Whitaker would quite force upon me: she would not take a denial. She said it must be such an amusement to me, as she understood I lived quite alone, to have a few living creatures of that sort; and so to be sure it will. I shall get the dairymaid to set them under the first spare hen, and if they come to good I can have them moved to my own house and borrow a coop; and it will be a great delight to me in my lonely hours to attend to them. And if I have good luck, your mother shall have some."

It was a beautiful evening, mild and still, and the drive was as pleasant as the serenity of Nature could make it; but when Mrs. Norris ceased speaking, it was altogether a silent drive to those within. Their spirits were in general exhausted; and to determine whether the day had afforded most pleasure or pain, might occupy the meditations of almost all.

Chapter 11

The day at Sotherton, with all its imperfections, afforded the Miss Bertrams much more agreeable feelings than were derived from the letters from Antigua, which soon afterwards reached Mansfield. It was much pleasanter to think of Henry Crawford than of their father; and to think of their father in England again within a certain period, which these letters obliged them to do, was a most unwelcome exercise.

November was the black month fixed for his return. Sir Thomas wrote of it with as much decision as experience and anxiety could authorise. His business was so nearly concluded as to justify him in proposing to take his passage in the September packet, and he consequently looked forward with the hope of being with his beloved family again early in November.

Maria was more to be pitied than Julia; for to her the father brought a husband, and the return of the friend most solicitous for her happiness would unite her to the lover, on whom she had chosen that happiness should depend. It was a gloomy prospect, and all she could do was to throw a mist over it, and hope when the mist cleared away she should see something else. It would hardly be *early* in November, there were generally delays, a bad passage or *something*; that favouring *something* which everybody who shuts their eyes while they look, or their understandings while they reason, feels the comfort of. It would probably be the middle of November at least; the middle of November was three months off. Three months comprised thirteen weeks. Much might happen in thirteen weeks.

Sir Thomas would have been deeply mortified by a suspicion of half that his daughters felt on the subject of his return, and would hardly have found consolation in a knowledge of the interest it excited in the breast of another young lady. Miss Crawford, on walking up with her brother to spend the evening at Mansfield Park, heard the good news; and though seeming to have no concern in the affair beyond politeness, and to have vented all her feelings in a quiet congratulation, heard it with an attention not so easily satisfied. Mrs. Norris gave the particulars of the letters, and the subject was dropt; but after tea, as Miss Crawford was standing at an open window with Edmund and Fanny looking out on a twilight scene, while the Miss Bertrams, Mr. Rushworth, and Henry Crawford were all busy with candles at the pianoforte, she suddenly revived it by turning round towards the group, and saying, "How happy Mr. Rushworth looks! He is thinking of November."

Edmund looked round at Mr. Rushworth too, but had nothing to say.

"Your father's return will be a very interesting event."

"It will, indeed, after such an absence; an absence not only long, but including so many dangers."

"It will be the forerunner also of other interesting events: your sister's marriage, and your taking orders."

"Yes."

"Don't be affronted," said she, laughing, "but it does put me in mind of some of the old heathen heroes, who, after performing great exploits in a foreign land, offered sacrifices to the gods on their safe return."

"There is no sacrifice in the case," replied Edmund, with a serious smile, and glancing at the pianoforte again; "it is entirely her own doing."

"Oh yes I know it is. I was merely joking. She has done no more than what every young woman would do; and I have no doubt of her being extremely happy. My other sacrifice, of course, you do not understand."

"My taking orders, I assure you, is quite as voluntary as Maria's marrying."

"It is fortunate that your inclination and your father's convenience should accord so well. There is a very good living kept for you, I understand, hereabouts."

"Which you suppose has biassed me?"

"But *that* I am sure it has not," cried Fanny.

"Thank you for your good word, Fanny, but it is more than I would affirm myself. On the contrary, the knowing that there was such a provision for me probably did bias me. Nor can I think it wrong that it should. There was no natural disinclination to be overcome, and I see no reason why a man should make a worse clergyman for knowing that he will have a competence early in life. I was in safe hands. I hope I should not have been influenced myself in a wrong way, and I am sure my father was too conscientious to have allowed it. I have no doubt that I was biased, but I think it was blamelessly."

"It is the same sort of thing," said Fanny, after a short pause, "as for the son of an admiral to go into the navy, or the son of a general to be in the army, and nobody sees anything wrong in that. Nobody wonders that they should prefer the line where their friends can serve them best, or suspects them to be less in earnest in it than they appear."

"No, my dear Miss Price, and for reasons good. The profession, either navy or army, is its own justification. It has everything in its favour: heroism, danger, bustle, fashion. Soldiers and sailors are always acceptable in society. Nobody can wonder that men are soldiers and sailors."

"But the motives of a man who takes orders with the certainty of preferment may be fairly suspected, you think?" said Edmund. "To be justified in your eyes, he must do it in the most complete uncertainty of any provision."

"What! take orders without a living! No; that is madness indeed; absolute madness."

"Shall I ask you how the church is to be filled, if a man is neither to take orders with a living nor without? No; for you certainly would not know what to say. But I must beg some advantage to the clergyman from your own argument. As he cannot be influenced by those feelings which you rank highly as temptation and reward to the soldier and sailor in their choice of a profession, as heroism, and noise, and fashion, are all against him, he ought to be less liable to the suspicion of wanting sincerity or good intentions in the choice of his."

"Oh! no doubt he is very sincere in preferring an income ready made, to the trouble of working for one; and has the best intentions of doing nothing all the rest of his days but eat, drink, and grow fat. It is indolence, Mr. Bertram, indeed. Indolence and love of ease; a want of all laudable ambition, of taste for good company, or of inclination to take the trouble of being agreeable, which make men clergymen. A clergyman has nothing to do but be slovenly and selfish—read the newspaper, watch the weather, and quarrel with his wife. His curate does all the work, and the business of his own life is to dine."

"There are such clergymen, no doubt, but I think they are not so common as to justify Miss Crawford in esteeming it their general character. I suspect that in this comprehensive and (may I say) commonplace censure, you are not judging from yourself, but from prejudiced persons, whose opinions you have been in the habit of hearing. It is impossible that your own observation can have given you much knowledge of the clergy. You can have been personally acquainted with very few of a set of men you condemn so conclusively. You are speaking what you have been told at your uncle's table."

"I speak what appears to me the general opinion; and where an opinion is general, it is usually correct. Though *I* have not seen much of the domestic lives of clergymen, it is seen by too many to leave any deficiency of information."

"Where any one body of educated men, of whatever denomination, are condemned indiscriminately, there must be a deficiency of information, or (smiling) of something else. Your uncle, and his brother admirals, perhaps knew little of clergymen beyond the chaplains whom, good or bad, they were always wishing away."

"Poor William! He has met with great kindness from the chaplain of the Antwerp," was a tender apostrophe of Fanny's, very much to the purpose of her own feelings if not of the conversation.

"I have been so little addicted to take my opinions from my uncle," said Miss Crawford, "that I can hardly suppose—and since you push me so hard, I must observe, that I am not entirely without the means of seeing what clergymen are, being at this present time the guest of my own brother, Dr. Grant. And though Dr. Grant is most kind and obliging to me, and though he is really a gentleman, and, I dare say, a good scholar and clever, and often preaches good sermons, and is very respectable, *I* see him to be an indolent, selfish *bon vivant*, who must have his palate consulted in everything; who will not stir a finger for the convenience of any one; and who, moreover, if the cook makes a blunder, is out of humour with his excellent wife. To own the truth, Henry and I were partly driven out this very evening by a disappointment about a green goose, which he could not get the better of. My poor sister was forced to stay and bear it."

"I do not wonder at your disapprobation, upon my word. It is a great defect of temper, made worse by a very faulty habit of self-indulgence; and to see your sister suffering from it must be exceedingly painful to such feelings as yours. Fanny, it goes against us. We cannot attempt to defend Dr. Grant."

"No," replied Fanny, "but we need not give up his profession for all that; because, whatever profession Dr. Grant had chosen, he would have taken a—not a good temper into it; and as he must, either in the navy or army, have had a great many more people under his command than he has now, I think more would have been made unhappy by him as a sailor or soldier than as a clergyman. Besides, I cannot but suppose that whatever there may be to wish otherwise in Dr. Grant would have been in a greater danger of becoming worse in a more active and worldly profession, where he would have had less time and obligation—where he might have escaped that knowledge of himself, the *frequency*, at least, of that knowledge which it is impossible he should escape as he is now. A man—a sensible man like Dr. Grant, cannot be in the habit of teaching others their duty every week, cannot go to church twice every Sunday, and preach such very good sermons in so good a manner as he does, without being the better for it himself. It must make him think; and I have no doubt that he oftener endeavours to restrain himself than he would if he had been anything but a clergyman."

"We cannot prove to the contrary, to be sure; but I wish you a better fate, Miss Price, than to be the wife of a man whose amiableness depends upon his own sermons; for though he may preach himself into a good-humour every Sunday, it will be bad enough to have him quarrelling about green geese from Monday morning till Saturday night."

"I think the man who could often quarrel with Fanny," said Edmund affectionately, "must be beyond the reach of any sermons."

Fanny turned farther into the window; and Miss Crawford had only time to say, in a pleasant manner, "I fancy Miss Price has been more used to deserve praise than to hear it"; when, being earnestly invited by the Miss Bertrams to join in a glee, she tripped off to the instrument, leaving Edmund looking after her in an ecstasy of admiration of all her many virtues, from her obliging manners down to her light and graceful tread.

"There goes good-humour, I am sure," said he presently. "There goes a temper which would never give pain! How well she walks! and how readily she falls in with the inclination of others! joining them the moment she is asked. What a pity," he added, after an instant's reflection, "that she should have been in such hands!"

Fanny agreed to it, and had the pleasure of seeing him continue at the window with her, in spite of the expected glee; and of having his eyes soon turned, like hers, towards the scene without, where all that was solemn, and soothing, and lovely, appeared in the brilliancy of an unclouded night, and the contrast of the deep shade of the woods. Fanny spoke her feelings. "Here's harmony!" said she; "here's repose! Here's what may leave all painting and all music behind, and what poetry only can attempt to describe! Here's what may tranquillise every care, and lift the heart to rapture! When I look out on such a night as this, I feel as if there could be neither wickedness nor sorrow in the world; and there certainly would be less of both if the sublimity of Nature were more attended to, and people were carried more out of themselves by contemplating such a scene."

"I like to hear your enthusiasm, Fanny. It is a lovely night, and they are much to be pitied who have not been taught to feel, in some degree, as you do; who have not, at least, been given a taste for Nature in early life. They lose a great deal."

"*You* taught me to think and feel on the subject, cousin."

"I had a very apt scholar. There's Arcturus looking very bright."

"Yes, and the Bear. I wish I could see Cassiopeia."

"We must go out on the lawn for that. Should you be afraid?"

"Not in the least. It is a great while since we have had any star-gazing."

"Yes; I do not know how it has happened." The glee began. "We will stay till this is finished, Fanny," said he, turning his back on the window; and as it advanced, she had the mortification of seeing him advance too, moving forward by gentle degrees towards the instrument, and when it ceased, he was close by the singers, among the most urgent in requesting to hear the glee again.

Fanny sighed alone at the window, imagining herself stargazing on the lawn with the one whose heart matched hers truly, his hand reaching for hers to point out some constellation or another, till scolded away by Mrs. Norris's threats of catching cold, and most grateful for the interruption.

Chapter 12

Sir Thomas was to return in November, and his eldest son had duties to call him earlier home. The approach of September brought tidings of Mr. Bertram, first in a letter to the gamekeeper and then in a letter to Edmund; and by the end of August he arrived himself, to be gay, agreeable, and gallant again as occasion served, or Miss Crawford demanded; to tell of races and Weymouth, and parties and friends, to which she might have listened six weeks before with some interest, and altogether to give her the fullest conviction, by the power of actual comparison, of her preferring his younger brother.

It was very vexatious, and she was heartily sorry for it; but so it was; and so far from now meaning to marry the elder, she did not even want to attract him beyond what the simplest claims of conscious beauty required: his lengthened absence from Mansfield, without anything but pleasure in view, and his own will to consult, made it perfectly clear that he did not care about her; and his indifference was so much more than equalled by her own, that were he now to step forth the owner of Mansfield Park, the Sir Thomas complete, which he was to be in time, she did not believe she could accept him.

The season and duties which brought Mr. Bertram back to Mansfield took Mr. Crawford into Norfolk. Everingham could not do without him in the beginning of September. He went for a fortnight—a fortnight of such dullness to the Miss Bertrams as ought to have put them both on their guard, and made even Julia admit, in her jealousy of her sister, the absolute necessity of distrusting his attentions, and wishing him not to return; and a fortnight of sufficient leisure, in the intervals of shooting and sleeping, to have convinced the gentleman that he ought to keep longer away, had he been more in the habit of examining his own motives, and of reflecting to what the indulgence of his idle vanity was tending; but, thoughtless and selfish from prosperity and bad example, he would not look beyond the present moment. The sisters, handsome, clever, and encouraging, were an amusement to his sated mind; and finding nothing in Norfolk to equal the social pleasures of Mansfield, he gladly returned to it at the time appointed, and was welcomed thither quite as gladly by those whom he came to trifle with further.

Maria, with only Mr. Rushworth to attend to her, and doomed to the repeated details of his day's sport, good or bad, his boast of his dogs, his jealousy of his neighbours, his doubts of their qualifications, and his zeal after poachers, subjects which will not find their way to female feelings without some talent on one side or some attachment on the other, had missed Mr. Crawford grievously; and Julia, unengaged and unemployed, felt all the right of missing him much more. Each sister believed herself the favourite. Julia might be justified in so doing by the hints of Mrs. Grant, inclined to credit what she wished, and Maria by the hints of Mr. Crawford himself. Everything returned into the same channel as before his absence; his manners being to each so animated and agreeable as to lose no ground with either, and just stopping short of the consistence, the steadiness, the solicitude, and the warmth which might excite general notice.

Fanny was the only one of the party who found anything to dislike; but since the day at Sotherton, she could never see Mr. Crawford with either sister without observation, and seldom without wonder or censure; and had her confidence in her own judgment been equal to her exercise of it in every other respect, had she been sure that she was seeing clearly, and judging candidly, she would probably have made some important communications to her usual confidant. As it was, however, she only hazarded a hint, and the hint was lost. "I am rather surprised," said she, "that Mr. Crawford should come back again so soon, after being here so long before, full seven weeks; for I had understood he was so very fond of change and moving about, that I thought something would certainly occur, when he was once gone, to take him elsewhere. He is used to much gayer places than Mansfield."

"It is to his credit," was Edmund's answer; "and I dare say it gives his sister pleasure. She does not like his unsettled habits."

"What a favourite he is with my cousins!"

"Yes, his manners to women are such as must please. Mrs. Grant, I believe, suspects him of a preference for Julia; I have never seen much symptom of it, but I wish it may be so. He has no faults but what a serious attachment would remove."

"If Miss Bertram were not engaged," said Fanny cautiously, "I could sometimes almost think that he admired her more than Julia."

"Which is, perhaps, more in favour of his liking Julia best, than you, Fanny, may be aware; for I believe it often happens that a man, before he has quite made up his own mind, will distinguish the sister or intimate friend of the woman he is really thinking of more than the woman herself. Crawford has too much sense to stay here if he found himself in any danger from Maria; and I am not at all afraid for her, after such a proof as she has given that her feelings are not strong."

Fanny supposed she must have been mistaken, and meant to think differently in future; but with all that submission to Edmund could do, and all the help of the coinciding looks and hints which she occasionally noticed in some of the others, and which seemed to say that Julia was Mr. Crawford's choice, she knew not always what to think. She was privy, one evening, to the hopes of her aunt Norris on the subject, as well as to her feelings, and the feelings of Mrs. Rushworth, on a point of some similarity, and could not help wondering as she listened; and glad would she have been not to be obliged to listen, for it was while all the other young people were dancing, and she sitting, most unwillingly, among the chaperons at the fire, longing for the re-entrance of her elder cousin, on whom all her own hopes of a partner then depended. It was Fanny's first ball, though without the preparation or splendour of many a young lady's first ball, being the thought only of the afternoon, built on the late acquisition of a violin player in the servants' hall, and the possibility of raising five couple with the help of Mrs. Grant and a new intimate friend of Mr. Bertram's just arrived on a visit. It had, however, been a very happy one to Fanny through four dances, and she was quite grieved to be losing even a quarter of an hour. While waiting and wishing, looking now at the dancers and now at the door, this dialogue between the two above-mentioned ladies was forced on her —

"I think, ma'am," said Mrs. Norris, her eyes directed towards Mr. Rushworth and Maria, who were partners for the second time, "we shall see some happy faces again now."

"Yes, ma'am, indeed," replied the other, with a stately simper, "there will be some satisfaction in looking on *now*, and I think it was rather a pity they should have been obliged to part. Young folks in their situation should be excused complying with the common forms. I wonder my son did not propose it."

"I dare say he did, ma'am. Mr. Rushworth is never remiss. But dear Maria has such a strict sense of propriety, so much of that true delicacy which one seldom meets with nowadays, Mrs. Rushworth—that wish of avoiding particularity! Dear ma'am, only look at her face at this moment; how different from what it was the two last dances!"

Miss Bertram did indeed look happy, her eyes were sparkling with pleasure, and she was speaking with great animation, for Julia and her partner, Mr. Crawford, were close to her; they were all in a cluster together. How she had looked before, Fanny could not recollect, for she had been dancing with Edmund herself, and had not thought about her.

Mrs. Norris continued, "It is quite delightful, ma'am, to see young people so properly happy, so well suited, and so much the thing! I cannot but think of dear Sir Thomas's delight. And what do you say, ma'am, to the chance of another match? Mr. Rushworth has set a good example, and such things are very catching."

Mrs. Rushworth, who saw nothing but her son, was quite at a loss.

"The couple above, ma'am. Do you see no symptoms there?"

"Oh dear! Miss Julia and Mr. Crawford. Yes, indeed, a very pretty match. What is his property?"

"Four thousand a year."

"Very well. Those who have not more must be satisfied with what they have. Four thousand a year is a pretty estate, and he seems a very genteel, steady young man, so I hope Miss Julia will be very happy."

"It is not a settled thing, ma'am, yet. We only speak of it among friends. But I have very little doubt it *will* be. He is growing extremely particular in his attentions."

Fanny could listen no farther. Listening and wondering were all suspended for a time, for Mr. Bertram was in the room again; and though feeling it would be a great honour to be asked by him, she thought it must happen. He came towards their little circle; but instead of asking her to dance, drew a chair near her, and gave her an account of the present state of a sick horse, and the opinion of the groom, from whom he had just parted. Fanny found that it was not to be, and in the modesty of her nature immediately felt that she had been unreasonable in expecting it. When he had told of his horse, he took a newspaper from the table, and looking over it, said in a languid way, "If you want to dance, Fanny, I will stand up with you." With more than equal civility the offer was declined; she did not wish to dance. "I am glad of it," said he, in a much brisker tone, and throwing down the newspaper again, "for I am tired to death. I only wonder how the good people can keep it up so long. They had need be *all* in love, to find any amusement in such folly; and so they are, I fancy. If you look at them you may see they are so many couple of lovers—all but Yates and Mrs. Grant—and, between ourselves, she, poor woman, must want a lover as much as any one of them. A desperate dull life hers must be with the doctor," making a sly face as he spoke towards the chair of the latter, who proving, however, to be close at his elbow, made so instantaneous a change of expression and subject necessary, as Fanny, in spite of everything, could hardly help laughing at. "A strange business this in America, Dr. Grant! What is your opinion? I always come to you to know what I am to think of public matters."

"My dear Tom," cried his aunt soon afterwards, "as you are not dancing, I dare say you will have no objection to join us in a rubber; shall you?" Then leaving her seat, and coming to him to enforce the proposal, added in a whisper, "We want to make a table for Mrs. Rushworth, you know. Your mother is quite anxious about it, but cannot very well spare time to sit down herself, because of her fringe. Now, you and I and Dr. Grant will just do; and though *we* play but half-crowns, you know, you may bet half-guineas with *him*."

"I should be most happy," replied he aloud, and jumping up with alacrity, "it would give me the greatest pleasure; but that I am this moment going to dance." Come, Fanny, taking her hand, "do not be dawdling any longer, or the dance will be over."

Fanny was led off very willingly, though it was impossible for her to feel much gratitude towards her cousin, or distinguish, as he certainly did, between the selfishness of another person and his own.

"A pretty modest request upon my word," he indignantly exclaimed as they walked away. "To want to nail me to a card-table for the next two hours with herself and Dr. Grant, who are always quarrelling, and that poking old woman, who knows no more of whist than of algebra. I wish my good aunt would be a little less busy! And to ask me in such a way too! without ceremony, before them all, so as to leave me no possibility of refusing. *That* is what I dislike most particularly. It raises my spleen more than anything, to have the pretence of being asked, of being given a choice, and at the same time addressed in such a way as to oblige one to do the very thing, whatever it be! If I had not luckily thought of standing up with you I could not have got out of it. It is a great deal too bad. But when my aunt has got a fancy in her head, nothing can stop her."

Chapter 13

The Honourable John Yates, this new friend, had not much to recommend him beyond habits of fashion and expense, and being the younger son of a lord with a tolerable independence; and Sir Thomas would probably have thought his introduction at Mansfield by no means desirable. Mr. Bertram's acquaintance with him had begun at Weymouth, where they had spent ten days together in the same society, and the friendship, if friendship it might be called, had been proved and perfected by Mr. Yates's being invited to take Mansfield in his way, whenever he could, and by his promising to come; and he did come rather earlier than had been expected, in consequence of the sudden breaking-up of a large party assembled for gaiety at the house of another friend, which he had left Weymouth to join. He came on the wings of disappointment, and with his head full of acting, for it had been a theatrical party; and the play in which he had borne a part was within two days of representation, when the sudden death of one of the nearest connexions of the family had destroyed the scheme and dispersed the performers. To be so near happiness, so near fame, so near the long paragraph in praise of the private theatricals at Ecclesford, the seat of the Right Hon. Lord Ravenshaw, in Cornwall, which would of course have immortalised the whole party for at least a twelvemonth! and being so near, to lose it all, was an injury to be keenly felt, and Mr. Yates could talk of nothing else. Ecclesford and its theatre, with its arrangements and dresses, rehearsals and jokes, was his never-failing subject, and to boast of the past his only consolation.

Happily for him, a love of the theatre is so general, an itch for acting so strong among young people, that he could hardly out-talk the interest of his hearers. From the first casting of the parts to the epilogue it was all bewitching, and there were few who did not wish to have been a party concerned, or would have hesitated to try their skill. The play had been Lovers' Vows, and Mr. Yates was to have been Count Cassel. "A trifling part," said he, "and not at all to my taste, and such a one as I certainly would not accept again; but I was determined to make no difficulties. Lord Ravenshaw and the duke had appropriated the only two characters worth playing before I reached Ecclesford; and though Lord Ravenshaw offered to resign his to me, it was impossible to take it, you know. I was sorry for *him* that he should have so mistaken his powers, for he was no more equal to the Baron—a little man with a weak voice, always hoarse after the first ten minutes. It must have injured the piece materially; but *I* was resolved to make no difficulties. Sir Henry thought the duke not equal to Frederick, but that was because Sir Henry wanted the part himself; whereas it was certainly in the best hands of the two. I was surprised to see Sir Henry such a stick. Luckily the strength of the piece did not depend upon him. Our Agatha was inimitable, and the duke was thought very great by many. And upon the whole, it would certainly have gone off wonderfully."

"It was a hard case, upon my word"; and, "I do think you were very much to be pitied," were the kind responses of listening sympathy.

"It is not worth complaining about; but to be sure the poor old dowager could not have died at a worse time; and it is impossible to help wishing that the news could have been suppressed for just the three days we wanted. It was but three days; and being only a grandmother, and all happening two hundred miles off, I think there would have been no great harm, and it was suggested, I know; but Lord Ravenshaw, who I suppose is one of the most correct men in England, would not hear of it."

"An afterpiece instead of a comedy," said Mr. Bertram. "*Lovers' Vows* were at an end, and Lord and Lady Ravenshaw left to act My

Grandmother by themselves. Well, the jointure may comfort *him*; and perhaps, between friends, he began to tremble for his credit and his lungs in the Baron, and was not sorry to withdraw; and to make *you* amends, Yates, I think we must raise a little theatre at Mansfield, and ask you to be our manager."

This, though the thought of the moment, did not end with the moment; for the inclination to act was awakened, and in no one more strongly than in him who was now master of the house; and who, having so much leisure as to make almost any novelty a certain good, had likewise such a degree of lively talents and comic taste, as were exactly adapted to the novelty of acting. The thought returned again and again. "Oh for the Ecclesford theatre and scenery to try something with." Each sister could echo the wish; and Henry Crawford, to whom, in all the riot of his gratifications it was yet an untasted pleasure, was quite alive at the idea. "I really believe," said he, "I could be fool enough at this moment to undertake any character that ever was written, from Shylock or Richard III down to the singing hero of a farce in his scarlet coat and cocked hat. I feel as if I could be anything or everything; as if I could rant and storm, or sigh or cut capers, in any tragedy or comedy in the English language. Let us be doing something. Be it only half a play, an act, a scene; what should prevent us? Not these countenances, I am sure," looking towards the Miss Bertrams; "and for a theatre, what signifies a theatre? We shall be only amusing ourselves. Any room in this house might suffice."

"We must have a curtain," said Tom Bertram; "a few yards of green baize for a curtain, and perhaps that may be enough."

"Oh, quite enough," cried Mr. Yates, "with only just a side wing or two run up, doors in flat, and three or four scenes to be let down; nothing more would be necessary on such a plan as this. For mere amusement among ourselves we should want nothing more."

"I believe we must be satisfied with *less*," said Maria. "There would not be time, and other difficulties would arise. We must rather adopt Mr. Crawford's views, and make the *performance*, not the *theatre*, our object. Many parts of our best plays are independent of scenery."

"Nay," said Edmund, who began to listen with alarm. "Let us do nothing by halves. If we are to act, let it be in a theatre completely fitted up with pit, boxes, and gallery, and let us have a play entire from beginning to end; so as it be a German play, no matter what, with a good tricking, shifting afterpiece, and a figure-dance, and a hornpipe, and a song between the acts. If we do not outdo Ecclesford, we do nothing."

"Now, Edmund, do not be disagreeable," said Julia. "Nobody loves a play better than you do, or can have gone much farther to see one."

"True, to see real acting, good hardened real acting; but I would hardly walk from this room to the next to look at the raw efforts of those who have not been bred to the trade: a set of gentlemen and ladies, who have all the disadvantages of education and decorum to struggle through."

After a short pause, however, the subject still continued, and was discussed with unabated eagerness, every one's inclination increasing by the discussion, and a knowledge of the inclination of the rest; and though nothing was settled but that Tom Bertram would prefer a comedy, and his sisters and Henry Crawford a tragedy, and that nothing in the world could be easier than to find a piece which would please them all, the resolution to act something or other seemed so decided as to make Edmund quite uncomfortable. He was determined to prevent it, if possible, though his mother, who equally heard the conversation which passed at table, did not evince the least disapprobation.

The same evening afforded him an opportunity of trying his strength. Maria, Julia, Henry Crawford, and Mr. Yates were in the billiard-room. Tom, returning from them into the drawing-room, where Edmund was standing thoughtfully by the fire, while Lady Bertram was on the sofa at a little distance, and Fanny close beside her arranging her work, thus began as he entered—"Such a horribly vile billiard-table as ours is not to be met with, I believe, above ground. I can stand it no longer, and I think, I may say, that nothing shall ever tempt me to it again; but one good thing I have just ascertained: it is the very room for a theatre, precisely the shape and length for it; and the doors at the farther end, communicating with each other, as they may be made to do in five minutes, by merely moving the bookcase in my father's room, is the very thing we could have desired, if we had sat down to wish for it; and my father's room will be an excellent greenroom. It seems to join the billiard-room on purpose."

"You are not serious, Tom, in meaning to act?" said Edmund, in a low voice, as his brother approached the fire.

"Not serious! never more so, I assure you. What is there to surprise you in it?"

"I think it would be very wrong. In a *general* light, private theatricals are open to some objections, but as *we* are circumstanced, I must think it would be highly injudicious, and more than injudicious to attempt anything of the kind. It would shew great want of feeling on my father's account, absent as he is, and in some degree of constant danger; and it would be imprudent, I think, with regard to Maria, whose situation is a very delicate one, considering everything, extremely delicate."

"You take up a thing so seriously! as if we were going to act three times a week till my father's return, and invite all the country. But it is not to be a display of that sort. We mean nothing but a little amusement among ourselves, just to vary the scene, and exercise our powers in something new. We want no audience, no publicity. We may be trusted, I think, in chusing some play most perfectly unexceptionable; and I can conceive no greater harm or danger to any of us in conversing in the elegant written language of some respectable author than in chattering in words of our own. I have no fears and no scruples. And as to my father's being absent, it is so far from an objection, that I consider it rather as a motive; for the expectation of his return must be a very anxious period to my mother; and if we can be the means of amusing that anxiety, and keeping up her spirits for the next few weeks, I shall think our time very well spent, and so, I am sure, will he. It is a *very* anxious period for her."

As he said this, each looked towards their mother. Lady Bertram, sunk back in one corner of the sofa, the picture of health, wealth, ease, and tranquillity, was just falling into a gentle doze, while Fanny was getting through the few difficulties of her work for her.

Edmund smiled and shook his head.

"By Jove! this won't do," cried Tom, throwing himself into a chair with a hearty laugh. "To be sure, my dear mother, your anxiety—I was unlucky there."

"What is the matter?" asked her ladyship, in the heavy tone of one half-roused; "I was not asleep."

"Oh dear, no, ma'am, nobody suspected you! Well, Edmund," he continued, returning to the former subject, posture, and voice, as soon as Lady Bertram began to nod again, "but *this* I *will* maintain, that we shall be doing no harm."

"I cannot agree with you; I am convinced that my father would totally disapprove it."

"And I am convinced to the contrary. Nobody is fonder of the exercise of talent in young people, or promotes it more, than my father, and for anything of the acting, spouting, reciting kind, I think he has always a decided taste. I am sure he encouraged it in us as boys. How many a time have we mourned over the dead body of Julius Caesar, and to *be'd* and not *to be'd*, in this very room, for his amusement? And I am sure, *my name was Norval*, every evening of my life through one Christmas holidays."

"It was a very different thing. You must see the difference yourself. My father wished us, as schoolboys, to speak well, but he would never wish his grown-up daughters to be acting plays. His sense of decorum is strict."

"I know all that," said Tom, displeased. "I know my father as well as you do; and I'll take care that his daughters do nothing to distress him. Manage your own concerns, Edmund, and I'll take care of the rest of the family."

"If you are resolved on acting," replied the persevering Edmund, "I must hope it will be in a very small and quiet way; and I think a theatre ought not to be attempted. It would be taking liberties with my father's house in his absence which could not be justified."

"For everything of that nature I will be answerable," said Tom, in a decided tone. "His house shall not be hurt. I have quite as great an interest in being careful of his house as you can have; and as to such alterations as I was suggesting just now, such as moving a bookcase, or unlocking a door, or even as using the billiard-room for the space of a week without playing at billiards in it, you might just as well suppose he would object to our sitting more in this room, and less in the breakfast-room, than we did before he went away, or to my sister's pianoforte being moved from one side of the room to the other. Absolute nonsense!"

"The innovation, if not wrong as an innovation, will be wrong as an expense."

"Yes, the expense of such an undertaking would be prodigious! Perhaps it might cost a whole twenty pounds. Something of a theatre we must have undoubtedly, but it will be on the simplest plan: a green curtain and a little carpenter's work, and that's all; and as the carpenter's work may be all done at home by Christopher Jackson himself, it will be too absurd to talk of expense; and as long as Jackson is employed, everything will be right with Sir Thomas. Don't imagine that nobody in this house can see or judge but yourself. Don't act yourself, if you do not like it, but don't expect to govern everybody else."

"No, as to acting myself," said Edmund, "*that* I absolutely protest against."

Tom walked out of the room as he said it, and Edmund was left to sit down and stir the fire in thoughtful vexation.

Fanny, who had heard it all, and borne Edmund company in every feeling throughout the whole, now ventured to say, in her anxiety to suggest some comfort, "Perhaps they may not be able to find any play to suit them. Your brother's taste and your sisters' seem very different."

"I have no hope there, Fanny. If they persist in the scheme, they will find something. I shall speak to my sisters and try to dissuade *them*, and that is all I can do."

"I should think my aunt Norris would be on your side."

"I dare say she would, but she has no influence with either Tom or my sisters that could be of any use; and if I cannot convince them myself, I shall let things take their course, without attempting it through her. Family squabbling is the greatest evil of all, and we had better do anything than be altogether by the ears."

His sisters, to whom he had an opportunity of speaking the next morning, were quite as impatient of his advice, quite as unyielding to his representation, quite as determined in the cause of pleasure, as Tom. Their mother had no objection to the plan, and they were not in the least afraid of their father's disapprobation. There could be no harm in what had been done in so many respectable families, and by so many women of the first consideration; and it must be scrupulousness run mad that could see anything to censure in a plan like theirs, comprehending only brothers and sisters and intimate friends, and which would never be heard of beyond themselves. Julia *did* seem inclined to admit that Maria's situation might require particular caution and delicacy—but that could not extend to *her*—she was at liberty; and Maria evidently considered her engagement as only raising her so much more above restraint, and leaving her less occasion than Julia to consult either father or mother. Edmund had little to hope, but he was still urging the subject when Henry Crawford entered the room, fresh from the Parsonage, calling out, "No want of hands in our theatre, Miss Bertram. No want of understrappers: my sister desires her love, and hopes to be admitted into the company, and will be happy to take the part of any old duenna or tame confidante, that you may not like to do yourselves."

Maria gave Edmund a glance, which meant, "What say you now? Can we be wrong if Mary Crawford feels the same?" And Edmund, silenced, was obliged to acknowledge that the charm of acting might well carry fascination to the mind of genius; and with the ingenuity of love, to dwell more on the obliging, accommodating purport of the message than on anything else.

The scheme advanced. Opposition was vain; and as to Mrs. Norris, he was mistaken in supposing she would wish to make any. She started no difficulties that were not talked down in five minutes by her eldest nephew and niece, who were all-powerful with her; and as the whole arrangement was to bring very little expense to anybody, and none at all to herself, as she foresaw in it all the comforts of hurry, bustle, and importance, and derived the immediate advantage of fancying herself obliged to leave her own house, where she had been living a month at her own cost, and take up her abode in theirs, that every hour might be spent in their service, she was, in fact, exceedingly delighted with the project.

Chapter 14

Fanny seemed nearer being right than Edmund had supposed. The business of finding a play that would suit everybody proved to be no trifle; and the carpenter had received his orders and taken his measurements, had suggested and removed at least two sets of difficulties, and having made the necessity of an enlargement of plan and expense fully evident, was already at work, while a play was still to seek. Other preparations were also in hand. An enormous roll of green baize had arrived from Northampton, and been cut out by Mrs. Norris (with a saving by her good management of full three-quarters of a yard), and was actually forming into a curtain by the housemaids, and still the play was wanting; and as two or three days passed away in this manner, Edmund began almost to hope that none might ever be found.

There were, in fact, so many things to be attended to, so many people to be pleased, so many best characters required, and, above all, such a need that the play should be at once both tragedy and comedy, that there did seem as little chance of a decision as anything pursued by youth and zeal could hold out.

On the tragic side were the Miss Bertrams, Henry Crawford, and Mr. Yates; on the comic, Tom Bertram, not *quite* alone, because it was evident that Mary Crawford's wishes, though politely kept back, inclined the same way: but his determinateness and his power seemed to make allies unnecessary; and, independent of this great irreconcilable difference, they wanted a piece containing very few characters in the whole, but every character first-rate, and three principal women. All the best plays were run over in vain. Neither *Hamlet*, nor *Macbeth*, nor *Othello*, nor *Douglas*, nor *The Gamester*, presented anything that could satisfy even the tragedians; and *The Rivals*, *The School for Scandal*, *Wheel of Fortune*,

Heir at Law, and a long et cetera, were successively dismissed with yet warmer objections. No piece could be proposed that did not supply somebody with a difficulty, and on one side or the other it was a continual repetition of, "Oh no, *that* will never do! Let us have no ranting tragedies. Too many characters. Not a tolerable woman's part in the play. Anything but *that*, my dear Tom. It would be impossible to fill it up. One could not expect anybody to take such a part. Nothing but buffoonery from beginning to end. *That* might do, perhaps, but for the low parts. If I *must* give my opinion, I have always thought it the most insipid play in the English language. *I* do not wish to make objections; I shall be happy to be of any use, but I think we could not chuse worse."

Fanny looked on and listened, not unamused to observe the selfishness which, more or less disguised, seemed to govern them all, and wondering how it would end. For her own gratification she could have wished that something might be acted, for she had never seen even half a play, but everything of higher consequence was against it.

"This will never do," said Tom Bertram at last. "We are wasting time most abominably. Something must be fixed on. No matter what, so that something is chosen. We must not be so nice. A few characters too many must not frighten us. We must *double* them. We must descend a little. If a part is insignificant, the greater our credit in making anything of it. From this moment I make no difficulties. I take any part you chuse to give me, so as it be comic. Let it but be comic, I condition for nothing more."

For about the fifth time he then proposed the *Heir at Law*, doubting only whether to prefer Lord Duberley or Dr. Pangloss for himself; and very earnestly, but very unsuccessfully, trying to persuade the others that there were some fine tragic parts in the rest of the dramatis personae.

The pause which followed this fruitless effort was ended by the same speaker, who, taking up one of the many volumes of plays

that lay on the table, and turning it over, suddenly exclaimed—
"*Lovers' Vows*! And why should not *Lovers' Vows* do for *us* as well as
for the Ravenshaws? How came it never to be thought of before?
It strikes me as if it would do exactly. What say you all? Here are
two capital tragic parts for Yates and Crawford, and here is the
rhyming Butler for me, if nobody else wants it; a trifling part, but
the sort of thing I should not dislike, and, as I said before, I am
determined to take anything and do my best. And as for the rest,
they may be filled up by anybody. It is only Count Cassel and
Anhalt."

The suggestion was generally welcome. Everybody was growing
weary of indecision, and the first idea with everybody was, that
nothing had been proposed before so likely to suit them all. Mr.
Yates was particularly pleased: he had been sighing and longing
to do the Baron at Ecclesford, had grudged every rant of Lord
Ravenshaw's, and been forced to re-rant it all in his own room. The
storm through Baron Wildenheim was the height of his theatrical
ambition; and with the advantage of knowing half the scenes
by heart already, he did now, with the greatest alacrity, offer his
services for the part. To do him justice, however, he did not resolve
to appropriate it; for remembering that there was some very good
ranting-ground in Frederick, he professed an equal willingness for
that. Henry Crawford was ready to take either. Whichever Mr.
Yates did not chuse would perfectly satisfy him, and a short parley
of compliment ensued. Miss Bertram, feeling all the interest of an
Agatha in the question, took on her to decide it, by observing to
Mr. Yates that this was a point in which height and figure ought
to be considered, and that *his* being the tallest, seemed to fit him
peculiarly for the Baron. She was acknowledged to be quite right,
and the two parts being accepted accordingly, she was certain
of the proper Frederick. Three of the characters were now cast,
besides Mr. Rushworth, who was always answered for by Maria as

willing to do anything; when Julia, meaning, like her sister, to be Agatha, began to be scrupulous on Miss Crawford's account.

"This is not behaving well by the absent," said she. "Here are not women enough. Amelia and Agatha may do for Maria and me, but here is nothing for your sister, Mr. Crawford."

Mr. Crawford desired *that* might not be thought of: he was very sure his sister had no wish of acting but as she might be useful, and that she would not allow herself to be considered in the present case. But this was immediately opposed by Tom Bertram, who asserted the part of Amelia to be in every respect the property of Miss Crawford, if she would accept it. "It falls as naturally, as necessarily to her," said he, "as Agatha does to one or other of my sisters. It can be no sacrifice on their side, for it is highly comic."

A short silence followed. Each sister looked anxious; for each felt the best claim to Agatha, and was hoping to have it pressed on her by the rest. Henry Crawford, who meanwhile had taken up the play, and with seeming carelessness was turning over the first act, soon settled the business.

"I must entreat Miss *Julia* Bertram," said he, "not to engage in the part of Agatha, or it will be the ruin of all my solemnity. You must not, indeed you must not" (turning to her). "I could not stand your countenance dressed up in woe and paleness. The many laughs we have had together would infallibly come across me, and Frederick and his knapsack would be obliged to run away."

Pleasantly, courteously, it was spoken; but the manner was lost in the matter to Julia's feelings. She saw a glance at Maria which confirmed the injury to herself: it was a scheme, a trick; she was slighted, Maria was preferred; the smile of triumph which Maria was trying to suppress shewed how well it was understood; and before Julia could command herself enough to speak, her brother gave his weight against her too, by saying, "Oh yes! Maria must be Agatha. Maria will be the best Agatha. Though Julia fancies she prefers tragedy, I would not trust her in it. There is nothing of tragedy about her. She has not the look of it. Her features are not tragic features, and she walks too quick, and speaks too quick, and would not keep her countenance. She had better do the old countrywoman: the Cottager's wife; you had, indeed, Julia. Cottager's wife is a very pretty part, I assure you. The old lady relieves the high-flown benevolence of her husband with a good deal of spirit. You shall be Cottager's wife."

"Cottager's wife!" cried Mr. Yates. "What are you talking of? The most trivial, paltry, insignificant part; the merest commonplace; not a tolerable speech in the whole. Your sister do that! It is an insult to propose it. At Ecclesford the governess was to have done it. We all agreed that it could not be offered to anybody else. A little more justice, Mr. Manager, if you please. You do not deserve the office, if you cannot appreciate the talents of your company a little better."

"Why, as to *that*, my good friend, till I and my company have really acted there must be some guesswork; but I mean no disparagement to Julia. We cannot have two Agathas, and we must have one Cottager's wife; and I am sure I set her the example of moderation myself in being satisfied with the old Butler. If the part is trifling she will have more credit in making something of it; and if she is so desperately bent against everything humorous, let her take Cottager's speeches instead of Cottager's wife's, and so change the parts all through; *he* is solemn and pathetic enough, I am sure. It could make no difference in the play, and as for Cottager himself, when he has got his wife's speeches, *I* would undertake him with all my heart."

"With all your partiality for Cottager's wife," said Henry Crawford, "it will be impossible to make anything of it fit for your sister, and we must not suffer her good-nature to be imposed on. We must not *allow* her to accept the part. She must not be left to her own complaisance. Her talents will be wanted in Amelia. Amelia is a character more difficult to be well represented than even Agatha. I consider Amelia is the most difficult character in the whole piece. It requires great powers, great nicety, to give her playfulness and simplicity without extravagance. I have seen good actresses fail in the part. Simplicity, indeed, is beyond the reach of almost every actress by profession. It requires a delicacy of feeling which they have not. It requires a gentlewoman—a Julia Bertram. You *will* undertake it, I hope?" turning to her with a look of anxious entreaty, which softened her a little; but while she hesitated what to say, her brother again interposed with Miss Crawford's better claim.

"No, no, Julia must not be Amelia. It is not at all the part for her. She would not like it. She would not do well. She is too tall and robust. Amelia should be a small, light, girlish, skipping figure. It is fit for Miss Crawford, and Miss Crawford only. She looks the part, and I am persuaded will do it admirably."

Without attending to this, Henry Crawford continued his supplication. "You must oblige us," said he, "indeed you must. When you have studied the character, I am sure you will feel it suit you. Tragedy may be your choice, but it will certainly appear that comedy chuses *you*. You will be to visit me in prison with a basket of provisions; you will not refuse to visit me in prison? I think I see you coming in with your basket."

The influence of his voice was felt. Julia wavered; but was he only trying to soothe and pacify her, and make her overlook the previous affront? She distrusted him. The slight had been most determined. He was, perhaps, but at treacherous play with her. She looked suspiciously at her sister; Maria's countenance was to decide it: if she were vexed and alarmed—but Maria looked all serenity and satisfaction, and Julia well knew that on this ground Maria could not be happy but at her expense. With hasty indignation, therefore, and a tremulous voice, she said to him, "You do not seem afraid of not keeping your countenance when I come in with a basket of provisions—though one might have supposed—but it is only as Agatha that I was to be so overpowering!" She stopped—Henry Crawford looked rather foolish, and as if he did not know what to say. Tom Bertram began again —

"Miss Crawford must be Amelia. She will be an excellent Amelia."

"Do not be afraid of *my* wanting the character," cried Julia, with angry quickness: "I am *not* to be Agatha, and I am sure I will do nothing else; and as to Amelia, it is of all parts in the world the most disgusting to me. I quite detest her. An odious, little, pert, unnatural, impudent girl. I have always protested against comedy, and this is comedy in its worst form." And so saying, she walked hastily out of the room, leaving awkward feelings to more than one, but exciting small compassion in any except Fanny, who had been a quiet auditor of the whole, and who could not think of her as under the agitations of *jealousy* without great pity.

A short silence succeeded her leaving them; but her brother soon returned to business and *Lovers' Vows*, and was eagerly looking over the play, with Mr. Yates's help, to ascertain what scenery would be necessary—while Maria and Henry Crawford conversed together in an under-voice, and the declaration with which she began of, "I am sure I would give up the part to Julia most willingly, but that though I shall probably do it very ill, I feel persuaded *she* would do it worse," was doubtless receiving all the compliments it called for.

When this had lasted some time, the division of the party was completed by Tom Bertram and Mr. Yates walking off together to consult farther in the room now beginning to be called *the Theatre*, and Miss Bertram's resolving to go down to the Parsonage herself with the offer of Amelia to Miss Crawford; and Fanny remained alone.

The first use she made of her solitude was to take up the volume which had been left on the table, and begin to acquaint herself with the play of which she had heard so much. Her curiosity was all awake, and she ran through it with an eagerness which was suspended only by intervals of astonishment, that it could be chosen in the present instance, that it could be proposed and accepted in a private theatre! Agatha and Amelia appeared to her in their different ways so totally improper for home representation—the situation of one, and the language of the other, so unfit to be expressed by any woman of modesty, that she could hardly suppose her cousins could be aware of what they were engaging in; and longed to have them roused as soon as possible by the remonstrance which Edmund would certainly make.

Chapter 15

Miss Crawford accepted the part very readily; and soon after Miss Bertram's return from the Parsonage, Mr. Rushworth arrived, and another character was consequently cast. He had the offer of Count Cassel and Anhalt, and at first did not know which to chuse, and wanted Miss Bertram to direct him; but upon being made to understand the different style of the characters, and which was which, and recollecting that he had once seen the play in London, and had thought Anhalt a very stupid fellow, he soon decided for the Count. Miss Bertram approved the decision, for the less he had to learn the better; and though she could not sympathise in his wish that the Count and Agatha might be to act together, nor wait very patiently while he was slowly turning over the leaves with the hope of still discovering such a scene, she very kindly took his part in hand, and curtailed every speech that admitted being shortened; besides pointing out the necessity of his being very much dressed, and chusing his colours. Mr. Rushworth liked the idea of his finery very well, though affecting to despise it; and was too much engaged with what his own appearance would be to think of the others, or draw any of those conclusions, or feel any of that displeasure which Maria had been half prepared for.

Thus much was settled before Edmund, who had been out all the morning, knew anything of the matter; but when he entered the drawing-room before dinner, the buzz of discussion was high between Tom, Maria, and Mr. Yates; and Mr. Rushworth stepped forward with great alacrity to tell him the agreeable news.

"We have got a play," said he. "It is to be *Lovers' Vows*; and I am to be Count Cassel, and am to come in first with a blue dress and a pink satin cloak, and afterwards am to have another fine fancy suit, by way of a shooting-dress. I do not know how I shall like it."

Fanny's eyes followed Edmund, and her heart beat for him as she heard this speech, and saw his look, and felt what his sensations must be.

"*Lovers' Vows*!" in a tone of the greatest amazement, was his only reply to Mr. Rushworth, and he turned towards his brother and sisters as if hardly doubting a contradiction.

"Yes," cried Mr. Yates. "After all our debatings and difficulties, we find there is nothing that will suit us altogether so well, nothing so unexceptionable, as *Lovers' Vows*. The wonder is that it should not have been thought of before. My stupidity was abominable, for here we have all the advantage of what I saw at Ecclesford; and it is so useful to have anything of a model! We have cast almost every part."

"But what do you do for women?" said Edmund gravely, and looking at Maria.

Maria blushed in spite of herself as she answered, "I take the part which Lady Ravenshaw was to have done, and" (with a bolder eye) "Miss Crawford is to be Amelia."

"I should not have thought it the sort of play to be so easily filled up, with *us*," replied Edmund, turning away to the fire, where sat his mother, aunt, and Fanny, and seating himself with a look of great vexation.

Mr. Rushworth followed him to say, "I come in three times, and have two-and-forty speeches. That's something, is not it? But I do not much like the idea of being so fine. I shall hardly know myself in a blue dress and a pink satin cloak."

Edmund could not answer him. In a few minutes Mr. Bertram was called out of the room to satisfy some doubts of the carpenter; and being accompanied by Mr. Yates, and followed soon afterwards by Mr. Rushworth, Edmund almost immediately took the opportunity of saying, "I cannot, before Mr. Yates, speak what I feel as to this play, without reflecting on his friends at Ecclesford; but I must now, my dear Maria, tell *you*, that I think it exceedingly unfit for private representation, and that I hope you will give it up. I cannot but suppose you *will* when you have read it carefully over. Read only the first act aloud to either your mother or aunt, and see how you can approve it. It will not be necessary to send you to your *father's* judgment, I am convinced."

"We see things very differently," cried Maria. "I am perfectly acquainted with the play, I assure you; and with a very few omissions, and so forth, which will be made, of course, I can see nothing objectionable in it; and *I* am not the *only* young woman you find who thinks it very fit for private representation."

"I am sorry for it," was his answer; "but in this matter it is *you* who are to lead. *You* must set the example. If others have blundered, it is your place to put them right, and shew them what true delicacy is. In all points of decorum *your* conduct must be law to the rest of the party."

This picture of her consequence had some effect, for no one loved better to lead than Maria; and with far more good-humour she answered, "I am much obliged to you, Edmund; you mean very well, I am sure: but I still think you see things too strongly; and I really cannot undertake to harangue all the rest upon a subject of this kind. *There* would be the greatest indecorum, I think."

"Do you imagine that I could have such an idea in my head? No; let your conduct be the only harangue. Say that, on examining the part, you feel yourself unequal to it; that you find it requiring more exertion and confidence than you can be supposed to have. Say this with firmness, and it will be quite enough. All who can distinguish will understand your motive. The play will be given up, and your delicacy honoured as it ought."

"Do not act anything improper, my dear," said Lady Bertram. "Sir Thomas would not like it.—Fanny, ring the bell; I must have my dinner.—To be sure, Julia is dressed by this time."

"I am convinced, madam," said Edmund, preventing Fanny, "that Sir Thomas would not like it."

"There, my dear, do you hear what Edmund says?"

"If I were to decline the part," said Maria, with renewed zeal, "Julia would certainly take it."

"What!" cried Edmund, "if she knew your reasons!"

"Oh! she might think the difference between us—the difference in our situations—that *she* need not be so scrupulous as *I* might feel necessary. I am sure she would argue so. No; you must excuse me; I cannot retract my consent; it is too far settled, everybody would be so disappointed, Tom would be quite angry; and if we are so very nice, we shall never act anything."

"I was just going to say the very same thing," said Mrs. Norris. "If every play is to be objected to, you will act nothing, and the preparations will be all so much money thrown away, and I am sure *that* would be a discredit to us all. I do not know the play; but, as Maria says, if there is anything a little too warm (and it is so with most of them) it can be easily left out. We must not be over-precise, Edmund. As Mr. Rushworth is to act too, there can be no harm. I only wish Tom had known his own mind when the carpenters began, for there was the loss of half a day's work about those side-doors. The curtain will be a good job, however. The maids do their work very well, and I think we shall be able to send back some dozens of the rings. There is no occasion to put them so very close together. I *am* of some use, I hope, in preventing waste and making the most of things. There should always be one steady head to superintend so many young ones. I forgot to tell Tom of something that happened to me this very day. I had been looking about me in the poultry-yard, and was just coming out, when who should I see but Dick Jackson making up to the servants' hall-door with two bits of deal board in his hand, bringing them to father, you may be sure; mother had chanced to send him of a message to father, and then father had bid him bring up them two bits of board, for he could not no how do without them. I knew what all this meant, for the servants' dinner-bell was ringing at the very moment over our heads; and as I hate such encroaching people (the Jacksons are very encroaching, I have always said so: just the sort of people to get all they can), I said to the boy directly (a great lubberly fellow of ten years old, you know, who ought to be ashamed of himself), '*I'll* take the boards to your father, Dick, so get you home again as fast as you can.' The boy looked very silly, and turned away without offering a word, for I believe I might speak pretty sharp; and I dare say it will cure him of coming marauding about the house for one while. I hate such greediness—so good as your father is to the family, employing the man all the year round!"

Nobody was at the trouble of an answer; the others soon returned; and Edmund found that to have endeavoured to set them right must be his only satisfaction.

Dinner passed heavily. Mrs. Norris related again her triumph over Dick Jackson, but neither play nor preparation were otherwise much talked of, for Edmund's disapprobation was felt even by his brother, though he would not have owned it. Maria, wanting Henry Crawford's animating support, thought the subject better avoided. Mr. Yates, who was trying to make himself agreeable to Julia, found her gloom less impenetrable on any topic than that of his regret at her secession from their company; and Mr. Rushworth, having only his own part and his own dress in his head, had soon talked away all that could be said of either.

But the concerns of the theatre were suspended only for an hour or two: there was still a great deal to be settled; and the spirits of evening giving fresh courage, Tom, Maria, and Mr. Yates, soon after their being reassembled in the drawing-room, seated themselves in committee at a separate table, with the play open before them, and were just getting deep in the subject when a most welcome interruption was given by the entrance of Mr. and

Miss Crawford, who, late and dark and dirty as it was, could not help coming, and were received with the most grateful joy.

"Well, how do you go on?" and "What have you settled?" and "Oh! we can do nothing without you," followed the first salutations; and Henry Crawford was soon seated with the other three at the table, while his sister made her way to Lady Bertram, and with pleasant attention was complimenting *her*. "I must really congratulate your ladyship," said she, "on the play being chosen; for though you have borne it with exemplary patience, I am sure you must be sick of all our noise and difficulties. The actors may be glad, but the bystanders must be infinitely more thankful for a decision; and I do sincerely give you joy, madam, as well as Mrs. Norris, and everybody else who is in the same predicament," glancing half fearfully, half slyly, beyond Fanny to Edmund.

She was very civilly answered by Lady Bertram, but Edmund said nothing. His being only a bystander was not disclaimed. After continuing in chat with the party round the fire a few minutes, Miss Crawford returned to the party round the table; and standing by them, seemed to interest herself in their arrangements till, as if struck by a sudden recollection, she exclaimed, "My good friends, you are most composedly at work upon these cottages and alehouses, inside and out; but pray let me know my fate in the meanwhile. Who is to be Anhalt? What gentleman among you am I to have the pleasure of making love to?"

For a moment no one spoke; and then many spoke together to tell the same melancholy truth, that they had not yet got any Anhalt. "Mr. Rushworth was to be Count Cassel, but no one had yet undertaken Anhalt."

"I had my choice of the parts," said Mr. Rushworth; "but I thought I should like the Count best, though I do not much relish the finery I am to have."

"You chose very wisely, I am sure," replied Miss Crawford, with a brightened look; "Anhalt is a heavy part."

"*The Count* has two-and-forty speeches," returned Mr. Rushworth, "which is no trifle."

"I am not at all surprised," said Miss Crawford, after a short pause, "at this want of an Anhalt. Amelia deserves no better. Such a forward young lady may well frighten the men."

"I should be but too happy in taking the part, if it were possible," cried Tom; "but, unluckily, the Butler and Anhalt are in together. I will not entirely give it up, however; I will try what can be done—I will look it over again."

"Your *brother* should take the part," said Mr. Yates, in a low voice. "Do not you think he would?"

"*I* shall not ask him," replied Tom, in a cold, determined manner.

Miss Crawford talked of something else, and soon afterwards rejoined the party at the fire.

"They do not want me at all," said she, seating herself. "I only puzzle them, and oblige them to make civil speeches. Mr. Edmund Bertram, as you do not act yourself, you will be a disinterested adviser; and, therefore, I apply to *you*. What shall we do for an Anhalt? Is it practicable for any of the others to double it? What is your advice?"

"My advice," said he calmly, "is that you change the play."

"*I* should have no objection," she replied; "for though I should not particularly dislike the part of Amelia if well supported, that is, if everything went well, I shall be sorry to be an inconvenience; but as they do not chuse to hear your advice at *that table*" (looking round), "it certainly will not be taken."

Edmund said no more.

"If *any* part could tempt *you* to act, I suppose it would be Anhalt," observed the lady archly, after a short pause; "for he is a clergyman, you know."

"*That* circumstance would by no means tempt me," he replied, "for I should be sorry to make the character ridiculous by bad acting.

It must be very difficult to keep Anhalt from appearing a formal, solemn lecturer; and the man who chuses the profession itself is, perhaps, one of the last who would wish to represent it on the stage."

Miss Crawford was silenced, and with some feelings of resentment and mortification, moved her chair considerably nearer the tea-table, and gave all her attention to Mrs. Norris, who was presiding there.

"Fanny," cried Tom Bertram, from the other table, where the conference was eagerly carrying on, and the conversation incessant, "we want your services."

Fanny was up in a moment, expecting some errand; for the habit of employing her in that way was not yet overcome, in spite of all that Edmund could do.

"Oh! we do not want to disturb you from your seat. We do not want your *present* services. We shall only want you in our play. You must be Cottager's wife."

"Me!" cried Fanny, sitting down again with a most frightened look. "Indeed you must excuse me. I could not act anything if you were to give me the world. No, indeed, I cannot act."

"Indeed, but you must, for we cannot excuse you. It need not frighten you: it is a nothing of a part, a mere nothing, not above half a dozen speeches altogether, and it will not much signify if nobody hears a word you say; so you may be as creep-mouse as you like, but we must have you to look at."

"If you are afraid of half a dozen speeches," cried Mr. Rushworth, "what would you do with such a part as mine? I have forty-two to learn."

"It is not that I am afraid of learning by heart," said Fanny, shocked to find herself at that moment the only speaker in the room, and to feel that almost every eye was upon her; "but I really cannot act."

"Yes, yes, you can act well enough for *us*. Learn your part, and we will teach you all the rest. You have only two scenes, and as I shall be Cottager, I'll put you in and push you about, and you will do it very well, I'll answer for it."

"No, indeed, Mr. Bertram, you must excuse me. You cannot have an idea. It would be absolutely impossible for me. If I were to undertake it, I should only disappoint you."

"Phoo! Phoo! Do not be so shamefaced. You'll do it very well. Every allowance will be made for you. We do not expect perfection. You must get a brown gown, and a white apron, and a mob cap, and we must make you a few wrinkles, and a little of the crowsfoot at the corner of your eyes, and you will be a very proper, little old woman."

"You must excuse me, indeed you must excuse me," cried Fanny, growing more and more red from excessive agitation, and looking distressfully at Edmund, who was kindly observing her; but unwilling to exasperate his brother by interference, gave her only an encouraging smile. Her entreaty had no effect on Tom: he only said again what he had said before; and it was not merely Tom, for the requisition was now backed by Maria, and Mr. Crawford, and Mr. Yates, with an urgency which differed from his but in being more gentle or more ceremonious, and which altogether was quite overpowering to Fanny; and before she could breathe after it, Mrs. Norris completed the whole by thus addressing her in a whisper at once angry and audible—"What a piece of work here is about nothing: I am quite ashamed of you, Fanny, to make such a difficulty of obliging your cousins in a trifle of this sort—so kind as they are to you! Take the part with a good grace, and let us hear no more of the matter, I entreat."

"Do not urge her, madam," said Edmund. "It is not fair to urge her in this manner. You see she does not like to act. Let her chuse for herself, as well as the rest of us. Her judgment may be quite as safely trusted. Do not urge her any more."

"I am not going to urge her," replied Mrs. Norris sharply; "but I shall think her a very obstinate, ungrateful girl, if she does not do what her aunt and cousins wish her—very ungrateful, indeed, considering who and what she is."

Edmund was too angry to speak; but Miss Crawford, looking for a moment with astonished eyes at Mrs. Norris, and then at Fanny, whose tears were beginning to shew themselves, immediately said, with some keenness, "I do not like my situation: this *place* is too hot for me," and moved away her chair to the opposite side of the table, close to Fanny, saying to her, in a kind, low whisper, as she placed herself, "Never mind, my dear Miss Price, this is a cross evening: everybody is cross and teasing, but do not let us mind them"; and with pointed attention continued to talk to her and endeavour to raise her spirits, in spite of being out of spirits herself. By a look at her brother she prevented any farther entreaty from the theatrical board, and the really good feelings by which she was almost purely governed were rapidly restoring her to all the little she had lost in Edmund's favour.

Fanny did not love Miss Crawford; but she felt very much obliged to her for her present kindness; and when, from taking notice of her work, and wishing *she* could work as well, and begging for the pattern, and supposing Fanny was now preparing for her *appearance*, as of course she would come out when her cousin was married, Miss Crawford proceeded to inquire if she had heard lately from her brother at sea, and said that she had quite a curiosity to see him, and imagined him a very fine young man, and advised Fanny to get his picture drawn before he went to sea again—she could not help admitting it to be very agreeable flattery, or help listening, and answering with more animation than she had intended.

The consultation upon the play still went on, and Miss Crawford's attention was first called from Fanny by Tom Bertram's telling her, with infinite regret, that he found it absolutely impossible for him to undertake the part of Anhalt in addition to the Butler: he had been most anxiously trying to make it out to be feasible, but it would not do; he must give it up. "But there will not be the smallest difficulty in filling it," he added. "We have but to speak the word; we may pick and chuse. I could name, at this moment, at least six young men within six miles of us, who are wild to be admitted into our company, and there are one or two that would not disgrace us: I should not be afraid to trust either of the Olivers or Charles Maddox. Tom Oliver is a very clever fellow, and Charles Maddox is as gentlemanlike a man as you will see anywhere, so I will take my horse early to-morrow morning and ride over to Stoke, and settle with one of them."

While he spoke, Maria was looking apprehensively round at Edmund in full expectation that he must oppose such an enlargement of the plan as this: so contrary to all their first protestations; but Edmund said nothing. After a moment's thought, Miss Crawford calmly replied, "As far as I am concerned, I can have no objection to anything that you all think eligible. Have I ever seen either of the gentlemen? Yes, Mr. Charles Maddox dined at my sister's one day, did not he, Henry? A quiet-looking young man. I remember him. Let *him* be applied to, if you please, for it will be less unpleasant to me than to have a perfect stranger."

Charles Maddox was to be the man. Tom repeated his resolution of going to him early on the morrow; and though Julia, who had scarcely opened her lips before, observed, in a sarcastic manner, and with a glance first at Maria and then at Edmund, that "the Mansfield theatricals would enliven the whole neighbourhood exceedingly," Edmund still held his peace, and shewed his feelings only by a determined gravity.

"I am not very sanguine as to our play," said Miss Crawford, in an undervoice to Fanny, after some consideration; "and I can tell Mr. Maddox that I shall shorten some of *his* speeches, and a great many of *my own*, before we rehearse together. It will be very disagreeable, and by no means what I expected."

Chapter 16

It was not in Miss Crawford's power to talk Fanny into any real forgetfulness of what had passed. When the evening was over, she went to bed full of it, her nerves still agitated by the shock of such an attack from her cousin Tom, so public and so persevered in, and her spirits sinking under her aunt's unkind reflection and reproach. To be called into notice in such a manner, to hear that it was but the prelude to something so infinitely worse, to be told that she must do what was so impossible as to act; and then to have the charge of obstinacy and ingratitude follow it, enforced with such a hint at the dependence of her situation, had been too distressing at the time to make the remembrance when she was alone much less so, especially with the superadded dread of what the morrow might produce in continuation of the subject. Miss Crawford had protected her only for the time; and if she were applied to again among themselves with all the authoritative urgency that Tom and Maria were capable of, and Edmund perhaps away, what should she do? She fell asleep before she could answer the question, and found it quite as puzzling when she awoke the next morning. The little white attic, which had continued her sleeping-room ever since her first entering the family, proving incompetent to suggest any reply, she had recourse, as soon as she was dressed, to another apartment more spacious and more meet for walking about in and thinking, and of which she had now for some time been almost equally mistress. It had been their school-room; so called till the Miss Bertrams would not allow it to be called so any longer, and inhabited as such to a later period. There Miss Lee had lived, and there they had read and written, and talked and laughed, till within the last three years, when she had quitted them. The room had then become useless, and for some time was quite deserted, except by Fanny, when she visited her plants, or wanted one of the books, which she was still glad to keep there, from the deficiency of space and accommodation in her little chamber above: but gradually, as her value for the comforts of it increased, she had added to her possessions, and spent more of her time there; and having nothing to oppose her, had so naturally and so artlessly worked herself into it, that it was now generally admitted to be hers. The East room, as it had been called ever since Maria Bertram was sixteen, was now considered Fanny's, almost as decidedly as the white attic: the smallness of the one making the use of the other so evidently reasonable that the Miss Bertrams, with every superiority in their own apartments which their own sense of superiority could demand, were entirely approving it; and Mrs. Norris, having stipulated for there never being a fire in it on Fanny's account, was tolerably resigned to her having the use of what nobody else wanted, though the terms in which she sometimes spoke of the indulgence seemed to imply that it was the best room in the house.

The aspect was so favourable that even without a fire it was habitable in many an early spring and late autumn morning to such a willing mind as Fanny's; and while there was a gleam of sunshine she hoped not to be driven from it entirely, even when winter came. The comfort of it in her hours of leisure was extreme. She could go there after anything unpleasant below, and find immediate consolation in some pursuit, or some train of thought at hand. Her plants, her books—of which she had been a collector from the first hour of her commanding a shilling—her writing-desk, and her works of charity and ingenuity, were all within her reach; or if indisposed for employment, if nothing but musing would do, she could scarcely see an object in that room which had not an interesting remembrance connected with it. Everything was a friend, or bore her thoughts to a friend; and though there had been sometimes much of suffering to her; though her motives had often been misunderstood, her feelings disregarded, and her comprehension undervalued; though she had known the pains of tyranny, of ridicule, and neglect, yet almost every recurrence of either had led to something consolatory: her aunt Bertram had spoken for her, or Miss Lee had been encouraging, or, what was yet more frequent or more dear, Edmund had been her champion and her friend: he had supported her cause or explained her meaning, he had told her not to cry, or had given her some proof of affection which made her tears delightful; and the whole was now so blended together, so harmonised by distance, that every former affliction had its charm. The room was most dear to her, and she would not have changed its furniture for the handsomest in the house, though what had been originally plain had suffered all the ill-usage of children; and its greatest elegancies and ornaments were a faded footstool of Julia's work, too ill done for the drawing-room, three transparencies, made in a rage for transparencies, for the three lower panes of one window, where Tintern Abbey held its station between a cave in Italy and a moonlight lake in Cumberland, a collection of family profiles, thought unworthy of being anywhere else, over the mantelpiece, and by their side, and pinned against the wall, a small sketch of a ship sent four years ago from the Mediterranean by William, with H.M.S. Antwerp at the bottom, in letters as tall as the mainmast.

To this nest of comforts Fanny now walked down to try its influence on an agitated, doubting spirit, to see if by looking at Edmund's profile she could catch any of his counsel, or by giving air to her geraniums she might inhale a breeze of mental strength herself. But she had more than fears of her own perseverance to remove: she had begun to feel undecided as to what she *ought to do*; and as she walked round the room her doubts were increasing. Was she *right* in refusing what was so warmly asked, so strongly wished for—what might be so essential to a scheme on which some of those to whom she owed the greatest complaisance had set their hearts? Was it not ill-nature, selfishness, and a fear of exposing herself? And would Edmund's judgment, would his persuasion of Sir Thomas's disapprobation of the whole, be enough to justify her in a determined denial in spite of all the rest? It would be so horrible to her to act that she was inclined to suspect the truth and purity of her own scruples; and as she looked around her, the claims of her cousins to being obliged were strengthened by the sight of present upon present that she had received from them. The table between the windows was covered with work-boxes and netting-boxes which had been given her at different times, principally by Tom; and she grew bewildered as to the amount of the debt which all these kind remembrances produced. A tap at the door roused her in the midst of this attempt to find her way to her duty, and her gentle "Come in" was answered by the appearance of one, before whom all her doubts were wont to be laid. Her eyes brightened at the sight of Edmund.

"Can I speak with you, Fanny, for a few minutes?" said he.

"Yes, certainly."

"I want to consult. I want your opinion."

"My opinion!" she cried, shrinking from such a compliment, highly as it gratified her. He drew closer in response to her excitement and his height was felt significantly in her attic room. She longed to reach upwards and touch his cheek and she could all but vow she also heard his heart race as well with their nearness.

"Yes, your advice and opinion. I do not know what to do. This acting scheme gets worse and worse, you see. They have chosen almost as bad a play as they could, and now, to complete the business, are going to ask the help of a young man very slightly known to any of us. This is the end of all the privacy and propriety which was talked about at first. I know no harm of Charles Maddox; but the excessive intimacy which must spring from his being admitted among us in this manner is highly objectionable, the *more* than intimacy—the familiarity. I cannot think of it with any patience; and it does appear to me an evil of such magnitude as must, *if possible*, be prevented. Do not you see it in the same light?"

"Yes; but what can be done? Your brother is so determined."

"There is but *one* thing to be done, Fanny. I must take Anhalt myself. I am well aware that nothing else will quiet Tom."

Fanny could not answer him.

"It is not at all what I like," he continued. "No man can like being driven into the *appearance* of such inconsistency. After being known to oppose the scheme from the beginning, there is absurdity in the face of my joining them *now*, when they are exceeding their first plan in every respect; but I can think of no other alternative. Can you, Fanny?"

"No," said Fanny slowly, "not immediately, but—"

"But what? I see your judgment is not with me. Think it a little over. Perhaps you are not so much aware as I am of the mischief that *may*, of the unpleasantness that *must* arise from a young man's being received in this manner: domesticated among us; authorised to come at all hours, and placed suddenly on a footing which must do away all restraints. To think only of the licence which every rehearsal must tend to create. It is all very bad! Put yourself in Miss Crawford's place, Fanny. Consider what it would be to act Amelia with a stranger. She has a right to be felt for, because she evidently feels for herself. I heard enough of what she said to you last night to understand her unwillingness to be acting with a stranger; and as she probably engaged in the part with different expectations—perhaps without considering the subject enough to know what was likely to be—it would be ungenerous, it would be really wrong to expose her to it. Her feelings ought to be respected. Does it not strike you so, Fanny? You hesitate."

"I am sorry for Miss Crawford; but I am more sorry to see you drawn in to do what you had resolved against, and what you are known to think will be disagreeable to my uncle. It will be such a triumph to the others!"

"They will not have much cause of triumph when they see how infamously I act. But, however, triumph there certainly will be, and I must brave it. But if I can be the means of restraining the publicity of the business, of limiting the exhibition, of concentrating our folly, I shall be well repaid. As I am now, I have no influence, I can do nothing: I have offended them, and they will not hear me; but when I have put them in good-humour by this concession, I am not without hopes of persuading them to confine the representation within a much smaller circle than they are now in the high road for. This will be a material gain. My object is to confine it to Mrs. Rushworth and the Grants. Will not this be worth gaining?"

"Yes, it will be a great point."

"But still it has not your approbation. Can you mention any other measure by which I have a chance of doing equal good?"

"No, I cannot think of anything else."

"Give me your approbation, then, Fanny. I am not comfortable without it."

"Oh, cousin!"

"If you are against me, I ought to distrust myself, and yet—But it is absolutely impossible to let Tom go on in this way, riding about the country in quest of anybody who can be persuaded to act—no matter whom: the look of a gentleman is to be enough. I thought *you* would have entered more into Miss Crawford's feelings."

"No doubt she will be very glad. It must be a great relief to her," said Fanny, trying for greater warmth of manner.

"She never appeared more amiable than in her behaviour to you last night. It gave her a very strong claim on my goodwill."

"She *was* very kind, indeed, and I am glad to have her spared" ...

She could not finish the generous effusion. Her conscience stopt her in the middle, but Edmund was satisfied.

"I shall walk down immediately after breakfast," said he, "and am sure of giving pleasure there. And now, dear Fanny, I will not interrupt you any longer. You want to be reading. But I could not be easy till I had spoken to you, and come to a decision. Sleeping or waking, my head has been full of this matter all night and it has been filled with anticipation of your valued response. It is an evil, but I am certainly making it less than it might be. If Tom is up, I shall go to him directly and get it over, and when we meet at breakfast we shall be all in high good-humour at the prospect of acting the fool together with such unanimity. *You*, in the meanwhile, will be taking a trip into China, I suppose. How does Lord Macartney go on?"—opening a volume on the table and then taking up some others. "And here are Crabbe's Tales, and the Idler, at hand to relieve you, if you tire of your great book. I admire your little establishment exceedingly; and as soon as I am gone, you will empty your head of all this nonsense of acting, and sit comfortably down to your table. But do not stay here to be cold."

He went; but there was no reading, no China, no composure for Fanny. He had told her the most extraordinary, the most inconceivable, the most unwelcome news; and she could think of nothing else. To be acting! After all his objections—objections so just and so public! After all that she had heard him say, and seen him look, and known him to be feeling. Could it be possible? Edmund so inconsistent! Was he not deceiving himself? Was he not wrong? Alas! it was all Miss Crawford's doing. She had seen her influence in every speech, and was miserable. The doubts and alarms as to her own conduct, which had previously distressed her, and which had all slept while she listened to him, were become of little consequence now. This deeper anxiety swallowed them up. Things should take their course; she cared not how it ended. Her cousins might attack, but could hardly tease her. She was beyond their reach; and if at last obliged to yield—no matter—it was all misery now.

Fanny could not help but find a large degree of pleasure knowing Edmund had thought of her all night, no matter she undoubtedly shared company in his thoughts, which she hoped turned out to be of equal measure.

Chapter 17

It was, indeed, a triumphant day to Mr. Bertram and Maria. Such a victory over Edmund's discretion had been beyond their hopes, and was most delightful. There was no longer anything to disturb them in their darling project, and they congratulated each other in private on the jealous weakness to which they attributed the change, with all the glee of feelings gratified in every way. Edmund might still look grave, and say he did not like the scheme in general, and must disapprove the play in particular; their point was gained: he was to act, and he was driven to it by the force of selfish inclinations only. Edmund had descended from that moral elevation which he had maintained before, and they were both as much the better as the happier for the descent.

They behaved very well, however, to *him* on the occasion, betraying no exultation beyond the lines about the corners of the mouth, and seemed to think it as great an escape to be quit of the intrusion of Charles Maddox, as if they had been forced into admitting him against their inclination. "To have it quite in their own family circle was what they had particularly wished. A stranger among them would have been the destruction of all their comfort"; and when Edmund, pursuing that idea, gave a hint of his hope as to the limitation of the audience, they were ready, in the complaisance of the moment, to promise anything. It was all good-humour and encouragement. Mrs. Norris offered to contrive his dress, Mr. Yates assured him that Anhalt's last scene with the Baron admitted a good deal of action and emphasis, and Mr. Rushworth undertook to count his speeches.

"Perhaps," said Tom, "Fanny may be more disposed to oblige us now. Perhaps you may persuade *her*."

"No, she is quite determined. She certainly will not act."

"Oh! very well." And not another word was said; but Fanny felt herself again in danger, and her indifference to the danger was beginning to fail her already.

There were not fewer smiles at the Parsonage than at the Park on this change in Edmund; Miss Crawford looked very lovely in hers, and entered with such an instantaneous renewal of cheerfulness into the whole affair as could have but one effect on him. "He was certainly right in respecting such feelings; he was glad he had determined on it." And the morning wore away in satisfactions very sweet, if not very sound. One advantage resulted from it to Fanny: at the earnest request of Miss Crawford, Mrs. Grant had, with her usual good-humour, agreed to undertake the part for which Fanny had been wanted; and this was all that occurred to gladden *her* heart during the day; and even this, when imparted by Edmund, brought a pang with it, for it was Miss Crawford to whom she was obliged—it was Miss Crawford whose kind exertions were to excite her gratitude, and whose merit in making them was spoken of with a glow of admiration. She was safe; but peace and safety were unconnected here. Her mind had been never farther from peace. She could not feel that she had done wrong herself, but she was disquieted in every other way. Her heart and her judgment were equally against Edmund's decision: she could not acquit his unsteadiness, and his happiness under it made her wretched. She was full of jealousy and agitation. Miss Crawford came with looks of gaiety which seemed an insult, with friendly expressions towards herself which she could hardly answer calmly. Everybody around her was gay and busy, prosperous and important; each had their object of interest, their part, their dress, their favourite scene, their friends and confederates: all were finding employment in consultations and comparisons, or diversion in the playful conceits they suggested. She alone was sad and insignificant: she had no share in anything; she might go or stay; she might be in the midst of their noise, or retreat from it to the solitude of the

East room, without being seen or missed. She could almost think anything would have been preferable to this. Mrs. Grant was of consequence: *her* good-nature had honourable mention; her taste and her time were considered; her presence was wanted; she was sought for, and attended, and praised; and Fanny was at first in some danger of envying her the character she had accepted. But reflection brought better feelings, and shewed her that Mrs. Grant was entitled to respect, which could never have belonged to *her*; and that, had she received even the greatest, she could never have been easy in joining a scheme which, considering only her uncle, she must condemn altogether.

Fanny's heart was not absolutely the only saddened one amongst them, as she soon began to acknowledge to herself. Julia was a sufferer too, though not quite so blamelessly.

Henry Crawford had trifled with her feelings; but she had very long allowed and even sought his attentions, with a jealousy of her sister so reasonable as ought to have been their cure; and now that the conviction of his preference for Maria had been forced on her, she submitted to it without any alarm for Maria's situation, or any endeavour at rational tranquillity for herself. She either sat in gloomy silence, wrapt in such gravity as nothing could subdue, no curiosity touch, no wit amuse; or allowing the attentions of Mr. Yates, was talking with forced gaiety to him alone, and ridiculing the acting of the others.

For a day or two after the affront was given, Henry Crawford had endeavoured to do it away by the usual attack of gallantry and compliment, but he had not cared enough about it to persevere against a few repulses; and becoming soon too busy with his play to have time for more than one flirtation, he grew indifferent to the quarrel, or rather thought it a lucky occurrence, as quietly putting an end to what might ere long have raised expectations in more than Mrs. Grant. She was not pleased to see Julia excluded from the play, and sitting by disregarded; but as it was not a matter which really involved her happiness, as Henry must be the best judge of his own, and as he did assure her, with a most persuasive smile, that neither he nor Julia had ever had a serious thought of each other, she could only renew her former caution as to the elder sister, entreat him not to risk his tranquillity by too much admiration there, and then gladly take her share in anything that brought cheerfulness to the young people in general, and that did so particularly promote the pleasure of the two so dear to her.

"I rather wonder Julia is not in love with Henry," was her observation to Mary.

"I dare say she is," replied Mary coldly. "I imagine both sisters are."

"Both! no, no, that must not be. Do not give him a hint of it. Think of Mr. Rushworth!"

"You had better tell Miss Bertram to think of Mr. Rushworth. It may do *her* some good. I often think of Mr. Rushworth's property and independence, and wish them in other hands; but I never think of him. A man might represent the county with such an estate; a man might escape a profession and represent the county."

"I dare say he *will* be in parliament soon. When Sir Thomas comes, I dare say he will be in for some borough, but there has been nobody to put him in the way of doing anything yet."

"Sir Thomas is to achieve many mighty things when he comes home," said Mary, after a pause. "Do you remember Hawkins Browne's 'Address to Tobacco,' in imitation of Pope?—

> *Blest leaf! whose aromatic gales dispense*
> *To Templars modesty, to Parsons sense.*

I will parody them —

> *Blest Knight! whose dictatorial looks dispense*
> *To Children affluence, to Rushworth sense.*

Will not that do, Mrs. Grant? Everything seems to depend upon Sir Thomas's return."

"You will find his consequence very just and reasonable when you see him in his family, I assure you. I do not think we do so well without him. He has a fine dignified manner, which suits the head of such a house, and keeps everybody in their place. Lady Bertram seems more of a cipher now than when he is at home; and nobody else can keep Mrs. Norris in order. But, Mary, do not fancy that Maria Bertram cares for Henry. I am sure *Julia* does not, or she would not have flirted as she did last night with Mr. Yates; and though he and Maria are very good friends, I think she likes Sotherton too well to be inconstant."

"I would not give much for Mr. Rushworth's chance if Henry stept in before the articles were signed."

"If you have such a suspicion, something must be done; and as soon as the play is all over, we will talk to him seriously and make him know his own mind; and if he means nothing, we will send him off, though he is Henry, for a time."

Julia *did* suffer, however, though Mrs. Grant discerned it not, and though it escaped the notice of many of her own family likewise. She had loved, she did love still, and she had all the suffering which a warm temper and a high spirit were likely to endure under the disappointment of a dear, though irrational hope, with a strong sense of ill-usage. Her heart was sore and angry, and she was capable only of angry consolations. The sister with whom she was used to be on easy terms was now become her greatest enemy: they were alienated from each other; and Julia was not superior to the hope of some distressing end to the attentions which were still carrying on there, some punishment to Maria for conduct so shameful towards herself as well as towards Mr. Rushworth. With no material fault of temper, or difference of opinion, to prevent their being very good friends while their interests were the same, the sisters, under such a trial as this, had not affection or principle enough to make them merciful or just, to give them honour or compassion. Maria felt her triumph, and pursued her purpose, careless of Julia; and Julia could never see Maria distinguished by Henry Crawford without trusting that it would create jealousy, and bring a public disturbance at last.

Fanny saw and pitied much of this in Julia; but there was no outward fellowship between them. Julia made no communication, and Fanny took no liberties. They were two solitary sufferers, or connected only by Fanny's consciousness.

The inattention of the two brothers and the aunt to Julia's discomposure, and their blindness to its true cause, must be imputed to the fullness of their own minds. They were totally preoccupied. Tom was engrossed by the concerns of his theatre, and saw nothing that did not immediately relate to it. Edmund, between his theatrical and his real part, between Miss Crawford's claims and his own conduct, between love and consistency, was equally unobservant; and Mrs. Norris was too busy in contriving and directing the general little matters of the company, superintending their various dresses with economical expedient, for which nobody thanked her, and saving, with delighted integrity, half a crown here and there to the absent Sir Thomas, to have leisure for watching the behaviour, or guarding the happiness of his daughters.

Chapter 18

Everything was now in a regular train: theatre, actors, actresses, and dresses, were all getting forward; but though no other great impediments arose, Fanny found, before many days were past, that it was not all uninterrupted enjoyment to the party themselves, and that she had not to witness the continuance of such unanimity and delight as had been almost too much for her at first. Everybody began to have their vexation. Edmund had many. Entirely against *his* judgment, a scene-painter arrived from town, and was at work, much to the increase of the expenses, and, what was worse, of the eclat of their proceedings; and his brother, instead of being really guided by him as to the privacy of the representation, was giving an invitation to every family who came in his way. Tom himself began to fret over the scene-painter's slow progress, and to feel the miseries of waiting. He had learned his part—all his parts, for he took every trifling one that could be united with the Butler, and began to be impatient to be acting; and every day thus unemployed was tending to increase his sense of the insignificance of all his parts together, and make him more ready to regret that some other play had not been chosen.

Fanny, being always a very courteous listener, and often the only listener at hand, came in for the complaints and the distresses of most of them. *She* knew that Mr. Yates was in general thought to rant dreadfully; that Mr. Yates was disappointed in Henry Crawford; that Tom Bertram spoke so quick he would be unintelligible; that Mrs. Grant spoiled everything by laughing; that Edmund was behindhand with his part, and that it was misery to have anything to do with Mr. Rushworth, who was wanting a prompter through every speech. She knew, also, that poor Mr. Rushworth could seldom get anybody to rehearse with him: *his* complaint came before her as well as the rest; and so decided to her eye was her cousin Maria's avoidance of him, and so needlessly often the rehearsal of the first scene between her and Mr. Crawford, that she had soon all the terror of other complaints from *him*. So far from being all satisfied and all enjoying, she found everybody requiring something they had not, and giving occasion of discontent to the others. Everybody had a part either too long or too short; nobody would attend as they ought; nobody would remember on which side they were to come in; nobody but the complainer would observe any directions.

Fanny believed herself to derive as much innocent enjoyment from the play as any of them; Henry Crawford acted well, and it was a pleasure to *her* to creep into the theatre, and attend the rehearsal of the first act, in spite of the feelings it excited in some speeches for Maria. Maria, she also thought, acted well, too well; and after the first rehearsal or two, Fanny began to be their only audience; and sometimes as prompter, sometimes as spectator, was often very useful. As far as she could judge, Mr. Crawford was considerably the best actor of all: he had more confidence than Edmund, more judgment than Tom, more talent and taste than Mr. Yates. She did not like him as a man, but she must admit him to be the best actor, and on this point there were not many who differed from her. Mr. Yates, indeed, exclaimed against his tameness and insipidity; and the day came at last, when Mr. Rushworth turned to her with a black look, and said, "Do you think there is anything so very fine in all this? For the life and soul of me, I cannot admire him; and, between ourselves, to see such an undersized, little, mean-looking man, set up for a fine actor, is very ridiculous in my opinion."

From this moment there was a return of his former jealousy, which Maria, from increasing hopes of Crawford, was at little pains to remove; and the chances of Mr. Rushworth's ever attaining to the knowledge of his two-and-forty speeches became much less.

As to his ever making anything *tolerable* of them, nobody had the smallest idea of that except his mother; *she*, indeed, regretted that his part was not more considerable, and deferred coming over to Mansfield till they were forward enough in their rehearsal to comprehend all his scenes; but the others aspired at nothing beyond his remembering the catchword, and the first line of his speech, and being able to follow the prompter through the rest. Fanny, in her pity and kindheartedness, was at great pains to teach him how to learn, giving him all the helps and directions in her power, trying to make an artificial memory for him, and learning every word of his part herself, but without his being much the forwarder.

Many uncomfortable, anxious, apprehensive feelings she certainly had; but with all these, and other claims on her time and attention, she was as far from finding herself without employment or utility amongst them, as without a companion in uneasiness; quite as far from having no demand on her leisure as on her compassion. The gloom of her first anticipations was proved to have been unfounded. She was occasionally useful to all; she was perhaps as much at peace as any.

There was a great deal of needlework to be done, moreover, in which her help was wanted; and that Mrs. Norris thought her quite as well off as the rest, was evident by the manner in which she claimed it—"Come, Fanny," she cried, "these are fine times for you, but you must not be always walking from one room to the other, and doing the lookings-on at your ease, in this way; I want you here. I have been slaving myself till I can hardly stand, to contrive Mr. Rushworth's cloak without sending for any more satin; and now I think you may give me your help in putting it together. There are but three seams; you may do them in a trice. It would be lucky for me if I had nothing but the executive part to do. *You* are best off, I can tell you: but if nobody did more than *you*, we should not get on very fast."

Fanny took the work very quietly, without attempting any defence; but her kinder aunt Bertram observed on her behalf —

"One cannot wonder, sister, that Fanny *should* be delighted: it is all new to her, you know; you and I used to be very fond of a play ourselves, and so am I still; and as soon as I am a little more at leisure, *I* mean to look in at their rehearsals too. What is the play about, Fanny? you have never told me."

"Oh! sister, pray do not ask her now; for Fanny is not one of those who can talk and work at the same time. It is about *Lovers' Vows*."

"I believe," said Fanny to her aunt Bertram, "there will be three acts rehearsed to-morrow evening, and that will give you an opportunity of seeing all the actors at once."

"You had better stay till the curtain is hung," interposed Mrs. Norris; "the curtain will be hung in a day or two—there is very little sense in a play without a curtain—and I am much mistaken if you do not find it draw up into very handsome festoons."

Lady Bertram seemed quite resigned to waiting. Fanny did not share her aunt's composure: she thought of the morrow a great deal, for if the three acts were rehearsed, Edmund and Miss Crawford would then be acting together for the first time; the third act would bring a scene between them which interested her most particularly, and which she was longing and dreading to see how they would perform. The whole subject of it was love—a marriage of love was to be described by the gentleman, and very little short of a declaration of love be made by the lady.

She had read and read the scene again with many painful, many wondering emotions, and looked forward to their representation of it as a circumstance almost too interesting. She did not *believe* they had yet rehearsed it, even in private.

The morrow came, the plan for the evening continued, and Fanny's consideration of it did not become less agitated. She worked very diligently under her aunt's directions, but her

diligence and her silence concealed a very absent, anxious mind; and about noon she made her escape with her work to the East room, that she might have no concern in another, and, as she deemed it, most unnecessary rehearsal of the first act, which Henry Crawford was just proposing, desirous at once of having her time to herself, and of avoiding the sight of Mr. Rushworth. A glimpse, as she passed through the hall, of the two ladies walking up from the Parsonage made no change in her wish of retreat, and she worked and meditated in the East room, undisturbed, for a quarter of an hour, when a gentle tap at the door was followed by the entrance of Miss Crawford.

"Am I right? Yes; this is the East room. My dear Miss Price, I beg your pardon, but I have made my way to you on purpose to entreat your help."

Fanny, quite surprised, endeavoured to shew herself mistress of the room by her civilities, and looked at the bright bars of her empty grate with concern.

"Thank you; I am quite warm, very warm. Allow me to stay here a little while, and do have the goodness to hear me my third act. I have brought my book, and if you would but rehearse it with me, I should be *so* obliged! I came here to-day intending to rehearse it with Edmund—by ourselves—against the evening, but he is not in the way; and if he *were*, I do not think I could go through it with *him*, till I have hardened myself a little; for really there is a speech or two. You will be so good, won't you?"

Fanny was most civil in her assurances, though she could not give them in a very steady voice.

"Have you ever happened to look at the part I mean?" continued Miss Crawford, opening her book. "Here it is. I did not think much of it at first—but, upon my word. There, look at *that* speech, and *that*, and *that*. How am I ever to look him in the face and say such things? Could you do it? But then he is your cousin, which makes all the difference. You must rehearse it with

me, that I may fancy *you* him, and get on by degrees. You *have* a look of *his* sometimes."

"Have I? I will do my best with the greatest readiness; but I must *read* the part, for I can say very little of it."

"*None* of it, I suppose. You are to have the book, of course. Now for it. We must have two chairs at hand for you to bring forward to the front of the stage. There—very good school-room chairs, not made for a theatre, I dare say; much more fitted for little girls to sit and kick their feet against when they are learning a lesson. What would your governess and your uncle say to see them used for such a purpose? Could Sir Thomas look in upon us just now, he would bless himself, for we are rehearsing all over the house. Yates is storming away in the dining-room. I heard him as I came upstairs, and the theatre is engaged of course by those indefatigable rehearsers, Agatha and Frederick. If *they* are not perfect, I *shall* be surprised. By the bye, I looked in upon them five minutes ago, and it happened to be exactly at one of the times when they were trying *not* to embrace, and Mr. Rushworth was with me. I thought he began to look a little queer, so I turned it off as well as I could, by whispering to him, 'We shall have an excellent Agatha; there is something so *maternal* in her manner, so completely *maternal* in her voice and countenance.' Was not that well done of me? He brightened up directly. Now for my soliloquy."

She began, and Fanny joined in with all the modest feeling which the idea of representing Edmund was so strongly calculated to inspire; but with looks and voice so truly feminine as to be no very good picture of a man. With such an Anhalt, however, Miss Crawford had courage enough; and they had got through half the scene, when a tap at the door brought a pause, and the entrance of Edmund, the next moment, suspended it all.

Surprise, consciousness, and pleasure appeared in each of the three on this unexpected meeting; and as Edmund was come on the very same business that had brought Miss Crawford, consciousness and pleasure were likely to be more than momentary in *them*. He too had his book, and was seeking Fanny, to ask her to rehearse with him, and help him to prepare for the evening, without knowing Miss Crawford to be in the house; and great was the joy and animation of being thus thrown together, of comparing schemes, and sympathising in praise of Fanny's kind offices.

She could not equal them in their warmth. *Her* spirits sank under the glow of theirs, and she felt herself becoming too nearly nothing to both to have any comfort in having been sought by either. They must now rehearse together. Edmund proposed, urged, entreated it, till the lady, not very unwilling at first, could refuse no longer, and Fanny was wanted only to prompt and observe them. She was invested, indeed, with the office of judge and critic, and earnestly desired to exercise it and tell them all their faults; but from doing so every feeling within her shrank—she could not, would not, dared not attempt it: had she been otherwise qualified for criticism, her conscience must have restrained her from venturing at disapprobation. She believed herself to feel too much of it in the aggregate for honesty or safety in particulars. To prompt them must be enough for her; and it was sometimes *more* than enough; for she could not always pay attention to the book. In watching them she forgot herself; and, agitated by the increasing spirit of Edmund's manner, had once closed the page and turned away exactly as he wanted help. It was imputed to very reasonable weariness, and she was thanked and pitied; but she deserved their pity more than she hoped they would ever surmise. At last the scene was over, and Fanny forced herself to add her praise to the compliments each was giving the other; and when again alone and able to recall the whole, she was inclined to believe their performance would, indeed, have such nature and feeling in it as must ensure their credit, and make it a very suffering exhibition to herself. Whatever might be its effect, however, she must stand the brunt of it again that very day.

The first regular rehearsal of the three first acts was certainly to take place in the evening: Mrs. Grant and the Crawfords were engaged to return for that purpose as soon as they could after dinner; and every one concerned was looking forward with eagerness. There seemed a general diffusion of cheerfulness on the occasion. Tom was enjoying such an advance towards the end; Edmund was in spirits from the morning's rehearsal, and little vexations seemed everywhere smoothed away. All were alert and impatient; the ladies moved soon, the gentlemen soon followed them, and with the exception of Lady Bertram, Mrs. Norris, and Julia, everybody was in the theatre at an early hour; and having lighted it up as well as its unfinished state admitted, were waiting only the arrival of Mrs. Grant and the Crawfords to begin.

They did not wait long for the Crawfords, but there was no Mrs. Grant. She could not come. Dr. Grant, professing an indisposition, for which he had little credit with his fair sister-in-law, could not spare his wife.

"Dr. Grant is ill," said she, with mock solemnity. "He has been ill ever since he did not eat any of the pheasant today. He fancied it tough, sent away his plate, and has been suffering ever since".

Here was disappointment! Mrs. Grant's non-attendance was sad indeed. Her pleasant manners and cheerful conformity made her always valuable amongst them; but *now* she was absolutely necessary. They could not act, they could not rehearse with any satisfaction without her. The comfort of the whole evening was destroyed. What was to be done? Tom, as Cottager, was in despair. After a pause of perplexity, some eyes began to be turned towards Fanny, and a voice or two to say, "If Miss Price would be so good as to *read* the part." She was immediately surrounded by supplications; everybody asked it; even Edmund said, "Do, Fanny, if it is not *very* disagreeable to you."

But Fanny still hung back. She could not endure the idea of it. Why was not Miss Crawford to be applied to as well? Or why had not she rather gone to her own room, as she had felt to be safest, instead of attending the rehearsal at all? She had known it would irritate and distress her; she had known it her duty to keep away. She was properly punished.

"You have only to *read* the part," said Henry Crawford, with renewed entreaty.

"And I do believe she can say every word of it," added Maria, "for she could put Mrs. Grant right the other day in twenty places. Fanny, I am sure you know the part."

Fanny could not say she did *not*; and as they all persevered, as Edmund repeated his wish, and with a look of even fond dependence on her good-nature, she must yield. She would do her best. Everybody was satisfied; and she was left to the tremors of a most palpitating heart, while the others prepared to begin.

They *did* begin; and being too much engaged in their own noise to be struck by an unusual noise in the other part of the house, had proceeded some way when the door of the room was thrown open, and Julia, appearing at it, with a face all aghast, exclaimed, "My father is come! He is in the hall at this moment."

Chapter 19

How is the consternation of the party to be described? To the greater number it was a moment of absolute horror. Sir Thomas in the house! All felt the instantaneous conviction. Not a hope of imposition or mistake was harboured anywhere. Julia's looks were an evidence of the fact that made it indisputable; and after the first starts and exclamations, not a word was spoken for half a minute: each with an altered countenance was looking at some other, and almost each was feeling it a stroke the most unwelcome, most ill-timed, most appalling! Mr. Yates might consider it only as a vexatious interruption for the evening, and Mr. Rushworth might imagine it a blessing; but every other heart was sinking under some degree of self-condemnation or undefined alarm, every other heart was suggesting, "What will become of us? what is to be done now?" It was a terrible pause; and terrible to every ear were the corroborating sounds of opening doors and passing footsteps.

Julia was the first to move and speak again. Jealousy and bitterness had been suspended: selfishness was lost in the common cause; but at the moment of her appearance, Frederick was listening with looks of devotion to Agatha's narrative, and pressing her hand to his heart; and as soon as she could notice this, and see that, in spite of the shock of her words, he still kept his station and retained her sister's hand, her wounded heart swelled again with injury, and looking as red as she had been white before, she turned out of the room, saying, "*I* need not be afraid of appearing before him."

Her going roused the rest; and at the same moment the two brothers stepped forward, feeling the necessity of doing something. A very few words between them were sufficient. The case admitted no difference of opinion: they must go to the drawing-room directly. Maria joined them with the same intent, just then the stoutest of the three; for the very circumstance which had driven Julia away was to her the sweetest support. Henry Crawford's retaining her hand at such a moment, a moment of such peculiar proof and importance, was worth ages of doubt and anxiety. She hailed it as an earnest of the most serious determination, and was equal even to encounter her father. They walked off, utterly heedless of Mr. Rushworth's repeated question of, "Shall I go too? Had not I better go too? Will not it be right for me to go too?" but they were no sooner through the door than Henry Crawford undertook to answer the anxious inquiry, and, encouraging him by all means to pay his respects to Sir Thomas without delay, sent him after the others with delighted haste.

Fanny was left with only the Crawfords and Mr. Yates. She had been quite overlooked by her cousins; and as her own opinion of her claims on Sir Thomas's affection was much too humble to give her any idea of classing herself with his children, she was glad to remain behind and gain a little breathing-time. Her agitation and alarm exceeded all that was endured by the rest, by the right of a disposition which not even innocence could keep from suffering. She was nearly fainting: all her former habitual dread of her uncle was returning, and with it compassion for him and for almost every one of the party on the development before him, with solicitude on Edmund's account indescribable. She had found a seat, where in excessive trembling she was enduring all these fearful thoughts, while the other three, no longer under any restraint, were giving vent to their feelings of vexation, lamenting over such an unlooked-for premature arrival as a most untoward event, and without mercy wishing poor Sir Thomas had been twice as long on his passage, or were still in Antigua.

The Crawfords were more warm on the subject than Mr. Yates, from better understanding the family, and judging more clearly of the mischief that must ensue. The ruin of the play was to them a certainty: they felt the total destruction of the scheme to be inevitably at hand; while Mr. Yates considered it only as a temporary interruption, a disaster for the evening, and could even suggest the possibility of the rehearsal being renewed after tea, when the bustle of receiving Sir Thomas were over, and he might be at leisure to be amused by it. The Crawfords laughed at the idea; and having soon agreed on the propriety of their walking quietly home and leaving the family to themselves, proposed Mr. Yates's accompanying them and spending the evening at the Parsonage. But Mr. Yates, having never been with those who thought much of parental claims, or family confidence, could not perceive that anything of the kind was necessary; and therefore, thanking them, said, "he preferred remaining where he was, that he might pay his respects to the old gentleman handsomely since he *was* come; and besides, he did not think it would be fair by the others to have everybody run away."

Fanny was just beginning to collect herself, and to feel that if she staid longer behind it might seem disrespectful, when this point was settled, and being commissioned with the brother and sister's apology, saw them preparing to go as she quitted the room herself to perform the dreadful duty of appearing before her uncle.

Too soon did she find herself at the drawing-room door; and after pausing a moment for what she knew would not come, for a courage which the outside of no door had ever supplied to her, she turned the lock in desperation, and the lights of the drawing-room, and all the collected family, were before her. As she entered, her own name caught her ear. Sir Thomas was at that moment looking round him, and saying, "But where is Fanny? Why do not I see my little Fanny?"—and on perceiving her, came forward with a kindness which astonished and penetrated her, calling her his dear Fanny, kissing her affectionately, and observing with decided pleasure how much she was grown! Fanny knew not how to feel, nor where to look. She was quite oppressed. He had never been so kind, so *very* kind to her in his life. His manner seemed changed, his voice was quick from the agitation of joy; and all that had been awful in his dignity seemed lost in tenderness. He led her nearer the light and looked at her again—inquired particularly after her health, and then, correcting himself, observed that he need not inquire, for her appearance spoke sufficiently on that point. A fine blush having succeeded the previous paleness of her face, he was justified in his belief of her equal improvement in health and beauty. He inquired next after her family, especially William: and his kindness altogether was such as made her reproach herself for loving him so little, and thinking his return a misfortune; and when, on having courage to lift her eyes to his face, she saw that he was grown thinner, and had the burnt, fagged, worn look of fatigue and a hot climate, every tender feeling was increased, and she was miserable in considering how much unsuspected vexation was probably ready to burst on him.

Sir Thomas was indeed the life of the party, who at his suggestion now seated themselves round the fire. He had the best right to be the talker; and the delight of his sensations in being again in his own house, in the centre of his family, after such a separation, made him communicative and chatty in a very unusual degree; and he was ready to give every information as to his voyage, and answer every question of his two sons almost before it was put. His business in Antigua had latterly been prosperously rapid, and he came directly from Liverpool, having had an opportunity of making his passage thither in a private vessel, instead of waiting for the packet; and all the little particulars of his proceedings and events, his arrivals and departures, were most promptly delivered, as he sat by Lady Bertram and looked with heartfelt satisfaction on the faces around him—most particularly his wife's—interrupting himself more than once, however, to remark on his good fortune in finding them all at home—coming unexpectedly as he did—all collected together exactly as he could have wished, but dared not depend on. Mr. Rushworth was not forgotten: a most friendly reception and warmth of hand-shaking had already met him, and with pointed attention he was now included in the objects most intimately connected with Mansfield. There was nothing disagreeable in Mr. Rushworth's appearance, and Sir Thomas was liking him already.

By not one of the circle was he listened to with such unbroken, unalloyed enjoyment as by his wife, who was really extremely happy to see him, and whose feelings were so warmed by his sudden arrival as to place her nearer agitation than she had been for the last twenty years. She had been *almost* fluttered for a few minutes, and still remained so sensibly animated as to put away her work, move Pug from her side, and give all her attention and all the rest of her sofa to her husband. She had no anxieties for anybody to cloud *her* pleasure: her own time had been irreproachably spent during his absence: she had done a great deal of carpet-work, and made many yards of fringe; and she would have answered as freely for the good conduct and useful pursuits of all the young people as for her own. It was so agreeable to her to see him again, and hear him talk, to have her ear amused and her whole comprehension filled by his narratives, that she began particularly to feel how dreadfully she must have missed him, and how impossible it would have been for her to bear a lengthened absence. She began to long for time alone with him in order to demonstrate the extent of her yearning.

Mrs. Norris was by no means to be compared in happiness to her sister. Not that *she* was incommoded by many fears of Sir Thomas's disapprobation when the present state of his house should be known, for her judgment had been so blinded that, except by the instinctive caution with which she had whisked away Mr. Rushworth's pink satin cloak as her brother-in-law entered, she could hardly be said to shew any sign of alarm; but she was vexed by the *manner* of his return. It had left her nothing to do.

Instead of being sent for out of the room, and seeing him first, and having to spread the happy news through the house, Sir Thomas, with a very reasonable dependence, perhaps, on the nerves of his wife and children, had sought no confidant but the butler, and had been following him almost instantaneously into the drawing-room. Mrs. Norris felt herself defrauded of an office on which she had always depended, whether his arrival or his death were to be the thing unfolded; and was now trying to be in a bustle without having anything to bustle about, and labouring to be important where nothing was wanted but tranquillity and silence. Would Sir Thomas have consented to eat, she might have gone to the housekeeper with troublesome directions, and insulted the footmen with injunctions of despatch; but Sir Thomas resolutely declined all dinner: he would take nothing, nothing till tea came—he would rather wait for tea. Still Mrs. Norris was at intervals urging something different; and in the most interesting moment of his passage to England, when the alarm of a French privateer was at the height, she burst through his recital with the proposal of soup. "Sure, my dear Sir Thomas, a basin of soup would be a much better thing for you than tea. Do have a basin of soup."

Sir Thomas could not be provoked. "Still the same anxiety for everybody's comfort, my dear Mrs. Norris," was his answer. "But indeed I would rather have nothing but tea."

"Well, then, Lady Bertram, suppose you speak for tea directly; suppose you hurry Baddeley a little; he seems behindhand to-night." She carried this point, and Sir Thomas's narrative proceeded.

At length there was a pause. His immediate communications were exhausted, and it seemed enough to be looking joyfully around him, now at one, now at another of the beloved circle; but the pause was not long: in the elation of her spirits Lady Bertram became talkative, and what were the sensations of her children upon hearing her say, "How do you think the young people have been amusing themselves lately, Sir Thomas? They have been acting. We have been all alive with acting."

"Indeed! and what have you been acting?"

"Oh! they'll tell you all about it."

"The *all* will soon be told," cried Tom hastily, and with affected unconcern; "but it is not worth while to bore my father with it now. You will hear enough of it to-morrow, sir. We have just been trying, by way of doing something, and amusing my mother, just within the last week, to get up a few scenes, a mere trifle. We have had such incessant rains almost since October began, that we have been nearly confined to the house for days together. I have hardly taken out a gun since the 3rd. Tolerable sport the first three days, but there has been no attempting anything since. The first day I went over Mansfield Wood, and Edmund took the copses beyond Easton, and we brought home six brace between us, and might each have killed six times as many, but we respect your pheasants, sir, I assure you, as much as you could desire. I do not think you will find your woods by any means worse stocked than they were. *I* never saw Mansfield Wood so full of pheasants in my life as this year. I hope you will take a day's sport there yourself, sir, soon."

For the present the danger was over, and Fanny's sick feelings subsided; but when tea was soon afterwards brought in, and Sir Thomas, getting up, said that he found that he could not be any longer in the house without just looking into his own dear room, every agitation was returning. He was gone before anything had been said to prepare him for the change he must find there; and a pause of alarm followed his disappearance. Edmund was the first to speak —

"Something must be done," said he.

"It is time to think of our visitors," said Maria, still feeling her hand pressed to Henry Crawford's heart, and caring little for anything else. "Where did you leave Miss Crawford, Fanny?"

Fanny told of their departure, and delivered their message.

"Then poor Yates is all alone," cried Tom. "I will go and fetch him. He will be no bad assistant when it all comes out."

To the theatre he went, and reached it just in time to witness the first meeting of his father and his friend. Sir Thomas had been a good deal surprised to find candles burning in his room; and on casting his eye round it, to see other symptoms of recent habitation and a general air of confusion in the furniture. The removal of the bookcase from before the billiard-room door struck him especially, but he had scarcely more than time to feel astonished at all this, before there were sounds from the billiard-room to astonish him still farther. Some one was talking there in a very loud accent; he did not know the voice—more than talking—almost hallooing. He stepped to the door, rejoicing at that moment in having the means of immediate communication, and, opening it, found himself on the stage of a theatre, and opposed to a ranting young man, who appeared likely to knock him down backwards. At the very moment of Yates perceiving Sir Thomas, and giving perhaps the very best start he had ever given in the whole course of his rehearsals, Tom Bertram entered at the other end of the room; and never had he found greater difficulty in keeping his countenance. His father's looks of solemnity and amazement on this his first appearance on any stage, and the gradual metamorphosis of the impassioned Baron Wildenheim into the well-bred and easy Mr. Yates, making his bow and apology to Sir Thomas Bertram, was such an exhibition, such a piece of true acting, as he would not have lost upon any account. It would be the last—in all probability—the last scene on that stage; but he was sure there could not be a finer. The house would close with the greatest eclat.

There was little time, however, for the indulgence of any images of merriment. It was necessary for him to step forward, too, and assist the introduction, and with many awkward sensations he did his best. Sir Thomas received Mr. Yates with all the appearance of cordiality which was due to his own character, but was really as far from pleased with the necessity of the acquaintance as with the manner of its commencement. Mr. Yates's family and connexions were sufficiently known to him to render his introduction as the "particular friend," another of the hundred particular friends of his son, exceedingly unwelcome; and it needed all the felicity of being again at home, and all the forbearance it could supply, to save Sir Thomas from anger on finding himself thus bewildered in his own house, making part of a ridiculous exhibition in the midst of theatrical nonsense, and forced in so untoward a moment to admit the acquaintance of a young man whom he felt sure of disapproving, and whose easy indifference and volubility in the course of the first five minutes seemed to mark him the most at home of the two.

Tom understood his father's thoughts, and heartily wishing he might be always as well disposed to give them but partial expression, began to see, more clearly than he had ever done before, that there might be some ground of offence, that there might be some reason for the glance his father gave towards the ceiling and stucco of the room; and that when he inquired with mild gravity after the fate of the billiard-table, he was not proceeding beyond a very allowable curiosity. A few minutes were enough for such unsatisfactory sensations on each side; and Sir Thomas having exerted himself so far as to speak a few words of calm approbation in reply to an eager appeal of Mr. Yates, as to the happiness of the arrangement, the three gentlemen returned to the drawing-room together, Sir Thomas with an increase of gravity which was not lost on all.

"I come from your theatre," said he composedly, as he sat down; "I found myself in it rather unexpectedly. Its vicinity to my own room—but in every respect, indeed, it took me by surprise, as I had not the smallest suspicion of your acting having assumed so serious a character. It appears a neat job, however, as far as I could judge by candlelight, and does my friend Christopher Jackson credit." And then he would have changed the subject, and sipped his coffee in peace over domestic matters of a calmer hue; but Mr. Yates, without discernment to catch Sir Thomas's meaning, or diffidence, or delicacy, or discretion enough to allow him to lead the discourse while he mingled among the others with the least obtrusiveness himself, would keep him on the topic of the theatre, would torment him with questions and remarks relative to it, and finally would make him hear the whole history of his disappointment at Ecclesford. Sir Thomas listened most politely, but found much to offend his ideas of decorum, and confirm his ill-opinion of Mr. Yates's habits of thinking, from the beginning to the end of the story; and when it was over, could give him no other assurance of sympathy than what a slight bow conveyed.

"This was, in fact, the origin of *our* acting," said Tom, after a moment's thought. "My friend Yates brought the infection from Ecclesford, and it spread—as those things always spread, you know, sir—the faster, probably, from *your* having so often encouraged the sort of thing in us formerly. It was like treading old ground again."

Mr. Yates took the subject from his friend as soon as possible, and immediately gave Sir Thomas an account of what they had done and were doing: told him of the gradual increase of their views, the happy conclusion of their first difficulties, and present promising state of affairs; relating everything with so blind an interest as made him not only totally unconscious of the uneasy movements of many of his friends as they sat, the change of countenance, the fidget, the hem! of unquietness, but prevented him even from seeing the expression of the face on which his own eyes were fixed—from seeing Sir Thomas's dark brow contract as he looked with inquiring earnestness at his daughters and Edmund, dwelling particularly on the latter, and speaking a language, a remonstrance, a reproof, which *he* felt at his heart. Not less acutely was it felt by Fanny, who had edged back her chair behind her aunt's end of the sofa, and, screened from notice herself, saw all that was passing before her. Such a look of reproach at Edmund from his father she could never have expected to witness; and to feel that it was in any degree deserved was an aggravation indeed. Sir Thomas's look implied, "On your judgment, Edmund, I depended; what have you been about?" She knelt in spirit to her uncle, and her bosom swelled to utter, "Oh, not to *him*! Look so to all the others, but not to *him*!" She looked towards Edmund, her heart overflowing.

Mr. Yates was still talking. "To own the truth, Sir Thomas, we were in the middle of a rehearsal when you arrived this evening. We were going through the three first acts, and not unsuccessfully upon the whole. Our company is now so dispersed, from the Crawfords being gone home, that nothing more can be done to-night; but if you will give us the honour of your company to-morrow evening, I should not be afraid of the result. We bespeak your indulgence, you understand, as young performers; we bespeak your indulgence."

"My indulgence shall be given, sir," replied Sir Thomas gravely, "but without any other rehearsal." And with a relenting smile, he added, "I come home to be happy and indulgent." Then turning away towards any or all of the rest, he tranquilly said, "Mr. and Miss Crawford were mentioned in my last letters from Mansfield. Do you find them agreeable acquaintance?"

Tom was the only one at all ready with an answer, but he being entirely without particular regard for either, without jealousy either in love or acting, could speak very handsomely of both. "Mr. Crawford was a most pleasant, gentleman-like man; his sister a sweet, pretty, elegant, lively girl."

Mr. Rushworth could be silent no longer. "I do not say he is not gentleman-like, considering; but you should tell your father he is not above five feet eight, or he will be expecting a well-looking man."

Sir Thomas did not quite understand this, and looked with some surprise at the speaker.

"If I must say what I think," continued Mr. Rushworth, "in my opinion it is very disagreeable to be always rehearsing. It is having too much of a good thing. I am not so fond of acting as I was at first. I think we are a great deal better employed, sitting comfortably here among ourselves, and doing nothing."

Sir Thomas looked again, and then replied with an approving smile, "I am happy to find our sentiments on this subject so much the same. It gives me sincere satisfaction. That I should be cautious and quick-sighted, and feel many scruples which my children do *not* feel, is perfectly natural; and equally so that my value for domestic tranquillity, for a home which shuts out noisy pleasures, should much exceed theirs. But at your time of life to feel all this, is a most favourable circumstance for yourself, and for everybody connected with you; and I am sensible of the importance of having an ally of such weight."

Sir Thomas meant to be giving Mr. Rushworth's opinion in better words than he could find himself. He was aware that he must not expect a genius in Mr. Rushworth; but as a well-judging, steady young man, with better notions than his elocution would do justice to, he intended to value him very highly. It was impossible for many of the others not to smile. Mr. Rushworth hardly knew what to do with so much meaning; but by looking, as he really felt, most exceedingly pleased with Sir Thomas's good opinion, and saying scarcely anything, he did his best towards preserving that good opinion a little longer.

And as the discussions of the evening appeared to reach a natural conclusion, it was Lady Bertram who gathered her pug with one arm, attached her free arm to her husband's and bid all a good-night on their behalf. Sir Thomas was not inclined to object to his wife's intervention.

Chapter 20

Edmund's first object the next morning was to see his father alone, and give him a fair statement of the whole acting scheme, defending his own share in it as far only as he could then, in a soberer moment, feel his motives to deserve, and acknowledging, with perfect ingenuousness, that his concession had been attended with such partial good as to make his judgment in it very doubtful. He was anxious, while vindicating himself, to say nothing unkind of the others: but there was only one amongst them whose conduct he could mention without some necessity of defence or palliation. "We have all been more or less to blame," said he, "every one of us, excepting Fanny. Fanny is the only one who has judged rightly throughout; who has been consistent. *Her* feelings have been steadily against it from first to last. She never ceased to think of what was due to you. You will find Fanny everything you could wish."

Sir Thomas saw all the impropriety of such a scheme among such a party, and at such a time, as strongly as his son had ever supposed he must; he felt it too much, indeed, for many words; and having shaken hands with Edmund, meant to try to lose the disagreeable impression, and forget how much he had been forgotten himself as soon as he could, after the house had been cleared of every object enforcing the remembrance, and restored to its proper state. He did not enter into any remonstrance with his other children: he was more willing to believe they felt their error than to run the risk of investigation. The reproof of an immediate conclusion of everything, the sweep of every preparation, would be sufficient.

There was one person, however, in the house, whom he could not leave to learn his sentiments merely through his conduct.

He could not help giving Mrs. Norris a hint of his having hoped that her advice might have been interposed to prevent what her judgment must certainly have disapproved. The young people had been very inconsiderate in forming the plan; they ought to have been capable of a better decision themselves; but they were young; and, excepting Edmund, he believed, of unsteady characters; and with greater surprise, therefore, he must regard her acquiescence in their wrong measures, her countenance of their unsafe amusements, than that such measures and such amusements should have been suggested. Mrs. Norris was a little confounded and as nearly being silenced as ever she had been in her life; for she was ashamed to confess having never seen any of the impropriety which was so glaring to Sir Thomas, and would not have admitted that her influence was insufficient—that she might have talked in vain. Her only resource was to get out of the subject as fast as possible, and turn the current of Sir Thomas's ideas into a happier channel. She had a great deal to insinuate in her own praise as to *general* attention to the interest and comfort of his family, much exertion and many sacrifices to glance at in the form of hurried walks and sudden removals from her own fireside, and many excellent hints of distrust and economy to Lady Bertram and Edmund to detail, whereby a most considerable saving had always arisen, and more than one bad servant been detected. But her chief strength lay in Sotherton. Her greatest support and glory was in having formed the connexion with the Rushworths. *There* she was impregnable. She took to herself all the credit of bringing Mr. Rushworth's admiration of Maria to any effect. "If I had not been active," said she, "and made a point of being introduced to his mother, and then prevailed on my sister to pay the first visit, I am as certain as I sit here that nothing would have come of it; for Mr. Rushworth is the sort of amiable modest young man who wants a great deal of encouragement, and there were girls enough on the catch for him if we had been idle. But I left no stone unturned. I was ready to move heaven and earth to persuade my sister, and at last I did persuade her. You know the distance to Sotherton; it was in the middle of winter, and the roads almost impassable, but I did persuade her."

"I know how great, how justly great, your influence is with Lady Bertram and her children, and am the more concerned that it should not have been."

"My dear Sir Thomas, if you had seen the state of the roads *that* day! I thought we should never have got through them, though we had the four horses of course; and poor old coachman would attend us, out of his great love and kindness, though he was hardly able to sit the box on account of the rheumatism which I had been doctoring him for ever since Michaelmas. I cured him at last; but he was very bad all the winter—and this was such a day, I could not help going to him up in his room before we set off to advise him not to venture: he was putting on his wig; so I said, 'Coachman, you had much better not go; your Lady and I shall be very safe; you know how steady Stephen is, and Charles has been upon the leaders so often now, that I am sure there is no fear.' But, however, I soon found it would not do; he was bent upon going, and as I hate to be worrying and officious, I said no more; but my heart quite ached for him at every jolt, and when we got into the rough lanes about Stoke, where, what with frost and snow upon beds of stones, it was worse than anything you can imagine, I was quite in an agony about him. And then the poor horses too! To see them straining away! You know how I always feel for the horses. And when we got to the bottom of Sandcroft Hill, what do you think I did? You will laugh at me; but I got out and walked up. I did indeed. It might not be saving them much, but it was something, and I could not bear to sit at my ease and be dragged up at the expense of those noble animals. I caught a dreadful cold, but *that* I did not regard. My object was accomplished in the visit."

"I hope we shall always think the acquaintance worth any trouble that might be taken to establish it. There is nothing very striking in Mr. Rushworth's manners, but I was pleased last night with what appeared to be his opinion on one subject: his decided preference of a quiet family party to the bustle and confusion of acting. He seemed to feel exactly as one could wish."

"Yes, indeed, and the more you know of him the better you will like him. He is not a shining character, but he has a thousand good qualities; and is so disposed to look up to you, that I am quite laughed at about it, for everybody considers it as my doing. 'Upon my word, Mrs. Norris,' said Mrs. Grant the other day, 'if Mr. Rushworth were a son of your own, he could not hold Sir Thomas in greater respect.'"

Sir Thomas gave up the point, foiled by her evasions, disarmed by her flattery; and was obliged to rest satisfied with the conviction that where the present pleasure of those she loved was at stake, her kindness did sometimes overpower her judgment.

It was a busy morning with him. Conversation with any of them occupied but a small part of it. He had to reinstate himself in all the wonted concerns of his Mansfield life: to see his steward and his bailiff; to examine and compute, and, in the intervals of business, to walk into his stables and his gardens, and nearest plantations; but active and methodical, he had not only done all this before he resumed his seat as master of the house at dinner, he had also set the carpenter to work in pulling down what had been so lately put up in the billiard-room, and given the scene-painter his dismissal long enough to justify the pleasing belief of his being then at least as far off as Northampton. The scene-painter was gone, having spoilt only the floor of one room, ruined all the coachman's sponges, and made five of the under-servants idle and dissatisfied; and Sir Thomas was in hopes that another day or two would suffice to wipe away every outward memento of what had been, even to the destruction of every unbound copy of *Lovers' Vows* in the house, for he was burning all that met his eye.

Mr. Yates was beginning now to understand Sir Thomas's intentions, though as far as ever from understanding their source. He and his friend had been out with their guns the chief of the morning, and Tom had taken the opportunity of explaining, with proper apologies for his father's particularity, what was to be expected. Mr. Yates felt it as acutely as might be supposed. To be a second time disappointed in the same way was an instance of very severe ill-luck; and his indignation was such, that had it not been for delicacy towards his friend, and his friend's youngest sister, he believed he should certainly attack the baronet on the absurdity of his proceedings, and argue him into a little more rationality. He believed this very stoutly while he was in Mansfield Wood, and all the way home; but there was a something in Sir Thomas, when they sat round the same table, which made Mr. Yates think it wiser to let him pursue his own way, and feel the folly of it without opposition. He had known many disagreeable fathers before, and often been struck with the inconveniences they occasioned, but never, in the whole course of his life, had he seen one of that class so unintelligibly moral, so infamously tyrannical as Sir Thomas. He was not a man to be endured but for his children's sake, and he might be thankful to his fair daughter Julia that Mr. Yates did yet mean to stay a few days longer under his roof.

The evening passed with external smoothness, though almost every mind was ruffled; and the music which Sir Thomas called for from his daughters helped to conceal the want of real harmony. Maria was in a good deal of agitation. It was of the utmost consequence to her that Crawford should now lose no time in declaring himself, and she was disturbed that even a day should be gone by without seeming to advance that point. She had been expecting to see him the whole morning, and all the evening, too, was still expecting him. Mr. Rushworth had set off early with the great news for Sotherton; and she had fondly hoped for such an immediate *eclaircissement* as might save him the trouble of ever coming back again. But they had seen no one from the Parsonage, not a creature, and had heard no tidings beyond a friendly note of congratulation and inquiry from Mrs. Grant to Lady Bertram. It was the first day for many, many weeks, in which the families had been wholly divided. Four-and-twenty hours had never passed before, since August began, without bringing them together in some way or other. It was a sad, anxious day; and the morrow, though differing in the sort of evil, did by no means bring less. A few moments of feverish enjoyment were followed by hours of acute suffering. Henry Crawford was again in the house: he walked up with Dr. Grant, who was anxious to pay his respects to Sir Thomas, and at rather an early hour they were ushered into the breakfast-room, where were most of the family. Sir Thomas soon appeared, and Maria saw with delight and agitation the introduction of the man she loved to her father. Her sensations were indefinable, and so were they a few minutes afterwards upon hearing Henry Crawford, who had a chair between herself and Tom, ask the latter in an undervoice whether there were any plans for resuming the play after the present happy interruption (with a courteous glance at Sir Thomas), because, in that case, he should make a point of returning to Mansfield at any time required by the party: he was going away immediately, being to meet his uncle at Bath without delay; but if there were any prospect of a renewal of *Lovers' Vows*, he should hold himself positively engaged, he should break through every other claim, he should absolutely condition with his uncle for attending them whenever he might be wanted. The play should not be lost by *his* absence.

"From Bath, Norfolk, London, York, wherever I may be," said he; "I will attend you from any place in England, at an hour's notice."

It was well at that moment that Tom had to speak, and not his sister. He could immediately say with easy fluency, "I am sorry you are going; but as to our play, *that* is all over—entirely at an end" (looking significantly at his father). "The painter was sent off yesterday, and very little will remain of the theatre to-morrow. I knew how *that* would be from the first. It is early for Bath. You will find nobody there."

"It is about my uncle's usual time."

"When do you think of going?"

"I may, perhaps, get as far as Banbury to-day."

"Whose stables do you use at Bath?" was the next question; and while this branch of the subject was under discussion, Maria, who wanted neither pride nor resolution, was preparing to encounter her share of it with tolerable calmness.

To her he soon turned, repeating much of what he had already said, with only a softened air and stronger expressions of regret. But what availed his expressions or his air? He was going, and, if not voluntarily going, voluntarily intending to stay away; for, excepting what might be due to his uncle, his engagements were all self-imposed. He might talk of necessity, but she knew his independence. The hand which had so pressed hers to his heart! the hand and the heart were alike motionless and passive now! Her spirit supported her, but the agony of her mind was severe. She had not long to endure what arose from listening to language which his actions contradicted, or to bury the tumult of her feelings under the restraint of society; for general civilities soon called his notice from her, and the farewell visit, as it then became openly acknowledged, was a very short one. He was gone—he had touched her hand for the last time, he had made his parting bow, and she might seek directly all that solitude could do for her. Henry Crawford was gone, gone from the house, and within two hours afterwards from the parish; and so ended all the hopes his selfish vanity had raised in Maria and Julia Bertram.

Julia could rejoice that he was gone. His presence was beginning to be odious to her; and if Maria gained him not, she was now cool enough to dispense with any other revenge. She did not want exposure to be added to desertion. Henry Crawford gone, she could even pity her sister.

With a purer spirit did Fanny rejoice in the intelligence. She heard it at dinner, and felt it a blessing. By all the others it was mentioned with regret; and his merits honoured with due gradation of feeling—from the sincerity of Edmund's too partial regard, to the unconcern of his mother speaking entirely by rote. Mrs. Norris began to look about her, and wonder that his falling in love with Julia had come to nothing; and could almost fear that she had been remiss herself in forwarding it; but with so many to care for, how was it possible for even *her* activity to keep pace with her wishes?

Another day or two, and Mr. Yates was gone likewise. In *his* departure Sir Thomas felt the chief interest: wanting to be alone with his family, the presence of a stranger superior to Mr. Yates must have been irksome; but of him, trifling and confident, idle and expensive, it was every way vexatious. In himself he was wearisome, but as the friend of Tom and the admirer of Julia he became offensive. Sir Thomas had been quite indifferent to Mr. Crawford's going or staying: but his good wishes for Mr. Yates's having a pleasant journey, as he walked with him to the hall-door, were given with genuine satisfaction. Mr. Yates had staid to see the destruction of every theatrical preparation at Mansfield, the removal of everything appertaining to the play: he left the house in all the soberness of its general character; and Sir Thomas hoped, in seeing him out of it, to be rid of the worst object connected with the scheme, and the last that must be inevitably reminding him of its existence.

Mrs. Norris contrived to remove one article from his sight that might have distressed him. The curtain, over which she had presided with such talent and such success, went off with her to her cottage, where she happened to be particularly in want of green baize.

Chapter 21

Sir Thomas's return made a striking change in the ways of the family, independent of *Lovers' Vows*. Under his government, Mansfield was an altered place. Some members of their society sent away, and the spirits of many others saddened—it was all sameness and gloom compared with the past—a sombre family party rarely enlivened. There was little intercourse with the Parsonage. Sir Thomas, drawing back from intimacies in general, was particularly disinclined, at this time, for any engagements but in one quarter. The Rushworths were the only addition to his own domestic circle which he could solicit.

Edmund did not wonder that such should be his father's feelings, nor could he regret anything but the exclusion of the Grants. "But they," he observed to Fanny, "have a claim. They seem to belong to us; they seem to be part of ourselves. I could wish my father were more sensible of their very great attention to my mother and sisters while he was away. I am afraid they may feel themselves neglected. But the truth is, that my father hardly knows them. They had not been here a twelvemonth when he left England. If he knew them better, he would value their society as it deserves; for they are in fact exactly the sort of people he would like. We are sometimes a little in want of animation among ourselves: my sisters seem out of spirits, and Tom is certainly not at his ease. Dr. and Mrs. Grant would enliven us, and make our evenings pass away with more enjoyment even to my father."

"Do you think so?" said Fanny: "in my opinion, my uncle would not like *any* addition. I think he values the very quietness you speak of, and that the repose of his own family circle is all he wants. And it does not appear to me that we are more serious than we used to be—I mean before my uncle went abroad. As well as I can recollect, it was always much the same. There was never much laughing in his presence; or, if there is any difference, it is not more, I think, than such an absence has a tendency to produce at first. There must be a sort of shyness; but I cannot recollect that our evenings formerly were ever merry, except when my uncle was in town. No young people's are, I suppose, when those they look up to are at home".

"I believe you are right, Fanny," was his reply, after a short consideration. "I believe our evenings are rather returned to what they were, than assuming a new character. The novelty was in their being lively. Yet, how strong the impression that only a few weeks will give! I have been feeling as if we had never lived so before."

"I suppose I am graver than other people," said Fanny. "The evenings do not appear long to me. I love to hear my uncle talk of the West Indies. I could listen to him for an hour together. It entertains *me* more than many other things have done; but then I am unlike other people, I dare say."

"Why should you dare say *that?*" (smiling). "Do you want to be told that you are only unlike other people in being more wise and discreet? But when did you, or anybody, ever get a compliment from me, Fanny? Go to my father if you want to be complimented. He will satisfy you. Ask your uncle what he thinks, and you will hear compliments enough: and though they may be chiefly on your person, you must put up with it, and trust to his seeing as much beauty of mind in time."

Such language was so new to Fanny that it quite embarrassed her.

"Your uncle thinks you very pretty, dear Fanny—and that is the long and the short of the matter. Anybody but myself would have made something more of it, and anybody but you would resent that you had not been thought very pretty before; but the truth is, that your uncle never did admire you till now—and now he does. Your complexion is so improved!—and you have gained so much countenance!—and your figure—nay, Fanny, do not turn away about it—it is but an uncle. If you cannot bear an uncle's admiration, what is to become of you? You must really begin to harden yourself to the idea of being worth looking at. You must try not to mind growing up into a pretty woman." And here Edmund paused to look at her for a great length, perhaps realising for the first time that she was indeed grown up and confirming that she was most certainly a pretty woman. When had her form become so round, her bosom so full?

"Oh! don't talk so, don't talk so," cried Fanny, distressed by more feelings than he was aware of; but seeing that she was distressed, he had done with the subject, and only added more seriously —

"Your uncle is disposed to be pleased with you in every respect; and I only wish you would talk to him more. You are one of those who are too silent in the evening circle."

"But I do talk to him more than I used. I am sure I do. Did not you hear me ask him about the slave-trade last night?"

"I did—and was in hopes the question would be followed up by others. It would have pleased your uncle to be inquired of farther."

"And I longed to do it—but there was such a dead silence! And while my cousins were sitting by without speaking a word, or seeming at all interested in the subject, I did not like—I thought it would appear as if I wanted to set myself off at their expense, by shewing a curiosity and pleasure in his information which he must wish his own daughters to feel."

"Miss Crawford was very right in what she said of you the other day: that you seemed almost as fearful of notice and praise as other women were of neglect. We were talking of you at the Parsonage, and those were her words. She has great discernment. I know nobody who distinguishes characters better. For so young a woman it is remarkable! She certainly understands *you* better than you are understood by the greater part of those who have known you so long; and with regard to some others, I can perceive, from occasional lively hints, the unguarded expressions of the moment, that she could define *many* as accurately, did not delicacy forbid it. I wonder what she thinks of my father! She must admire him as a fine-looking man, with most gentlemanlike, dignified, consistent manners; but perhaps, having seen him so seldom, his reserve may be a little repulsive. Could they be much together, I feel sure of their liking each other. He would enjoy her liveliness and she has talents to value his powers. I wish they met more frequently! I hope she does not suppose there is any dislike on his side."

"She must know herself too secure of the regard of all the rest of you," said Fanny, with half a sigh, "to have any such apprehension. And Sir Thomas's wishing just at first to be only with his family, is so very natural, that she can argue nothing from that. After a little while, I dare say, we shall be meeting again in the same sort of way, allowing for the difference of the time of year."

"This is the first October that she has passed in the country since her infancy. I do not call Tunbridge or Cheltenham the country; and November is a still more serious month, and I can see that Mrs. Grant is very anxious for her not finding Mansfield dull as winter comes on."

Fanny could have said a great deal, but it was safer to say nothing, and leave untouched all Miss Crawford's resources—her accomplishments, her spirits, her importance, her friends, lest it should betray her into any observations seemingly unhandsome. Miss Crawford's kind opinion of herself deserved at least a grateful forbearance, and she began to talk of something else.

"To-morrow, I think, my uncle dines at Sotherton, and you and Mr. Bertram too. We shall be quite a small party at home. I hope my uncle may continue to like Mr. Rushworth."

"That is impossible, Fanny. He must like him less after to-morrow's visit, for we shall be five hours in his company. I should dread the stupidity of the day, if there were not a much greater evil to follow—the impression it must leave on Sir Thomas. He cannot much longer deceive himself. I am sorry for them all, and would give something that Rushworth and Maria had never met."

In this quarter, indeed, disappointment was impending over Sir Thomas. Not all his good-will for Mr. Rushworth, not all Mr. Rushworth's deference for him, could prevent him from soon discerning some part of the truth—that Mr. Rushworth was an inferior young man, as ignorant in business as in books, with opinions in general unfixed, and without seeming much aware of it himself.

He had expected a very different son-in-law; and beginning to feel grave on Maria's account, tried to understand *her* feelings. Little observation there was necessary to tell him that indifference was the most favourable state they could be in. Her behaviour to Mr. Rushworth was careless and cold. She could not, did not like him. Sir Thomas resolved to speak seriously to her. Advantageous as would be the alliance, and long standing and public as was the engagement, her happiness must not be sacrificed to it. Mr. Rushworth had, perhaps, been accepted on too short an acquaintance, and, on knowing him better, she was repenting.

With solemn kindness Sir Thomas addressed her: told her his fears, inquired into her wishes, entreated her to be open and sincere, and assured her that every inconvenience should be braved, and the connexion entirely given up, if she felt herself unhappy in the prospect of it. He would act for her and release her. Maria had a moment's struggle as she listened, and only a moment's: when her father ceased, she was able to give her answer immediately, decidedly, and with no apparent agitation. She thanked him for his great attention, his paternal kindness, but he was quite mistaken in supposing she had the smallest desire of breaking through her engagement, or was sensible of any change of opinion or inclination since her forming it. She had the highest esteem for Mr. Rushworth's character and disposition, and could not have a doubt of her happiness with him.

Sir Thomas was satisfied; too glad to be satisfied, perhaps, to urge the matter quite so far as his judgment might have dictated to others. It was an alliance which he could not have relinquished without pain; and thus he reasoned. Mr. Rushworth was young enough to improve. Mr. Rushworth must and would improve in good society; and if Maria could now speak so securely of her happiness with him, speaking certainly without the prejudice, the blindness of love, she ought to be believed. Her feelings, probably, were not acute; he had never supposed them to be so; but her comforts might not be less on that account; and if she could dispense with seeing her husband a leading, shining character, there would certainly be everything else in her favour. A well-disposed young woman, who did not marry for love, was in general but the more attached to her own family; and the nearness of Sotherton to Mansfield must naturally hold out the greatest temptation, and would, in all probability, be a continual supply of the most amiable and innocent enjoyments. Such and such-like were the reasonings of Sir Thomas, happy to escape the embarrassing evils of a rupture, the wonder, the reflections, the reproach that must attend it; happy to secure a marriage which would bring him such an addition of respectability and influence, and very happy to think anything of his daughter's disposition that was most favourable for the purpose.

To her the conference closed as satisfactorily as to him. She was in a state of mind to be glad that she had secured her fate beyond recall: that she had pledged herself anew to Sotherton; that she was safe from the possibility of giving Crawford the triumph of governing her actions, and destroying her prospects; and retired in proud resolve, determined only to behave more cautiously to Mr. Rushworth in future, that her father might not be again suspecting her.

Had Sir Thomas applied to his daughter within the first three or four days after Henry Crawford's leaving Mansfield, before her feelings were at all tranquillised, before she had given up every hope of him, or absolutely resolved on enduring his rival, her answer might have been different; but after another three or four days, when there was no return, no letter, no message, no symptom of a softened heart, no hope of advantage from separation, her mind became cool enough to seek all the comfort that pride and self revenge could give.

Henry Crawford had destroyed her happiness, but he should not know that he had done it; he should not destroy her credit, her appearance, her prosperity, too. He should not have to think of her as pining in the retirement of Mansfield for *him*, rejecting Sotherton and London, independence and splendour, for *his* sake. Independence was more needful than ever; the want of it at Mansfield more sensibly felt. She was less and less able to endure the restraint which her father imposed. The liberty which his absence had given was now become absolutely necessary. She must escape from him and Mansfield as soon as possible, and find consolation in fortune and consequence, bustle and the world, for a wounded spirit. Her mind was quite determined, and varied not.

To such feelings delay, even the delay of much preparation, would have been an evil, and Mr. Rushworth could hardly be more impatient for the marriage than herself. In all the important preparations of the mind she was complete: being prepared for matrimony by an hatred of home, restraint, and tranquillity; by the misery of disappointed affection, and contempt of the man she was to marry. The rest might wait. The preparations of new carriages and furniture might wait for London and spring, when her own taste could have fairer play.

The principals being all agreed in this respect, it soon appeared that a very few weeks would be sufficient for such arrangements as must precede the wedding.

Mrs. Rushworth was quite ready to retire, and make way for the fortunate young woman whom her dear son had selected; and very early in November removed herself, her maid, her footman, and her chariot, with true dowager propriety, to Bath, there to parade over the wonders of Sotherton in her evening parties; enjoying them as thoroughly, perhaps, in the animation of a card-table, as she had ever done on the spot; and before the middle of the same month the ceremony had taken place which gave Sotherton another mistress.

It was a very proper wedding. The bride was elegantly dressed; the two bridesmaids were duly inferior; her father gave her away; her mother stood with salts in her hand, expecting to be agitated; her aunt tried to cry; and the service was impressively read by Dr. Grant. Nothing could be objected to when it came under the discussion of the neighbourhood, except that the carriage which conveyed the bride and bridegroom and Julia from the church-door to Sotherton was the same chaise which Mr. Rushworth had used for a twelvemonth before. In everything else the etiquette of the day might stand the strictest investigation.

It was done, and they were gone. Sir Thomas felt as an anxious father must feel, and was indeed experiencing much of the agitation which his wife had been apprehensive of for herself, but had fortunately escaped. Mrs. Norris, most happy to assist in the duties of the day, by spending it at the Park to support her sister's spirits, and drinking the health of Mr. and Mrs. Rushworth in a supernumerary glass or two, was all joyous delight; for she had made the match; she had done everything; and no one would have supposed, from her confident triumph, that she had ever heard of conjugal infelicity in her life, or could have the smallest insight into the disposition of the niece who had been brought up under her eye.

The plan of the young couple was to proceed, after a few days, to Brighton, and take a house there for some weeks. Every public place was new to Maria, and Brighton is almost as gay in winter as in summer. When the novelty of amusement there was over, it would be time for the wider range of London.

Julia was to go with them to Brighton. Since rivalry between the sisters had ceased, they had been gradually recovering much of their former good understanding; and were at least sufficiently friends to make each of them exceedingly glad to be with the other at such a time. Some other companion than Mr. Rushworth was of the first consequence to his lady; and Julia was quite as eager for novelty and pleasure as Maria, though she might not have struggled through so much to obtain them, and could better bear a subordinate situation.

Their departure made another material change at Mansfield, a chasm which required some time to fill up. The family circle became greatly contracted; and though the Miss Bertrams had latterly added little to its gaiety, they could not but be missed. Even their mother missed them; and how much more their tenderhearted cousin, who wandered about the house, and thought of them, and felt for them, with a degree of affectionate regret which they had never done much to deserve!

Chapter 22

Fanny's consequence increased on the departure of her cousins. Becoming, as she then did, the only young woman in the drawing-room, the only occupier of that interesting division of a family in which she had hitherto held so humble a third, it was impossible for her not to be more looked at, more thought of and attended to, than she had ever been before; and "Where is Fanny?" became no uncommon question, even without her being wanted for any one's convenience.

Not only at home did her value increase, but at the Parsonage too. In that house, which she had hardly entered twice a year since Mr. Norris's death, she became a welcome, an invited guest, and in the gloom and dirt of a November day, most acceptable to Mary Crawford. Her visits there, beginning by chance, were continued by solicitation. Mrs. Grant, really eager to get any change for her sister, could, by the easiest self-deceit, persuade herself that she was doing the kindest thing by Fanny, and giving her the most important opportunities of improvement in pressing her frequent calls.

Fanny, having been sent into the village on some errand by her aunt Norris, was overtaken by a heavy shower close to the Parsonage; and being descried from one of the windows endeavouring to find shelter under the branches and lingering leaves of an oak just beyond their premises, was forced, though not without some modest reluctance on her part, to come in. A civil servant she had withstood; but when Dr. Grant himself went out with an umbrella, there was nothing to be done but to be very much ashamed, and to get into the house as fast as possible; and to poor Miss Crawford, who had just been contemplating the dismal rain in a very desponding state of mind, sighing over the ruin of all her plan of exercise for that morning, and of every chance of seeing a single creature beyond themselves for the next twenty-four hours, the sound of a little bustle at the front door, and the sight of Miss Price dripping with wet in the vestibule, was delightful. The value of an event on a wet day in the country was most forcibly brought before her. She was all alive again directly, and among the most active in being useful to Fanny, in detecting her to be wetter than she would at first allow, and providing her with dry clothes; and Fanny, after being obliged to submit to all this attention, and to being assisted and waited on by mistresses and maids, being also obliged, on returning downstairs, to be fixed in their drawing-room for an hour while the rain continued, the blessing of something fresh to see and think of was thus extended to Miss Crawford, and might carry on her spirits to the period of dressing and dinner.

The two sisters were so kind to her, and so pleasant, that Fanny might have enjoyed her visit could she have believed herself not in the way, and could she have foreseen that the weather would certainly clear at the end of the hour, and save her from the shame of having Dr. Grant's carriage and horses out to take her home, with which she was threatened. As to anxiety for any alarm that her absence in such weather might occasion at home, she had nothing to suffer on that score; for as her being out was known only to her two aunts, she was perfectly aware that none would be felt, and that in whatever cottage aunt Norris might chuse to establish her during the rain, her being in such cottage would be indubitable to aunt Bertram.

It was beginning to look brighter, when Fanny, observing a harp in the room, asked some questions about it, which soon led to an acknowledgment of her wishing very much to hear it, and a confession, which could hardly be believed, of her having never yet heard it since its being in Mansfield. To Fanny herself it appeared a very simple and natural circumstance. She had scarcely ever been at the Parsonage since the instrument's arrival, there had been no reason that she should; but Miss Crawford, calling to mind an early expressed wish on the subject, was concerned at her own neglect; and "Shall I play to you now?" and "What will you have?" were questions immediately following with the readiest good-humour.

She played accordingly; happy to have a new listener, and a listener who seemed so much obliged, so full of wonder at the performance, and who shewed herself not wanting in taste. She played till Fanny's eyes, straying to the window on the weather's being evidently fair, spoke what she felt must be done.

"Another quarter of an hour," said Miss Crawford, "and we shall see how it will be. Do not run away the first moment of its holding up. Those clouds look alarming."

"But they are passed over," said Fanny. "I have been watching them. This weather is all from the south."

"South or north, I know a black cloud when I see it; and you must not set forward while it is so threatening. And besides, I want to play something more to you—a very pretty piece—and your cousin Edmund's prime favourite. You must stay and hear your cousin's favourite."

Fanny felt that she must; and though she had not waited for that sentence to be thinking of Edmund, such a memento made her particularly awake to his idea, and she fancied him sitting in that room again and again, perhaps in the very spot where she sat now, listening with constant delight to the favourite air, played, as it appeared to her, with superior tone and expression; and though pleased with it herself, and glad to like whatever was liked by him, she was more sincerely impatient to go away at the conclusion of it than she had been before; and on this being evident, she was so kindly asked to call again, to take them in her walk whenever she could, to come and hear more of the harp, that she felt it necessary to be done, if no objection arose at home.

Such was the origin of the sort of intimacy which took place between them within the first fortnight after the Miss Bertrams' going away—an intimacy resulting principally from Miss Crawford's desire of something new, and which had little reality in Fanny's feelings. Fanny went to her every two or three days: it seemed a kind of fascination: she could not be easy without going, and yet it was without loving her, without ever thinking like her, without any sense of obligation for being sought after now when nobody else was to be had; and deriving no higher pleasure from her conversation than occasional amusement, and *that* often at the expense of her judgment, when it was raised by pleasantry on people or subjects which she wished to be respected. She went, however, and they sauntered about together many an half-hour in Mrs. Grant's shrubbery, the weather being unusually mild for the time of year, and venturing sometimes even to sit down on one of the benches now comparatively unsheltered, remaining there perhaps till, in the midst of some tender ejaculation of Fanny's on the sweets of so protracted an autumn, they were forced, by the sudden swell of a cold gust shaking down the last few yellow leaves about them, to jump up and walk for warmth.

"This is pretty, very pretty," said Fanny, looking around her as they were thus sitting together one day; "every time I come into this shrubbery I am more struck with its growth and beauty. Three years ago, this was nothing but a rough hedgerow along the upper side of the field, never thought of as anything, or capable of becoming anything; and now it is converted into a walk, and it would be difficult to say whether most valuable as a convenience or an ornament; and perhaps, in another three years, we may be forgetting—almost forgetting what it was before. How wonderful, how very wonderful the operations of time, and the changes of the human mind!" And following the latter train of thought, she soon afterwards added: "If any one faculty of our nature may be called *more* wonderful than the rest, I do think it is memory.

There seems something more speakingly incomprehensible in the powers, the failures, the inequalities of memory, than in any other of our intelligences. The memory is sometimes so retentive, so serviceable, so obedient; at others, so bewildered and so weak; and at others again, so tyrannic, so beyond control! We are, to be sure, a miracle every way; but our powers of recollecting and of forgetting do seem peculiarly past finding out."

Miss Crawford, untouched and inattentive, had nothing to say; and Fanny, perceiving it, brought back her own mind to what she thought must interest.

"It may seem impertinent in *me* to praise, but I must admire the taste Mrs. Grant has shewn in all this. There is such a quiet simplicity in the plan of the walk! Not too much attempted!"

"Yes," replied Miss Crawford carelessly, "it does very well for a place of this sort. One does not think of extent *here*; and between ourselves, till I came to Mansfield, I had not imagined a country parson ever aspired to a shrubbery, or anything of the kind."

"I am so glad to see the evergreens thrive!" said Fanny, in reply. "My uncle's gardener always says the soil here is better than his own, and so it appears from the growth of the laurels and evergreens in general. The evergreen! How beautiful, how welcome, how wonderful the evergreen! When one thinks of it, how astonishing a variety of nature! In some countries we know the tree that sheds its leaf is the variety, but that does not make it less amazing that the same soil and the same sun should nurture plants differing in the first rule and law of their existence. You will think me rhapsodising; but when I am out of doors, especially when I am sitting out of doors, I am very apt to get into this sort of wondering strain. One cannot fix one's eyes on the commonest natural production without finding food for a rambling fancy."

"To say the truth," replied Miss Crawford, "I am something like the famous Doge at the court of Lewis XIV.; and may declare that I see no wonder in this shrubbery equal to seeing myself in it. If anybody had told me a year ago that this place would be my home, that I should be spending month after month here, as I have done, I certainly should not have believed them. I have now been here nearly five months; and, moreover, the quietest five months I ever passed."

"*Too* quiet for you, I believe."

"I should have thought so *theoretically* myself, but," and her eyes brightened as she spoke, "take it all and all, I never spent so happy a summer. But then," with a more thoughtful air and lowered voice, "there is no saying what it may lead to."

Fanny's heart beat quick, and she felt quite unequal to surmising or soliciting anything more. Miss Crawford, however, with renewed animation, soon went on —

"I am conscious of being far better reconciled to a country residence than I had ever expected to be. I can even suppose it pleasant to spend *half* the year in the country, under certain circumstances, very pleasant. An elegant, moderate-sized house in the centre of family connexions; continual engagements among them; commanding the first society in the neighbourhood; looked up to, perhaps, as leading it even more than those of larger fortune, and turning from the cheerful round of such amusements to nothing worse than a *tete-a-tete* with the person one feels most agreeable in the world. There is nothing frightful in such a picture, is there, Miss Price? One need not envy the new Mrs. Rushworth with such a home as *that*."

"Envy Mrs. Rushworth!" was all that Fanny attempted to say. "Come, come, it would be very un-handsome in us to be severe on Mrs. Rushworth, for I look forward to our owing her a great many gay, brilliant, happy hours. I expect we shall be all very much at Sotherton another year. Such a match as Miss Bertram has made is a public blessing; for the first pleasures of Mr. Rushworth's wife must be to fill her house, and give the best balls in the country."

Fanny was silent, and Miss Crawford relapsed into thoughtfulness, till suddenly looking up at the end of a few minutes, she exclaimed, "Ah! here he is." It was not Mr. Rushworth, however, but Edmund, who then appeared walking towards them with Mrs. Grant. "My sister and Mr. Bertram. I am so glad your eldest cousin is gone, that he may be Mr. Bertram again. There is something in the sound of Mr. *Edmund* Bertram so formal, so pitiful, so younger-brother-like, that I detest it."

"How differently we feel!" cried Fanny. "To me, the sound of *Mr.* Bertram is so cold and nothing-meaning, so entirely without warmth or character! It just stands for a gentleman, and that's all. But there is nobleness in the name of Edmund. It is a name of heroism and renown; of kings, princes, and knights; and seems to breathe the spirit of chivalry and warm affections."

"I grant you the name is good in itself, and *Lord* Edmund or *Sir* Edmund sound delightfully; but sink it under the chill, the annihilation of a Mr., and Mr. Edmund is no more than Mr. John or Mr. Thomas. Well, shall we join and disappoint them of half their lecture upon sitting down out of doors at this time of year, by being up before they can begin?"

Edmund met them with particular pleasure. It was the first time of his seeing them together since the beginning of that better acquaintance which he had been hearing of with great satisfaction. A friendship between two so very dear to him was exactly what he could have wished: and to the credit of the lover's understanding, be it stated, that he did not by any means consider Fanny as the only, or even as the greater gainer by such a friendship.

"Well," said Miss Crawford, "and do you not scold us for our imprudence? What do you think we have been sitting down for but to be talked to about it, and entreated and supplicated never to do so again?"

"Perhaps I might have scolded," said Edmund, "if either of you had been sitting down alone; but while you do wrong together, I can overlook a great deal."

"They cannot have been sitting long," cried Mrs. Grant, "for when I went up for my shawl I saw them from the staircase window, and then they were walking."

"And really," added Edmund, "the day is so mild, that your sitting down for a few minutes can be hardly thought imprudent. Our weather must not always be judged by the calendar. We may sometimes take greater liberties in November than in May."

"Upon my word," cried Miss Crawford, "you are two of the most disappointing and unfeeling kind friends I ever met with! There is no giving you a moment's uneasiness. You do not know how much we have been suffering, nor what chills we have felt! But I have long thought Mr. Bertram one of the worst subjects to work on, in any little manoeuvre against common sense, that a woman could be plagued with. I had very little hope of *him* from the first; but you, Mrs. Grant, my sister, my own sister, I think I had a right to alarm you a little."

"Do not flatter yourself, my dearest Mary. You have not the smallest chance of moving me. I have my alarms, but they are quite in a different quarter; and if I could have altered the weather, you would have had a good sharp east wind blowing on you the whole time—for here are some of my plants which Robert *will* leave out because the nights are so mild, and I know the end of it will be, that we shall have a sudden change of weather, a hard frost setting in all at once, taking everybody (at least Robert) by surprise, and I shall lose every one; and what is worse, cook has just been telling me that the turkey, which I particularly wished not to be dressed till Sunday, because I know how much more Dr. Grant would enjoy it on Sunday after the fatigues of the day, will not keep beyond to-morrow. These are something like grievances, and make me think the weather most unseasonably close."

"The sweets of housekeeping in a country village!" said Miss Crawford archly. "Commend me to the nurseryman and the poulterer."

"My dear child, commend Dr. Grant to the deanery of Westminster or St. Paul's, and I should be as glad of your nurseryman and poulterer as you could be. But we have no such people in Mansfield. What would you have me do?"

"Oh! you can do nothing but what you do already: be plagued very often, and never lose your temper."

"Thank you; but there is no escaping these little vexations, Mary, live where we may; and when you are settled in town and I come to see you, I dare say I shall find you with yours, in spite of the nurseryman and the poulterer, perhaps on their very account. Their remoteness and unpunctuality, or their exorbitant charges and frauds, will be drawing forth bitter lamentations."

"I mean to be too rich to lament or to feel anything of the sort. A large income is the best recipe for happiness I ever heard of. It certainly may secure all the myrtle and turkey part of it."

"You intend to be very rich?" said Edmund, with a look which, to Fanny's eye, had a great deal of serious meaning.

"To be sure. Do not you? Do not we all?"

"I cannot intend anything which it must be so completely beyond my power to command. Miss Crawford may chuse her degree of wealth. She has only to fix on her number of thousands a year, and there can be no doubt of their coming. My intentions are only not to be poor."

"By moderation and economy, and bringing down your wants to your income, and all that. I understand you—and a very proper plan it is for a person at your time of life, with such limited means and indifferent connexions. What can *you* want but a decent maintenance? You have not much time before you; and your relations are in no situation to do anything for you, or to mortify you by the contrast of their own wealth and consequence. Be honest and poor, by all means—but I shall not envy you; I do not much think I shall even respect you. I have a much greater respect for those that are honest and rich."

"Your degree of respect for honesty, rich or poor, is precisely what I have no manner of concern with. I do not mean to be poor. Poverty is exactly what I have determined against. Honesty, in the something between, in the middle state of worldly circumstances, is all that I am anxious for your not looking down on."

"But I do look down upon it, if it might have been higher. I must look down upon anything contented with obscurity when it might rise to distinction."

"But how may it rise? How may my honesty at least rise to any distinction?"

This was not so very easy a question to answer, and occasioned an "Oh!" of some length from the fair lady before she could add, "You ought to be in parliament, or you should have gone into the army ten years ago."

"*That* is not much to the purpose now; and as to my being in parliament, I believe I must wait till there is an especial assembly for the representation of younger sons who have little to live on. No, Miss Crawford," he added, in a more serious tone, "there *are* distinctions which I should be miserable if I thought myself without any chance—absolutely without chance or possibility of obtaining—but they are of a different character."

A look of consciousness as he spoke, and what seemed a consciousness of manner on Miss Crawford's side as she made some laughing answer, was sorrowfull food for Fanny's observation; and finding herself quite unable to attend as she ought to Mrs. Grant, by whose side she was now following the others, she had nearly resolved on going home immediately, and only waited for courage to say so, when the sound of the great clock at Mansfield Park, striking three, made her feel that she had really been much longer absent than usual, and brought the previous self-inquiry of whether she should take leave or not just then, and how, to a very speedy issue. With undoubting decision she directly began her adieus; and Edmund began at the same time to recollect that his mother had been inquiring for her, and that he had walked down to the Parsonage on purpose to bring her back.

Fanny's hurry increased; and without in the least expecting Edmund's attendance, she would have hastened away alone; but the general pace was quickened, and they all accompanied her into the house, through which it was necessary to pass. Dr. Grant was in the vestibule, and as they stopt to speak to him she found, from Edmund's manner, that he *did* mean to go with her. He too was taking leave. She could not but be thankful. In the moment of parting, Edmund was invited by Dr. Grant to eat his mutton with him the next day; and Fanny had barely time for an unpleasant feeling on the occasion, when Mrs. Grant, with sudden recollection, turned to her and asked for the pleasure of her company too. This was so new an attention, so perfectly new a circumstance in the events of Fanny's life, that she was all surprise and embarrassment; and while stammering out her great obligation, and her "but she did not suppose it would be in her power," was looking at Edmund for his opinion and help. But Edmund, delighted with her having such an happiness offered, and ascertaining with half a look, and half a sentence, that she had no objection but on her aunt's account, could not imagine that his mother would make any difficulty of sparing her, and therefore gave his decided open advice that the invitation should be accepted; and though Fanny would not venture, even on his encouragement, to such a flight of audacious independence, it was soon settled, that if nothing were heard to the contrary, Mrs. Grant might expect her.

"And you know what your dinner will be," said Mrs. Grant, smiling—"the turkey, and I assure you a very fine one; for, my dear," turning to her husband, "cook insists upon the turkey's being dressed to-morrow."

"Very well, very well," cried Dr. Grant, "all the better; I am glad to hear you have anything so good in the house. But Miss Price and Mr. Edmund Bertram, I dare say, would take their chance. We none of us want to hear the bill of fare. A friendly meeting, and not a fine dinner, is all we have in view. A turkey, or a goose, or a leg of mutton, or whatever you and your cook chuse to give us."

The two cousins walked home together; and, except in the immediate discussion of this engagement, which Edmund spoke of with the warmest satisfaction, as so particularly desirable for her in the intimacy which he saw with so much pleasure established, it was a silent walk; for having finished that subject, he grew thoughtful and indisposed for any other. Yet it occurred to Fanny that more was said in their silence than could have been spoken in words as she occasionally allowed herself to turn to look up at his face and whenever she did so he held her gaze and smiled, and it was a lovely smile; it was a smile that said if Fanny had been feeling vexed before they shared a quiet walk she was all the more so now.

Chapter 23

"But why should Mrs. Grant ask Fanny?" said Lady Bertram. "How came she to think of asking Fanny? Fanny never dines there, you know, in this sort of way. I cannot spare her, and I am sure she does not want to go. Fanny, you do not want to go, do you?"

"If you put such a question to her," cried Edmund, preventing his cousin's speaking, "Fanny will immediately say No; but I am sure, my dear mother, she would like to go; and I can see no reason why she should not."

"I cannot imagine why Mrs. Grant should think of asking her? She never did before. She used to ask your sisters now and then, but she never asked Fanny."

"If you cannot do without me, ma'am—" said Fanny, in a self-denying tone.

"But my mother will have my father with her all the evening."

"To be sure, so I shall."

"Suppose you take my father's opinion, ma'am."

"That's well thought of. So I will, Edmund. I will ask Sir Thomas, as soon as he comes in, whether I can do without her."

"As you please, ma'am, on that head; but I meant my father's opinion as to the *propriety* of the invitation's being accepted or not; and I think he will consider it a right thing by Mrs. Grant, as well as by Fanny, that being the *first* invitation it should be accepted."

"I do not know. We will ask him. But he will be very much surprised that Mrs. Grant should ask Fanny at all."

There was nothing more to be said, or that could be said to any purpose, till Sir Thomas were present; but the subject involving, as it did, her own evening's comfort for the morrow, was so much uppermost in Lady Bertram's mind, that half an hour afterwards, on his looking in for a minute in his way from his plantation to his dressing-room, she called him back again, when he had almost closed the door, with "Sir Thomas, stop a moment—I have something to say to you."

Her tone of calm languor, for she never took the trouble of raising her voice, was always heard and attended to; and Sir Thomas came back. Her story began; and Fanny immediately slipped out of the room; for to hear herself the subject of any discussion with her uncle was more than her nerves could bear. She was anxious, she knew—more anxious perhaps than she ought to be—for what was it after all whether she went or staid? but if her uncle were to be a great while considering and deciding, and with very grave looks, and those grave looks directed to her, and at last decide against her, she might not be able to appear properly submissive and indifferent. Her cause, meanwhile, went on well. It began, on Lady Bertram's part, with—"I have something to tell you that will surprise you. Mrs. Grant has asked Fanny to dinner."

"Well," said Sir Thomas, as if waiting more to accomplish the surprise.

"Edmund wants her to go. But how can I spare her?"

"She will be late," said Sir Thomas, taking out his watch; "but what is your difficulty?"

Edmund found himself obliged to speak and fill up the blanks in his mother's story. He told the whole; and she had only to add, "So strange! for Mrs. Grant never used to ask her."

"But is it not very natural," observed Edmund, "that Mrs. Grant should wish to procure so agreeable a visitor for her sister?"

"Nothing can be more natural," said Sir Thomas, after a short deliberation; "nor, were there no sister in the case, could anything, in my opinion, be more natural. Mrs. Grant's shewing civility to Miss Price, to Lady Bertram's niece, could never want explanation. The only surprise I can feel is, that this should be the *first* time of its being paid. Fanny was perfectly right in giving only a conditional answer. She appears to feel as she ought. But as I conclude that she must wish to go, since all young people like to be together, I can see no reason why she should be denied the indulgence."

"But can I do without her, Sir Thomas?"

"Indeed I think you may."

"She always makes tea, you know, when my sister is not here."

"Your sister, perhaps, may be prevailed on to spend the day with us, and I shall certainly be at home."

"Very well, then, Fanny may go, Edmund."

The good news soon followed her. Edmund knocked at her door in his way to his own.

"Well, Fanny, it is all happily settled, and without the smallest hesitation on your uncle's side. He had but one opinion. You are to go."

"Thank you, I am *so* glad," was Fanny's instinctive reply; though when she had turned from him and shut the door, she could not help feeling, "And yet why should I be glad? for am I not certain of seeing or hearing something there to pain me?"

In spite of this conviction, however, she was glad. Simple as such an engagement might appear in other eyes, it had novelty and importance in hers, for excepting the day at Sotherton, she had scarcely ever dined out before; and though now going only half a mile, and only to three people, still it was dining out, and all the little interests of preparation were enjoyments in themselves. She had neither sympathy nor assistance from those who ought to have entered into her feelings and directed her taste; for Lady Bertram never thought of being useful to anybody, and Mrs. Norris, when she came on the morrow, in consequence of an early call and invitation from Sir Thomas, was in a very ill humour, and seemed intent only on lessening her niece's pleasure, both present and future, as much as possible.

"Upon my word, Fanny, you are in high luck to meet with such attention and indulgence! You ought to be very much obliged to

Mrs. Grant for thinking of you, and to your aunt for letting you go, and you ought to look upon it as something extraordinary; for I hope you are aware that there is no real occasion for your going into company in this sort of way, or ever dining out at all; and it is what you must not depend upon ever being repeated. Nor must you be fancying that the invitation is meant as any particular compliment to *you*; the compliment is intended to your uncle and aunt and me. Mrs. Grant thinks it a civility due to *us* to take a little notice of you, or else it would never have come into her head, and you may be very certain that, if your cousin Julia had been at home, you would not have been asked at all."

Mrs. Norris had now so ingeniously done away all Mrs. Grant's part of the favour, that Fanny, who found herself expected to speak, could only say that she was very much obliged to her aunt Bertram for sparing her, and that she was endeavouring to put her aunt's evening work in such a state as to prevent her being missed.

"Oh! depend upon it, your aunt can do very well without you, or you would not be allowed to go. *I* shall be here, so you may be quite easy about your aunt. And I hope you will have a very *agreeable* day, and find it all mighty *delightful*. But I must observe that five is the very awkwardest of all possible numbers to sit down to table; and I cannot but be surprised that such an *elegant* lady as Mrs. Grant should not contrive better! And round their enormous great wide table, too, which fills up the room so dreadfully! Had the doctor been contented to take my dining-table when I came away, as anybody in their senses would have done, instead of having that absurd new one of his own, which is wider, literally wider than the dinner-table here, how infinitely better it would have been! and how much more he would have been respected! for people are never respected when they step out of their proper sphere. Remember that, Fanny. Five—only five to be sitting round that table. However, you will have dinner enough on it for ten, I dare say."

Mrs. Norris fetched breath, and went on again.

"The nonsense and folly of people's stepping out of their rank and trying to appear above themselves, makes me think it right to give *you* a hint, Fanny, now that you are going into company without any of us; and I do beseech and entreat you not to be putting yourself forward, and talking and giving your opinion as if you were one of your cousins—as if you were dear Mrs. Rushworth or Julia. *That* will never do, believe me. Remember, wherever you are, you must be the lowest and last; and though Miss Crawford is in a manner at home at the Parsonage, you are not to be taking place of her. And as to coming away at night, you are to stay just as long as Edmund chuses. Leave him to settle *that*."

"Yes, ma'am, I should not think of anything else."

"And if it should rain, which I think exceedingly likely, for I never saw it more threatening for a wet evening in my life, you must manage as well as you can, and not be expecting the carriage to be sent for you. I certainly do not go home to-night, and, therefore, the carriage will not be out on my account; so you must make up your mind to what may happen, and take your things accordingly."

Her niece thought it perfectly reasonable. She rated her own claims to comfort as low even as Mrs. Norris could; and when Sir Thomas soon afterwards, just opening the door, said, "Fanny, at what time would you have the carriage come round?" she felt a degree of astonishment which made it impossible for her to speak.

"My dear Sir Thomas!" cried Mrs. Norris, red with anger, "Fanny can walk."

"Walk!" repeated Sir Thomas, in a tone of most unanswerable dignity, and coming farther into the room. "My niece walk to a dinner engagement at this time of the year! Will twenty minutes after four suit you?"

"Yes, sir," was Fanny's humble answer, given with the feelings almost of a criminal towards Mrs. Norris; and not bearing to remain with her in what might seem a state of triumph, she followed her uncle out of the room, having staid behind him only long enough to hear these words spoken in angry agitation —

"Quite unnecessary! a great deal too kind! But Edmund goes; true, it is upon Edmund's account. I observed he was hoarse on Thursday night."

But this could not impose on Fanny. She felt that the carriage was for herself, and herself alone: and her uncle's consideration of her, coming immediately after such representations from her aunt, cost her some tears of gratitude when she was alone.

The coachman drove round to a minute; another minute brought down the gentleman; and as the lady had, with a most scrupulous fear of being late, been many minutes seated in the drawing-room, Sir Thomas saw them off in as good time as his own correctly punctual habits required.

"Now I must look at you, Fanny," said Edmund, with the kind smile of an affectionate brother, "and tell you how I like you; and as well as I can judge by this light, you look very nicely indeed. What have you got on?"

"The new dress that my uncle was so good as to give me on my cousin's marriage." Fanny was most happy to have the distraction of describing her dress as he studied her carefully amidst his many compliments. She reminded herself he was taking such care as to give her the practise he insisted upon concerning others deeming her a pretty young woman. "I hope it is not too fine; but I thought I ought to wear it as soon as I could, and that I might not have such another opportunity all the winter. I hope you do not think me too fine."

"A woman can never be too fine while she is all in white. No, I see no finery about you; nothing but what is perfectly proper. Your gown seems very pretty. I like these glossy spots. Has not Miss Crawford a gown something the same?"

In approaching the Parsonage they passed close by the stable-yard and coach-house.

"Heyday!" said Edmund, "here's company, here's a carriage! who have they got to meet us?" And letting down the side-glass to distinguish, "'Tis Crawford's, Crawford's barouche, I protest! There are his own two men pushing it back into its old quarters. He is here, of course. This is quite a surprise, Fanny. I shall be very glad to see him."

There was no occasion, there was no time for Fanny to say how very differently she felt; but the idea of having such another to observe her was a great increase of the trepidation with which she performed the very awful ceremony of walking into the drawing-room.

In the drawing-room Mr. Crawford certainly was, having been just long enough arrived to be ready for dinner; and the smiles and pleased looks of the three others standing round him, shewed how welcome was his sudden resolution of coming to them for a few days on leaving Bath. A very cordial meeting passed between him and Edmund; and with the exception of Fanny, the pleasure was general; and even to *her* there might be some advantage in his presence, since every addition to the party must rather forward her favourite indulgence of being suffered to sit silent and unattended to. She was soon aware of this herself; for though she must submit, as her own propriety of mind directed, in spite of her aunt Norris's opinion, to being the principal lady in company, and to all the little distinctions consequent thereon, she found, while they were at table, such a happy flow of conversation prevailing, in which she was not required to take any part—there was so much to be said between the brother and sister about Bath, so much between the two young men about hunting, so much of politics between Mr. Crawford and Dr. Grant, and of everything and all together between Mr. Crawford and Mrs. Grant, as to leave her the fairest prospect of having only to listen in quiet, and of passing a very agreeable day. She could not compliment the newly arrived gentleman, however, with any appearance of interest, in a scheme for extending his stay at Mansfield, and sending for his hunters from Norfolk, which, suggested by Dr. Grant, advised by Edmund, and warmly urged by the two sisters, was soon in possession of his mind, and which he seemed to want to be encouraged even by her to resolve on. Her opinion was sought as to the probable continuance of the open weather, but her answers were as short and indifferent as civility allowed. She could not wish him to stay, and would much rather not have him speak to her.

Her two absent cousins, especially Maria, were much in her thoughts on seeing him; but no embarrassing remembrance affected *his* spirits. Here he was again on the same ground where all had passed before, and apparently as willing to stay and be happy without the Miss Bertrams, as if he had never known Mansfield in any other state. She heard them spoken of by him only in a general way, till they were all re-assembled in the drawing-room, when Edmund, being engaged apart in some matter of business with Dr. Grant, which seemed entirely to engross them, and Mrs. Grant occupied at the tea-table, he began talking of them with more particularity to his other sister. With a significant smile, which made Fanny quite hate him, he said, "So! Rushworth and his fair bride are at Brighton, I understand; happy man!"

"Yes, they have been there about a fortnight, Miss Price, have they not? And Julia is with them."

"And Mr. Yates, I presume, is not far off."

"Mr. Yates! Oh! we hear nothing of Mr. Yates. I do not imagine he figures much in the letters to Mansfield Park; do you, Miss Price? I think my friend Julia knows better than to entertain her father with Mr. Yates."

"Poor Rushworth and his two-and-forty speeches!" continued Crawford. "Nobody can ever forget them. Poor fellow! I see him now—his toil and his despair. Well, I am much mistaken if his lovely Maria will ever want him to make two-and-forty speeches to her"; adding, with a momentary seriousness, "She is too good for him—much too good." And then changing his tone again to one of gentle gallantry, and addressing Fanny, he said, "You were Mr. Rushworth's best friend. Your kindness and patience can never be forgotten, your indefatigable patience in trying to make it possible for him to learn his part—in trying to give him a brain which nature had denied—to mix up an understanding for him out of the superfluity of your own! *He* might not have sense enough himself to estimate your kindness, but I may venture to say that it had honour from all the rest of the party."

Fanny coloured, and said nothing.

"It is as a dream, a pleasant dream!" he exclaimed, breaking forth again, after a few minutes' musing. "I shall always look back on our theatricals with exquisite pleasure. There was such an interest, such an animation, such a spirit diffused. Everybody felt it. We were all alive. There was employment, hope, solicitude, bustle, for every hour of the day. Always some little objection, some little doubt, some little anxiety to be got over. I never was happier."

With silent indignation Fanny repeated to herself, "Never happier!—never happier than when doing what you must know was not justifiable!—never happier than when behaving so dishonourably and unfeelingly! Oh! what a corrupted mind!"

"We were unlucky, Miss Price," he continued, in a lower tone, to avoid the possibility of being heard by Edmund, and not at all aware of her feelings, "we certainly were very unlucky. Another week, only one other week, would have been enough for us. I think if we had had the disposal of events—if Mansfield Park had had the government of the winds just for a week or two, about the equinox, there would have been a difference. Not that we would have endangered his safety by any tremendous weather—but only by a steady contrary wind, or a calm. I think, Miss Price, we would have indulged ourselves with a week's calm in the Atlantic at that season."

He seemed determined to be answered; and Fanny, averting her face, said, with a firmer tone than usual, "As far as *I* am concerned, sir, I would not have delayed his return for a day. My uncle disapproved it all so entirely when he did arrive, that in my opinion everything had gone quite far enough."

She had never spoken so much at once to him in her life before, and never so angrily to any one; and when her speech was over, she trembled and blushed at her own daring. He was surprised; but after a few moments' silent consideration of her, replied in a calmer, graver tone, and as if the candid result of conviction, "I believe you are right. It was more pleasant than prudent. We were getting too noisy." And then turning the conversation, he would have engaged her on some other subject, but her answers were so shy and reluctant that he could not advance in any.

Miss Crawford, who had been repeatedly eyeing Dr. Grant and Edmund, now observed, "Those gentlemen must have some very interesting point to discuss."

"The most interesting in the world," replied her brother— "how to make money; how to turn a good income into a better. Dr. Grant is giving Bertram instructions about the living he is to step into so soon. I find he takes orders in a few weeks. They were at it in the dining-parlour. I am glad to hear Bertram will be so well off. He will have a very pretty income to make ducks and drakes with, and earned without much trouble. I apprehend he will not have less than seven hundred a year. Seven hundred a year is a fine thing for a younger brother; and as of course he will still live at home, it will be all for his *menus plaisirs*; and a sermon at Christmas and Easter, I suppose, will be the sum total of sacrifice."

His sister tried to laugh off her feelings by saying, "Nothing amuses me more than the easy manner with which everybody settles the abundance of those who have a great deal less than themselves. You would look rather blank, Henry, if your *menus plaisirs* were to be limited to seven hundred a year."

"Perhaps I might; but all *that* you know is entirely comparative. Birthright and habit must settle the business. Bertram is certainly well off for a cadet of even a baronet's family. By the time he is four or five and twenty he will have seven hundred a year, and nothing to do for it."

Miss Crawford *could* have said that there would be a something to do and to suffer for it, which she could not think lightly of; but she checked herself and let it pass; and tried to look calm and unconcerned when the two gentlemen shortly afterwards joined them.

"Bertram," said Henry Crawford, "I shall make a point of coming to Mansfield to hear you preach your first sermon. I shall come on purpose to encourage a young beginner. When is it to be? Miss Price, will not you join me in encouraging your cousin? Will not you engage to attend with your eyes steadily fixed on him the whole time—as I shall do—not to lose a word; or only looking off just to note down any sentence preeminently beautiful? We will provide ourselves with tablets and a pencil. When will it be? You must preach at Mansfield, you know, that Sir Thomas and Lady Bertram may hear you."

"I shall keep clear of you, Crawford, as long as I can," said Edmund; "for you would be more likely to disconcert me, and I should be more sorry to see you trying at it than almost any other man."

"Will he not feel this?" thought Fanny. "No, he can feel nothing as he ought."

The party being now all united, and the chief talkers attracting each other, she remained in tranquillity; and as a whist-table was formed after tea—formed really for the amusement of Dr. Grant, by his attentive wife, though it was not to be supposed so—and Miss Crawford took her harp, she had nothing to do but to listen;

and her tranquillity remained undisturbed the rest of the evening, except when Mr. Crawford now and then addressed to her a question or observation, which she could not avoid answering. Miss Crawford was too much vexed by what had passed to be in a humour for anything but music. With that she soothed herself and amused her friend.

The assurance of Edmund's being so soon to take orders, coming upon her like a blow that had been suspended, and still hoped uncertain and at a distance, was felt with resentment and mortification. She was very angry with him. She had thought her influence more. She *had* begun to think of him; she felt that she had, with great regard, with almost decided intentions; but she would now meet him with his own cool feelings. It was plain that he could have no serious views, no true attachment, by fixing himself in a situation which he must know she would never stoop to. She would learn to match him in his indifference. She would henceforth admit his attentions without any idea beyond immediate amusement. If *he* could so command his affections, *hers* should do her no harm.

Chapter 24

Henry Crawford had quite made up his mind by the next morning to give another fortnight to Mansfield, and having sent for his hunters, and written a few lines of explanation to the Admiral, he looked round at his sister as he sealed and threw the letter from him, and seeing the coast clear of the rest of the family, said, with a smile, "And how do you think I mean to amuse myself, Mary, on the days that I do not hunt? I am grown too old to go out more than three times a week; but I have a plan for the intermediate days, and what do you think it is?"

"To walk and ride with me, to be sure."

"Not exactly, though I shall be happy to do both, but *that* would be exercise only to my body, and I must take care of my mind. Besides, *that* would be all recreation and indulgence, without the wholesome alloy of labour, and I do not like to eat the bread of idleness. No, my plan is to make Fanny Price in love with me."

"Fanny Price! Nonsense! No, no. You ought to be satisfied with her two cousins."

"But I cannot be satisfied without Fanny Price, without making a small hole in Fanny Price's heart. You do not seem properly aware of her claims to notice. When we talked of her last night, you none of you seemed sensible of the wonderful improvement that has taken place in her looks within the last six weeks. You see her every day, and therefore do not notice it; but I assure you she is quite a different creature from what she was in the autumn. She was then merely a quiet, modest, not plain-looking girl, but she is now absolutely pretty. I used to think she had neither complexion nor countenance; but in that soft skin of hers, so frequently tinged with a blush as it was yesterday, there is decided beauty; and from what I observed of her eyes and mouth, I do not despair of their being capable of expression enough when she has anything to express. And then, her air, her manner, her *tout ensemble*, is so indescribably improved! She must be grown two inches, at least, since October."

"Phoo! phoo! This is only because there were no tall women to compare her with, and because she has got a new gown, and you never saw her so well dressed before. She is just what she was in October, believe me. The truth is, that she was the only girl in company for you to notice, and you must have a somebody. I have always thought her pretty—not strikingly pretty—but 'pretty enough,' as people say; a sort of beauty that grows on one. Her eyes should be darker, but she has a sweet smile; but as for this wonderful degree of improvement, I am sure it may all be resolved into a better style of dress, and your having nobody else to look at; and therefore, if you do set about a flirtation with her, you never will persuade me that it is in compliment to her beauty, or that it proceeds from anything but your own idleness and folly."

Her brother gave only a smile to this accusation, and soon afterwards said, "I do not quite know what to make of Miss Fanny. I do not understand her. I could not tell what she would be at yesterday. What is her character? Is she solemn? Is she queer? Is she prudish? Why did she draw back and look so grave at me? I could hardly get her to speak. I never was so long in company with a girl in my life, trying to entertain her, and succeed so ill! Never met with a girl who looked so grave on me! I must try to get the better of this. Her looks say, 'I will not like you, I am determined not to like you'; and I say she shall."

"Foolish fellow! And so this is her attraction after all! This it is, her not caring about you, which gives her such a soft skin, and makes her so much taller, and produces all these charms and graces! I do desire that you will not be making her really unhappy; a *little* love, perhaps, may animate and do her good, but I will not have you plunge her deep, for she is as good a little creature as ever lived, and has a great deal of feeling."

"It can be but for a fortnight," said Henry; "and if a fortnight can kill her, she must have a constitution which nothing could save. No, I will not do her any harm, dear little soul! only want her to look kindly on me, to give me smiles as well as blushes, to keep a chair for me by herself wherever we are, and be all animation when I take it and talk to her; to think as I think, be interested in all my possessions and pleasures, try to keep me longer at Mansfield, and feel when I go away that she shall be never happy again. I want nothing more."

"Moderation itself!" said Mary. "I can have no scruples now. Well, you will have opportunities enough of endeavouring to recommend yourself, for we are a great deal together."

And without attempting any farther remonstrance, she left Fanny to her fate, a fate which, had not Fanny's heart been guarded in a way unsuspected by Miss Crawford, might have been a little harder than she deserved; for although there doubtless are such unconquerable young ladies of eighteen (or one should not read about them) as are never to be persuaded into love against their judgment by all that talent, manner, attention, and flattery can do, I have no inclination to believe Fanny one of them, or to think that with so much tenderness of disposition, and so much taste as belonged to her, she could have escaped heart-whole from the courtship (though the courtship only of a fortnight) of such a man as Crawford, in spite of there being some previous ill opinion of him to be overcome, had not her affection been engaged elsewhere. With all the security which love of another and disesteem of him could give to the peace of mind he was attacking, his continued attentions—continued, but not obtrusive, and adapting themselves more and more to the gentleness and delicacy of her character—obliged her very soon to dislike him less than formerly. She had by no means forgotten the past, and she thought as ill of him as ever;

but she felt his powers: he was entertaining; and his manners were so improved, so polite, so seriously and blamelessly polite, that it was impossible not to be civil to him in return.

A very few days were enough to effect this; and at the end of those few days, circumstances arose which had a tendency rather to forward his views of pleasing her, inasmuch as they gave her a degree of happiness which must dispose her to be pleased with everybody. William, her brother, the so long absent and dearly loved brother, was in England again. She had a letter from him herself, a few hurried happy lines, written as the ship came up Channel, and sent into Portsmouth with the first boat that left the Antwerp at anchor in Spithead; and when Crawford walked up with the newspaper in his hand, which he had hoped would bring the first tidings, he found her trembling with joy over this letter, and listening with a glowing, grateful countenance to the kind invitation which her uncle was most collectedly dictating in reply.

It was but the day before that Crawford had made himself thoroughly master of the subject, or had in fact become at all aware of her having such a brother, or his being in such a ship, but the interest then excited had been very properly lively, determining him on his return to town to apply for information as to the probable period of the Antwerp's return from the Mediterranean, etc.; and the good luck which attended his early examination of ship news the next morning seemed the reward of his ingenuity in finding out such a method of pleasing her, as well as of his dutiful attention to the Admiral, in having for many years taken in the paper esteemed to have the earliest naval intelligence. He proved, however, to be too late. All those fine first feelings, of which he had hoped to be the exciter, were already given. But his intention, the kindness of his intention, was thankfully acknowledged: quite thankfully and warmly, for she was elevated beyond the common timidity of her mind by the flow of her love for William.

This dear William would soon be amongst them. There could be no doubt of his obtaining leave of absence immediately, for he was still only a midshipman; and as his parents, from living on the spot, must already have seen him, and be seeing him perhaps daily, his direct holidays might with justice be instantly given to the sister, who had been his best correspondent through a period of seven years, and the uncle who had done most for his support and advancement; and accordingly the reply to her reply, fixing a very early day for his arrival, came as soon as possible; and scarcely ten days had passed since Fanny had been in the agitation of her first dinner-visit, when she found herself in an agitation of a higher nature, watching in the hall, in the lobby, on the stairs, for the first sound of the carriage which was to bring her a brother.

It came happily while she was thus waiting; and there being neither ceremony nor fearfulness to delay the moment of meeting, she was with him as he entered the house, and the first minutes of exquisite feeling had no interruption and no witnesses, unless the servants chiefly intent upon opening the proper doors could be called such. This was exactly what Sir Thomas and Edmund had been separately conniving at, as each proved to the other by the sympathetic alacrity with which they both advised Mrs. Norris's continuing where she was, instead of rushing out into the hall as soon as the noises of the arrival reached them.

William and Fanny soon shewed themselves; and Sir Thomas had the pleasure of receiving, in his protege, certainly a very different person from the one he had equipped seven years ago, but a young man of an open, pleasant countenance, and frank, unstudied, but feeling and respectful manners, and such as confirmed him his friend.

It was long before Fanny could recover from the agitating happiness of such an hour as was formed by the last thirty minutes of expectation, and the first of fruition; it was some time even before her happiness could be said to make her happy, before the disappointment inseparable from the alteration of person had vanished, and she could see in him the same William as before, and talk to him, as her heart had been yearning to do through many a past year. That time, however, did gradually come, forwarded by an affection on his side as warm as her own, and much less encumbered by refinement or self-distrust. She was the first object of his love, but it was a love which his stronger spirits, and bolder temper, made it as natural for him to express as to feel. On the morrow they were walking about together with true enjoyment, and every succeeding morrow renewed a *tete-a-tete* which Sir Thomas could not but observe with complacency, even before Edmund had pointed it out to him.

Excepting the moments of peculiar delight, which any marked or unlooked-for instance of Edmund's consideration of her in the last few months had excited, Fanny had never known so much felicity in her life, as in this unchecked, equal, fearless intercourse with the brother and friend who was opening all his heart to her, telling her all his hopes and fears, plans, and solicitudes respecting that long thought of, dearly earned, and justly valued blessing of promotion; who could give her direct and minute information of the father and mother, brothers and sisters, of whom she very seldom heard; who was interested in all the comforts and all the little hardships of her home at Mansfield; ready to think of every member of that home as she directed, or differing only by a less scrupulous opinion, and more noisy abuse of their aunt Norris, and with whom (perhaps the dearest indulgence of the whole) all the evil and good of their earliest years could be gone over again, and every former united pain and pleasure retraced with the fondest recollection. An advantage this, a strengthener of love, in which even the conjugal tie is beneath the fraternal. Children of the same family, the same blood, with the same first associations and habits, have some means of enjoyment in their power, which no subsequent connexions can supply; and it must be by a long and unnatural estrangement, by a divorce which no subsequent connexion can justify, if such precious remains of the earliest attachments are ever entirely outlived. Too often, alas! it is so. Fraternal love, sometimes almost everything, is at others worse than nothing. But with William and Fanny Price it was still a sentiment in all its prime and freshness, wounded by no opposition of interest, cooled by no separate attachment, and feeling the influence of time and absence only in its increase.

An affection so amiable was advancing each in the opinion of all who had hearts to value anything good. Henry Crawford was as much struck with it as any. He honoured the warm-hearted, blunt fondness of the young sailor, which led him to say, with his hands stretched towards Fanny's head, "Do you know, I begin to like that queer fashion already, though when I first heard of such things being done in England, I could not believe it; and when Mrs. Brown, and the other women at the Commissioner's at Gibraltar, appeared in the same trim, I thought they were mad; but Fanny can reconcile me to anything"; and saw, with lively admiration, the glow of Fanny's cheek, the brightness of her eye, the deep interest, the absorbed attention, while her brother was describing any of the imminent hazards, or terrific scenes, which such a period at sea must supply.

It was a picture which Henry Crawford had moral taste enough to value. Fanny's attractions increased—increased twofold; for the sensibility which beautified her complexion and illumined her countenance was an attraction in itself. He was no longer in doubt of the capabilities of her heart. She had feeling, genuine feeling. It would be something to be loved by such a girl, to excite the first ardours of her young unsophisticated mind! She interested him more than he had foreseen. A fortnight was not enough. His stay became indefinite.

William was often called on by his uncle to be the talker. His recitals were amusing in themselves to Sir Thomas, but the chief object in seeking them was to understand the reciter, to know the young man by his histories; and he listened to his clear, simple, spirited details with full satisfaction, seeing in them the proof of good principles, professional knowledge, energy, courage, and cheerfulness, everything that could deserve or promise well. Young as he was, William had already seen a great deal. He had been in the Mediterranean; in the West Indies; in the Mediterranean again; had been often taken on shore by the favour of his captain, and in the course of seven years had known every variety of danger which sea and war together could offer. With such means in his power he had a right to be listened to; and though Mrs. Norris could fidget about the room, and disturb everybody in quest of two needlefuls of thread or a second-hand shirt button, in the midst of her nephew's account of a shipwreck or an engagement, everybody else was attentive; and even Lady Bertram could not hear of such horrors unmoved, or without sometimes lifting her eyes from her work to say, "Dear me! how disagreeable! I wonder anybody can ever go to sea."

To Henry Crawford they gave a different feeling. He longed to have been at sea, and seen and done and suffered as much. His heart was warmed, his fancy fired, and he felt the highest respect for a lad who, before he was twenty, had gone through such bodily hardships and given such proofs of mind. The glory of heroism, of usefulness, of exertion, of endurance, made his own habits of selfish indulgence appear in shameful contrast; and he wished he had been a William Price, distinguishing himself and working his way to fortune and consequence with so much self-respect and happy ardour, instead of what he was!

The wish was rather eager than lasting. He was roused from the reverie of retrospection and regret produced by it, by some inquiry from Edmund as to his plans for the next day's hunting; and he found it was as well to be a man of fortune at once with horses and grooms at his command. In one respect it was better, as it gave him the means of conferring a kindness where he wished to oblige. With spirits, courage, and curiosity up to anything, William expressed an inclination to hunt; and Crawford could mount him without the slightest inconvenience to himself, and with only some scruples to obviate in Sir Thomas, who knew better than his nephew the value of such a loan, and some alarms to reason away in Fanny. She feared for William; by no means convinced by all that he could relate of his own horsemanship in various countries, of the scrambling parties in which he had been engaged, the rough horses and mules he had ridden, or his many narrow escapes from dreadful falls, that he was at all equal to the management of a high-fed hunter in an English fox-chase; nor till he returned safe and well, without accident or discredit, could she be reconciled to the risk, or feel any of that obligation to Mr. Crawford for lending the horse which he had fully intended it should produce. When it was proved, however, to have done William no harm, she could allow it to be a kindness, and even reward the owner with a smile when the animal was one minute tendered to his use again; and the next, with the greatest cordiality, and in a manner not to be resisted, made over to his use entirely so long as he remained in Northamptonshire.

About the Authors

Jane Austen was born in Steventon, United Kingdom in 1775. Arguably one of the most loved and respected English writers, she published six critically acclaimed novels that have been translated into more than thirty languages.

Nina Mitchell lives with her family in Texas. She read her first Jane Austen novel as a teenager and has read them repeatedly ever since.

A Sneak Peek from Crimson Romance
(From *A Room With a View* by Coco Rousseau and E. M. Forster)

"The Signora had no business to do it," said Miss Bartlett, "no business at all. She promised us south rooms with a view close together, instead of which here are north rooms, looking into a courtyard, and a long way apart. Oh, Lucy!"

"And a Cockney, besides!" said Lucy to her cousin, Miss Bartlett, who had been further saddened by the Signora's unexpected accent. "It might be London," Lucy continued. Then she looked at the two rows of English people who were sitting at the table; at the row of white bottles of water and red bottles of wine that ran between the English people; at the portraits of the late Queen and the late Poet Laureate that hung behind the English people, heavily framed; at the notice of the English church (Rev. Cuthbert Eager, M. A. Oxon.), that was the only other decoration of the wall; and she might have remained saddened had her eyes not swept past an older gentleman and come to rest upon the dashingly handsome face of a young man. She studied the lines of his face, absorbing all of his features at once. There was a softness to his fair complexion and cerulean eyes, yet the man in him was strong and exuded all that was masculine, all that she so longed to know.

Lucy's bosom swelled, her heart began to flutter, and her breath hastened. She was utterly mesmerized, unable to break her gaze, though she lingered a measure too long because the young man suddenly met her stare

Bursting from within, Lucy's heart pulsed against its cage: a cage that she had never once been allowed to escape.

The couple stared longingly into each other's eyes as though they shared a secret: one of intimacy, one that might have revealed they had been lovers from the birth of time. Despite her attempt to stay calm, she felt her cheeks flush with heat and her pulse quicken. When a fork clinked loudly against the older man's plate, Lucy quickly cast her eyes down and toward her own plate. Searching for her breath, she could hardly believe her boldness, a brazenness that had sprung from hidden depths inside her that she had not even known existed. How could she have permitted herself to be partner to this surreptitious exchange with a stranger?

Was she to blame for these strange new feelings that were beginning to stir deep within her—feelings that glided like lightning from the tips of her bosoms through her loins and down to the very ends of her toes.

How could she feel such yearning desire to be in the arms of a man she had never once laid eyes upon before this day in her life? She felt as though she was possessed by some inexplicable and captivating allure. She questioned whether she would be able to eat another bite much less converse with the others while they took their evening meal.

She could not stop herself. Her imagination sprang forth and began to roam through the wilds of her mind. The handsome young man lying next to her; her body cradled in his. Their breath as one. Their hands freely exploring. Her legs slowly unfolding to allow his caressing hand to know her intimate flesh.

"Ah." The very thought of his touch befell Lucy with such an intense sensation that a surge of lust shot through her loins. Try as she might, she could not calm her nerves. She felt the urge to run.

All aflutter, she placed a hand on her Cousin Charlotte's lap. "I must fetch my handkerchief from the room, I will return shortly," Lucy whispered.

"My dear Lucia, can it not wait?" Miss Bartlett said in an attempt to suppress her young cousin.

"No, I am quite sorry. Pardon me. I won't be long."

Lucy quickly slipped away from her chaperon and hurried from the dining room hall. As she rounded the corner, she hurried to stairs, which led to the sleeping quarters upstairs. The clock in the hallway struck; the surprise of it almost shattered her nerves. Her head spinning, Lucy hastened to an unexpected stop and braced herself against the wall. Closing her eyes, she took a moment to catch her breath as she listened to the clock wend its way through its chords.

"Is it possible to be love-struck?" she thought. "Hit by a bolt of lightning clapping the earth?"

Lucy felt an overwhelming urge to be taken, to be ravaged, to be made love to in the most intimate and devouring of manners. Although what did she know of these matters? She knew nothing of such delicacies; these affairs were not to be spoken of till the bedroom door closed on one's wedding night; though, the primal urge could not be denied.

"What's come over me?" she thought. "Perhaps it's just fatigue." Lucy brought her hands to her raised bosom. "That must be it, only tiredness from travel." She drew in a long savoring breath. "To be sure, that must be it, nothing more."

The clock reached its final stanza and the only sound that remained was the faint echoes of the bells. Breathing more steadily, Lucy opened her eyes and leaned over to straighten her skirts. She would forego the handkerchief and return to the dining room instead.

Only as she turned to go, the very gentleman who had stolen her breath completely away was standing right there, in front of her, unnaturally close, in this lone hallway. It was just the two of them. Man and woman. He was so close.

Could it be a dream? Did her eyes deceive her?

It could not be. No, it could not. She felt the heat radiating from his body and pouring into her soul.

The air in the hallway instantly drained.

Frightened and filled with insatiable desire, Lucy gasped, trying desperately to draw in a breath, trying to scream, although the presence of this man had shaken her to down to her innermost core, stealing not only her breath but also her words.

Surely, his intentions were not …

Without uttering a word, without asking for permission, he grasped her arms and held her firm. He stared deeply into her eyes. Still, he spoke not a word, although his labored breath was hot against hers.

Braced against the wall, she could not escape. There was nowhere to go. Her heart beat uncontrollably. Inside she ached, her legs weakened. And then he took his liberty. He leaned closer and before she could form a word, her face was in his hands. His strong, warm hands, holding her ever so gently. He paused for a moment to study her face, and then softly touched his lips against hers.

Lucy was unable to resist. Never before kissed, she relinquished every bit of control to this man. With his tongue, he parted her lips to slip inside and find her tongue. Soft and delicate, he began sliding his tongue against hers in a rhythm that played like a sonata.

As if tasting honey for the first time in his life, he kissed her ever so gently till the beast in him emerged unfettered. All at once, he closed the distance between them till he pressed himself against her skirts. There was no mistaking his intention. He kissed her harder. More wildly. Passionately. She could not have stopped him had she wanted to—and she did not want him to stop.

His hands released from her face and slid over the fabric of her dress toward her bosom, where he grasped the fullness of each breast in his hands. He found the aroused tips of her bosom pressing against the cloth and began to circle them with his fingertips.

Through their kisses, Lucy surrendered a light sigh. His touch was so pleasureful, she began to purr until the purr became a moan. A moan filled with such indulgence that it begged for him to lift her skirts. If only his hands would find her intimate flesh. Oh, the pleasure she had longed for—the desire to be caressed, the need to be released. Oh my love, don't stop.

He lifted his lips from hers and began kissing the line of her jaw, moving ever so slowly toward her neck. Unable to speak, she could only gasp with that unspeakable desire. Not asking, he slipped his fingers through her blouse, but just as he was about to clasp the buds of her bosoms, footsteps pattered across the wooden floors downstairs and toward the staircase.

Charlotte!

The young man straightened, and then whispered into Lucy's ear, "Please do not think ill of me, Your beauty drew me to you, my darling."

The stranger drew back, parted himself from her, and rushed toward the stairs.

Bewildered, Lucy raced to her room, and before she closed her door, she heard the voice of Charlotte speaking to the Signora.

Safe inside the sleeping quarters, Lucy hurried to settle herself. She raced to her looking glass mirror and saw that her face was flushed a crimson red. Reaching quickly for her powder brush, she began painting her face.

There was a rap on the door.

Lucy was straightening her hair just as the door burst open..

"Are you quite all right, my dear, Lucia?" Miss Bartlett inquired of her young cousin.

"Of course. Shall we go back down?"

Without waiting for a reply, Lucy hurried past Miss Bartlett, and before long, the two were once again situated at the dining room table with all of its members assembled exactly as they had left them, including the handsome young man who had so intimately descended upon Lucy in that upper hallway only moments ago. Had the two of them been left there alone for a moment longer, pray tell what would have become of her chaste virtue?

Lucy was a shambles, confused, and filled with unspeakable thoughts. How would he dare? Should she feel shame? She glimpsed at the young man, but what she saw astonished her; he appeared exactly as she had left him when he was seated at the table—untouched.

"Lucia," said Miss Bartlett. "Do eat."

Sweeping her eyes past the young man, Lucy forced herself to speak pleasantly to her cousin. "Charlotte," she said, "don't you feel, too, that we might be in London?? I can hardly believe that all kinds of other things are just outside. I suppose it is one's being so tired."

"This meat has surely been used for soup," said Miss Bartlett, laying down her fork.

"I want so to see the Arno. The rooms the Signora promised us in her letter would have looked over the Arno. The Signora had no business to do it at all. Oh, it is a shame!"

"Any nook does for me," Miss Bartlett continued; "but it does seem hard that you shouldn't have a view."

Lucy felt that she had been selfish. "Charlotte, you mustn't spoil me: of course, you must look over the Arno, too. I meant that. The first vacant room in the front—"

"You must have it," said Miss Bartlett, part of whose travelling expenses were paid by Lucy's mother—a piece of generosity to which she made many a tactful allusion.

"No, no. You must have it."

"I insist on it. Your mother would never forgive me, Lucy."

"She would never forgive me."

The ladies' voices grew animated, and—if the sad truth be owned—a little peevish. They were tired, and under the guise of unselfishness they wrangled. Some of their neighbours interchanged glances, and one of them—one of the ill-bred people whom one does meet abroad—leant forward over the table and actually intruded into their argument. He said:

"I have a view, I have a view."

Miss Bartlett was startled. Generally at a pension people looked them over for a day or two before speaking, and often did not find out that they would "do" till they had gone. She knew that the intruder was ill-bred, even before she glanced at him. He was an old man, of heavy build, with a fair, shaven face and large eyes. There was something childish in those eyes, though it was not the childishness of senility. What exactly it was Miss Bartlett did not stop to consider, for her glance passed on to his clothes. These did not attract her. He was probably trying to become acquainted with them before they got into the swim. So she assumed a dazed expression when he spoke to her, and then said: "A view? Oh, a view! How delightful a view is!"

"This is my son," said the old man; "his name's George. He has a view too."

"Ah," said Miss Bartlett, repressing Lucy, who was about to speak.

"Ah, the name. He has a name," Lucy thought. "One wouldn't simply be a handsome young man who took liberties to kiss a complete stranger; he must of course have a name: George. Her Dear George."

For a better definition, Lucy considered George at length. He was not only a handsome young man who sat contentedly, appearing quite untouched as though it were perfectly natural to go about seducing another's affections without speaking a word. He was genuinely the most desirable man she had ever set eyes upon in her life.

The kiss—the very kiss—they shared just moments ago thrilled Lucy so that her toes still tingled. She knew she had to restrain her desire, but it was only heightened.

"What I mean," the older man continued, "is that you can have our rooms, and we'll have yours. We'll change."

The better class of tourist was shocked at this, and sympathized with the new-comers. Miss Bartlett, in reply, opened her mouth as little as possible, and said "Thank you very much indeed; that is out of the question."

Lucy wriggled her toes at the very thought of lying in the same bed in which George had slept.

"Why?" said the old man, with both fists on the table.

"Because it is quite out of the question, thank you," replied Miss Bartlett.

"You see, we don't like to take——" began Lucy. Her cousin again repressed her.

"But why?" he persisted. "Women like looking at a view; men don't." And he thumped with his fists like a naughty child, and turned to his son, saying, "George, persuade them!"

"It's so obvious they should have the rooms," said the son. "There's nothing else to say … "

Though calm on the outside, George did not look at Lucy for fear that his desires would be laid upon the table for all to inspect. His hands moistened at the thought of touching her bare breasts, separated only by the thin cloth of her dress. He had been so close to claiming his prize, so close to making her his own. His fingers hungered at the thought of finding the tips of her bare breasts, the very act which had been denied.

George's heart began to pound within the confines of his chest. The young woman had bedazzled him like no other. Her beauty had allured him, compelled him to act upon impulse. He wanted her. The touch of her soft lips against his, to feel her, to know her quiet sighs, to see her blissful expression.

He turned toward the window, stealing a lingering glance at Lucy's voluptuous bosom. He would have her, but if he did not regain his inner composure this instant, their secret was sure to be discovered.

"Yes," George said, "we insist."

Still, he did not look at the ladies as he spoke, but his voice was perplexed and sorrowful.

He forced himself to slow his breathing and continued to gaze out the window. The view was lush and flawless as Italy, herself, would have it; the canvas lacked only the merged flesh of a man and a woman. If only he could take Lucy now, the two might escape the mundane and meld into an eternal perfection …

Lucy, too, was perplexed; but she saw that they were in for what is known as "quite a scene," and she had an odd feeling that whenever these ill-bred tourists spoke the contest widened and deepened till it dealt, not with rooms and views, but with— well, with something quite different, whose existence she had not realized before. Now the old man attacked Miss Bartlett almost violently: Why should she not change? What possible objection had she? They would clear out in half an hour.

Miss Bartlett, though skilled in the delicacies of conversation, was powerless in the presence of brutality. It was impossible to snub any one so gross. Her face reddened with displeasure. She looked around as much as to say, "Are you all like this?" And two little old ladies, who were sitting further up the table, with shawls hanging over the backs of the chairs, looked back, clearly indicating "We are not; we are genteel."

"Eat your dinner, dear," she said to Lucy, and began to toy again with the meat that she had once censured.

Lucy mumbled that those seemed very odd people opposite, excepting George, of course. She would most certainly have to give the thought of him more consideration.

"Eat your dinner, dear. This pension is a failure. To-morrow we will make a change," said Miss Bartlett.

Lucy felt her heart twist. To be forced to leave George whom she had only just met was simply unthinkable. How could Charlotte take her away from him? She would not stand for it.

Hardly had Miss Bartlett announced this fell decision when she reversed it. She felt her breath catch in her throat as soon as the curtains at the end of the room parted, and revealed a clergyman, stout but pleasingly attractive, who hurried forward to take his place at the table, cheerfully apologizing for his lateness. Lucy, who had not yet acquired decency, at once rose to her feet, exclaiming: "Oh, oh! Why, it's Mr. Beebe! Oh, how perfectly lovely! Oh, Charlotte, we must stop now, however bad the rooms are. Oh!"

Miss Bartlett whose head was now beginning to spin with thoughts she had never known said, forcing herself to profess with more restraint:

"How do you do, Mr. Beebe? I expect that you have forgotten us: Miss Bartlett and Miss Honeychurch, who were at Tunbridge Wells when you helped the Vicar of St. Peter's that very cold Easter."

The clergyman, who had the air of one on a holiday, did not remember the ladies quite as clearly as they remembered him. But he came forward pleasantly enough and accepted the chair into which he was beckoned by Lucy.

"I AM so glad to see you," said the girl, who was in a state of spiritual starvation, and would have been glad to see the waiter, if her cousin had permitted it had George not been present. "Just fancy how small the world is. Summer Street, too, makes it so specially funny." Lucy knew Miss Bartlett would never take her away from the Bertolini, not now, not with the presentation of their new vicar so close at hand.

"Miss Honeychurch lives in the parish of Summer Street," said Miss Bartlett, filling up the gap for fear that she might give way to swooning like some silly young girl. "And," Miss Bartlett continued, "she happened to tell me in the course of conversation that you have just accepted the living—"

"Yes, I heard from mother so last week. She didn't know that I knew you at Tunbridge Wells; but I wrote back at once, and I said: 'Mr. Beebe is—'"

"Quite right," said the clergyman. "I move into the Rectory at Summer Street next June. I am lucky to be appointed to such a charming neighbourhood."

"Oh, how glad I am! The name of our house is Windy Corner." Mr. Beebe bowed.

"There is mother and me generally, and my brother, though it's not often we get him to ch—The church is rather far off, I mean."

"Lucy, dearest, let Mr. Beebe eat his dinner." At hearing Lucy prattle on with the vicar, Miss Bartlett had now regained her countenance as her young cousin's chaperon.

"I am eating it, thank you, and enjoying it." Mr. Beebe stole a glance Miss Barlett's way. A careful observer might have gleaned an added twinkle in his eye, though the vicar was sure to mask any gesture that might appear untoward in polite society.

To be safe at present, he preferred to talk to Lucy, whose playing he remembered, rather than to Miss Bartlett, who probably remembered his sermons. He asked the girl whether she knew Florence well, and was informed at some length that she had never been there before. It is delightful to advise a newcomer, and he was first in the field. "Don't neglect the country round," his advice concluded. "The first fine afternoon drive up to Fiesole, and round by Settignano, or something of that sort."

"No!" cried a voice from the top of the table. "Mr. Beebe, you are wrong. The first fine afternoon your ladies must go to Prato."

"That lady looks so clever," whispered Miss Bartlett to her cousin. "We are in luck."

And, indeed, a perfect torrent of information burst on them. People told them what to see, when to see it, how to stop the electric trams, how to get rid of the beggars, how much to give for a vellum blotter, how much the place would grow upon them. The Pension Bertolini had decided, almost enthusiastically, that they would do. Whichever way they looked, kind ladies smiled and shouted at them. And above all rose the voice of the clever lady, crying: "Prato! They must go to Prato. That place is too sweetly squalid for words. I love it; I revel in shaking off the trammels of respectability, as you know."

The young man named George glanced at the clever lady, and then returned moodily to his plate. Obviously he and his father did not do. Lucy, in the midst of her success, found time to wish they did. It gave her no extra pleasure that any one should be left in the cold: especially George, whom she so longed to be near. When she rose to go, she turned back and gave the two outsiders a nervous little bow.

The father did not see it; the son acknowledged it, not by another bow, but by raising his eyebrows and smiling; he seemed to be smiling across something, and Lucy knew exactly why—their kiss.

She hastened after her cousin, who had already disappeared through the curtains—curtains which smote one in the face, and seemed heavy with more than cloth. Beyond them stood the unreliable Signora, bowing good-evening to her guests, and supported by 'Enery, her little boy, and Victorier, her daughter. It made a curious little scene, this attempt of the Cockney to convey the grace and geniality of the South. And even more curious was the drawing-room, which attempted to rival the solid comfort of a Bloomsbury boarding-house. Was this really Italy?

Miss Bartlett was already seated on a tightly stuffed arm-chair, which had the colour and the contours of a tomato. She was talking to Mr. Beebe, and as she spoke, her long narrow head drove backwards and forwards, slowly, regularly, as though she were demolishing some invisible obstacle. "We are most grateful to you," she was saying. "The first evening means so much. When you arrived we were in for a peculiarly mauvais quart d'heure."

He expressed his regret.

"I must say it is so delightful to see a friendly face." Miss Bartlett's eyes met Mr. Beebe's and before she thought to check herself, she released a delicate smile.

Nodding, Mr. Beebe returned the smile.

Charlotte felt her bosom swell. Again, she was struck with fanciful thoughts usually reserved exclusively for young girls.

"Do you, by any chance, know the name of an old man who sat opposite us at dinner?" she asked, forcing herself back into her role of restraint.

"Emerson."

"Is he a friend of yours?"

"We are friendly—as one is in pensions."

"Then I will say no more."

He pressed her very slightly, and she said more.

"I am, as it were," she concluded, "the chaperon of my young cousin, Lucy, and it would be a serious thing if I put her under an obligation to people of whom we know nothing. His manner was somewhat unfortunate. I hope I acted for the best."

"You acted very naturally," said he. He seemed thoughtful, and after a few moments added: "All the same, I don't think much harm would have come of accepting."

"No harm, of course. But we could not be under an obligation." His rather casual response to their becoming obliged to the wrong sort of person beckoned Charlotte to steal dangerous, impure glances at Mr. Beebe. She wondered what knowledge of the world he might harbor. But then she looked away when shame overtook her.

She scolded herself for allowing her thoughts of the clergyman to roam beyond the boundaries of decent society. Then she forced herself to glance at the severest of paintings mounted on the wall off to the side of Mr. Beebe. Straightening her posture, she smoothed the arm of the chair and reclaimed her matronly position by resting her hands on her lap.

The vicar continued. "He is rather a peculiar man." Again he hesitated, and then said gently: "I think he would not take advantage of your acceptance," he gave Charlotte a peculiar smile, which she did her best to ignore before he continued to say, "nor would he expect you to show gratitude. He has the merit—if it is one—of saying exactly what he means. He has rooms he does not value, and he thinks you would value them. He no more thought of putting you under an obligation than he thought of being polite. It is so difficult—at least, I find it difficult—to understand people who speak the truth."

Charlotte stiffened, but spoke not.

Lucy was pleased, and said: "I was hoping that he was nice; I do so always hope that people will be nice." Moreover, if Lucy were to sleep in the bed where George slept, she would have heavenly dreams. Lucy felt herself becoming aroused again by the thought of sharing his bed. Was it wrong to think like this when the thoughts came so naturally to her?

The vicar continued. "I think he is; nice and tiresome. I differ from him on almost every point of any importance, and so, I expect—I may say I hope—you will differ. But his is a type one disagrees with rather than deplores. When he first came here he not unnaturally put people's backs up. He has no tact and no manners—I don't mean by that that he has bad manners—and he will not keep his opinions to himself. We nearly complained about him to our depressing Signora, but I am glad to say we thought better of it."

"Am I to conclude," said Miss Bartlett, "that he is a Socialist?"

Mr. Beebe accepted the convenient word, not without a slight twitching of the lips.

"And presumably he has brought up his son to be a Socialist, too?"

"I hardly know George, for he hasn't learnt to talk yet." Lucy listened in silence, but she smiled inwardly when she thought, "he may not know how to talk but he has learnt how to kiss. "He seems a nice creature, and I think he has brains. Of course, he has all his father's mannerisms, and it is quite possible that he, too, may be a Socialist."

"Oh, you relieve me," said Miss Bartlett. "So you think I ought to have accepted their offer? You feel I have been narrow-minded and suspicious?"

"Not at all," he answered; "I never suggested that."

"But ought I not to apologize, at all events, for my apparent rudeness?"

He replied, with some irritation, that it would be quite unnecessary, and got up from his seat to go to the smoking-room.

"Was I a bore?" said Miss Bartlett, as soon as he had disappeared, surprising herself at this sudden, unfamiliar desire for a man's attention. "Why didn't you talk, Lucy? He prefers young people, I'm sure. I do hope I haven't monopolized him. I hoped you would have him all the evening, as well as all dinner-time."

"He is nice," exclaimed Lucy. "Just what I remember. He seems to see good in every one. No one would take him for a clergyman." Lucy thought how delightful it was that the vicar had seemed so playful, that he would not be one to stand in the way of her having fun with George; but, oh dear, least he should discover her secret. It would be most uncivil, scandalous, to discuss the matter. But this was all assuming Dear George would return to her. Lucy fretted. Oh surely —

"My dear Lucia—"

"Well," Lucy quickly recovered herself and promptly addressed her cousin's concerns, "you know what I mean. And you know how clergymen generally laugh; Mr. Beebe laughs just like an ordinary man."

"Funny girl! How you do remind me of your mother. I wonder if she will approve of Mr. Beebe." She secretly hoped so, although she must remember in future to keep such thoughts in check.

"I'm sure she will; and so will Freddy."

"I think every one at Windy Corner will approve; it is the fashionable world. I am used to Tunbridge Wells, where we are all hopelessly behind the times."

"Yes," said Lucy despondently.

There was a haze of disapproval in the air, but whether the disapproval was of herself, or of Mr. Beebe, or of the fashionable world at Windy Corner, or of the narrow world at Tunbridge Wells, she could not determine. She tried to locate it, but as usual she blundered. Miss Bartlett sedulously denied disapproving of any one, and added, "I am afraid you are finding me a very depressing companion."

And the girl again thought: "I must have been selfish or unkind; I must be more careful. It is so dreadful for Charlotte, being poor, and I am certain she has never once in her entire solitary life had a kiss; certainly not like the one I received from my Dear George."

Fortunately one of the little old ladies, who for some time had been smiling very benignly, now approached and asked if she might be allowed to sit where Mr. Beebe had sat. Permission granted, she began to chatter gently about Italy, the plunge it had been to come there, the gratifying success of the plunge, the improvement in her sister's health, the necessity of closing the bed-room windows at night, and of thoroughly emptying the water-bottles in the morning. She handled her subjects agreeably, and they were, perhaps, more worthy of attention than the high discourse upon Guelfs and Ghibellines which was proceeding tempestuously at the other end of the room. It was a real catastrophe, not a mere episode, that evening of hers at Venice, when she had found in her bedroom something that is one worse than a flea, though one better than something else.

"But here you are as safe as in England. Signora Bertolini is so English."

"Yet our rooms smell," said poor Lucy. "We dread going to bed," although to bed was exactly where Lucy wanted to go—to George's bed.

"Ah, then you look into the court." She sighed. "If only Mr. Emerson was more tactful! We were so sorry for you at dinner."

"I think he was meaning to be kind."

"Undoubtedly he was," said Miss Bartlett.

"Mr. Beebe has just been scolding me for my suspicious nature. Of course, I was holding back on my cousin's account."

"Of course," said the little old lady; and they murmured that one could not be too careful with a young girl.

Lucy tried to look demure, but could not help feeling a great fool. No one was careful with her at home; or, at all events, she had not noticed it. And now, Charlotte would spoil her opportunity by trying to do what she thought right.

"About old Mr. Emerson—I hardly know. No, he is not tactful; yet, have you ever noticed that there are people who do things which are most indelicate, and yet at the same time—beautiful?"

"Beautiful?" said Miss Bartlett, puzzled at the word. "Are not beauty and delicacy the same?"

"So one would have thought," said the other helplessly. "But things are so difficult, I sometimes think." Or do we make them difficult by not following our feelings, thought Lucy.

She proceeded no further into things, for Mr. Beebe reappeared, looking extremely pleasant.

"Miss Bartlett," he cried, "it's all right about the rooms. I'm so glad. Mr. Emerson was talking about it in the smoking-room, and knowing what I did, I encouraged him to make the offer again. He has let me come and ask you. He would be so pleased."

"Oh, Charlotte," cried Lucy to her cousin, "we must have the rooms now. The old man is just as nice and kind as he can be."

Miss Bartlett was silent.

"I fear," said Mr. Beebe, after a pause, "that I have been officious. I must apologize for my interference."

Gravely displeased, he turned to go. Not till then did Miss Bartlett reply: "My own wishes, dearest Lucy, are unimportant in comparison with yours. It would be hard indeed if I stopped you doing as you liked at Florence, when I am only here through your kindness. If you wish me to turn these gentlemen out of their rooms, I will do it. Would you then, Mr. Beebe, kindly tell Mr. Emerson that I accept his kind offer, and then conduct him to me, in order that I may thank him personally?"

She raised her voice as she spoke; it was heard all over the drawing room, and silenced the Guelfs and the Ghibellines. The clergyman, inwardly cursing the female sex, but only for his lack of knowing what pleasures the intimate company of the right woman might bring, bowed, glanced at Charlotte, and then departed the room with her message.

"Remember, Lucy, I alone am implicated in this. I do not wish the acceptance to come from you. Grant me that, at all events."

Mr. Beebe was back, saying rather nervously:

"Mr. Emerson is engaged, but here is his son instead."

The young man gazed down on the three ladies, who felt seated on the floor at the intensity of his eyes, so low were their chairs.

Lucy held her breath as she sat motionless, waiting for George to speak. His presence caused her heart to flutter, and she wondered if he noticed the blood rushing to her cheeks.

"My father," he said, "is in his bath, so you cannot thank him personally. But any message given by you to me will be given by me to him as soon as he comes out." George glimpsed at Lucy, a glint of light shone from his fiery eyes, and then he quickly looked away.

Indeed, George would return to her. She clearly saw his intentions in that fleeting expression of his; he was so apparent to her, but thank goodness to her alone. Lucy's heart raced, her bosom rose higher with each and every breath, and she felt the buds of her bosom beginning to flower.

To feel his touch, those fingers of his reaching for her ...

Miss Bartlett was unequal to the bath. All her barbed civilities came forth wrong end first. Young Mr. Emerson scored a notable triumph to the delight of Mr. Beebe and to the secret delight of Lucy.

"Poor young man!" said Miss Bartlett, as soon as he had gone.

"How angry he is with his father about the rooms! It is all he can do to keep polite."

Or not, as Lucy secretly knew. Not anger. It was that beast in him, anticipating what joy they would share together.

"In half an hour or so your rooms will be ready," said Mr. Beebe. Then looking rather thoughtfully at the two cousins, he retired to his own rooms, to write up his philosophic diary.

"Oh, dear!" breathed the little old lady, and shuddered as if all the winds of heaven had entered the apartment. "Gentlemen sometimes do not realize—" Her voice faded away, but Miss Bartlett seemed to understand and a conversation developed, in which gentlemen who did not thoroughly realize played a principal part. Lucy, not realizing either, was reduced to literature. Taking up Baedeker's Handbook to Northern Italy, she committed to memory the most important dates of Florentine History. For she was determined to enjoy herself on the morrow. Thus the half-hour crept profitably away, and at last Miss Bartlett rose with a sigh, and said:

"I think one might venture now. No, Lucy, do not stir. I will superintend the move."

"How you do everything," said Lucy.

"Naturally, dear. It is my affair."

"But I would like to help you."

"No, dear."

Charlotte's energy! And her unselfishness! She had been thus all her life, but really, on this Italian tour, she was surpassing herself. So Lucy felt, or strove to feel. And yet—there was a rebellious spirit in her brought about by George's kiss, which wondered whether the acceptance might not have been less delicate and more beautiful. At all events, she entered her own room without any feeling of joy.

"I want to explain," said Miss Bartlett, "why it is that I have taken the largest room. Naturally, of course, I should have given it to you; but I happen to know that it belongs to the young man, and I was sure your mother would not like it."

Lucy was bewildered. She felt deprived of not being able to lie in the bed that George had slept.

"If you are to accept a favour it is more suitable you should be under an obligation to his father than to him. I am a woman of the world, in my small way, and I know where things lead to. However, Mr. Beebe is a guarantee of a sort that they will not presume on this."

"Mother wouldn't mind I'm sure," said Lucy, but again had the sense of larger and unsuspected, as yet unlabeled issues.

Miss Bartlett only sighed, and enveloped her in a protecting embrace as she wished her good-night. It gave Lucy the sensation of a fog, and when she reached her own room she opened the window and breathed the clean night air, thinking of the kind old man who had enabled her to see the lights dancing in the Arno and the cypresses of San Miniato, and the foot-hills of the Apennines, black against the rising moon. As Lucy drew in a deep breath, savoring the pristine air, she longed to escape through the window with her Dear George and experience life.

Miss Bartlett, in her room, fastened the window-shutters and locked the door, and then made a tour of the apartment to see where the cupboards led, and whether there were any oubliettes or secret entrances. It was then that she saw, pinned up over the washstand, a sheet of paper on which was scrawled an enormous note of interrogation. Nothing more.

"What does it mean?" she thought, and she examined it carefully by the light of a candle. Meaningless at first, it gradually became menacing, obnoxious, portentous with evil. She was seized with an impulse to destroy it, but fortunately remembered that she had no right to do so, since it must be the property of young Mr. Emerson. So she unpinned it carefully, and put it between two pieces of blotting-paper to keep it clean for him. Then she completed her inspection of the room, sighed heavily according to her habit, and went to bed, knowing within her bosom that her window to life was closing, if not already closed.

In the mood for more Crimson Romance?
Check out *Dracula: The Wild and Wanton Editon,*
Vol. 1 and *Vol. 2*
by Lucy Hartbury and Bram Stoker
at *CrimsonRomance.com.*